Readers love the Forbes Mates series by GRACE R. DUNCAN

Devotion

"Shifter fans are going to flock t⌐   ⌐
much more to the story."

—MM Good Book Reviews

"I really, really loved this book. It was awesome… I devoured this from start to finish."

—The Blogger Girls

Patience

"This book was beautifully written and I could see the connection strengthening between them."

—Two Chicks Obsessed

"I really loved it… it was a fantastic read and I'll be pre-ordering every book still to come in this series."

—*Divine Magazine*

Acceptance

"I can't recommend this series or this book any higher—it's truly wonderful. Any fans of shifter romances should consider this a MUST READ."

—Open Skye Book Reviews

"If you loved the first two books of this series, *Devotion* and *Patience*, you will want to pick this one up! If you haven't read them yet…well, why not? Go do it now!"

—Diverse Reader

By GRACE R. DUNCAN

Beautiful boy
Love Wins (Dreamspinner Anthology)
No Sacrifice
One Pulse (Dreamspinner Anthology)
Turning His Life Around
What About Now

FORBES MATES
Devotion
Patience
Acceptance
Forgiveness

GOLDEN COLLAR SERIES
Choices
Coronation
Deception

PANDEMUS CHRONICLES
Celebrating You
Healing

Published by DREAMSPINNER PRESS
www.dreamspinnerpress.com

Forgiveness

GRACE R. DUNCAN

Published by
DREAMSPINNER PRESS

5032 Capital Circle SW, Suite 2, PMB# 279, Tallahassee, FL 32305-7886 USA
www.dreamspinnerpress.com

This is a work of fiction. Names, characters, places, and incidents either are the product of author imagination or are used fictitiously, and any resemblance to actual persons, living or dead, business establishments, events, or locales is entirely coincidental.

Forgiveness
© 2018 Grace R. Duncan.

Cover Art
© 2018 Reese Dante.
http://www.reesedante.com
Cover content is for illustrative purposes only and any person depicted on the cover is a model.

Trade Paperback ISBN: 978-1-64080-269-8
Digital ISBN: 978-1-64080-270-4
Library of Congress Control Number: 2017916218
Trade Paperback published March 2018
v. 1.0

Printed in the United States of America
∞
This paper meets the requirements of
ANSI/NISO Z39.48-1992 (Permanence of Paper).

To everyone who's ever needed a second chance.

To Tricia, who has the patience of a saint with my grammatical shenanigans.

And to Joe, Sara, Phyllis, Wendy, Robin, Vic, Tempe, and Lex for being my cheering squad and reminding me the words are still in there, even if they don't want to come out as fast as I'd like them to.

Chapter 1

SHE SMELLED funny. Or rather, she didn't smell like anything he recognized. She *looked* human, but she didn't *smell* human, which confused him. And she walked across the forest floor in her bare feet.

He tilted his head as she approached, trying to figure out the puzzle. She wore simple dark pants, a plain tunic-like top, and had a bow slung over her shoulder with a quiver of arrows on her back. Instinct told him, however, he had nothing to fear from her.

She knelt in front of him, her long dark hair spilling over one shoulder, and reached out to brush her fingers over his head. "My poor lost wolf," she murmured, tilting her head in a mimic of him, considering him. "I understand your pain, but you are not ready to be wolf all the time. You have more to do in your human form, and you need your pack. My wolves aren't meant to be alone, not like this. It is time—past time— for you to return to your pack and those who love you."

Even though the soft touch soothed him, he whined quietly, not liking the words. He'd left for a reason. There was nothing for him back there. He'd turned his back on them. They wouldn't want him now.

"Oh, Eric, that's not true," she said, shaking her head.

Eric. He'd forgotten that name, perhaps deliberately, years ago. He shied away from the reminder of the human side of him, away from the echo of old pain.

"They miss you, more than you know. And there are others now. Others who will understand you in a way you weren't understood back then." She laid a hand on his head, and his eyes slid closed.

An image floated into his mind of a house at the edge of a stream, near a waterfall. The scent of someone very familiar joined the image, and Eric whined again. He didn't want it, that scent, didn't want to acknowledge he missed it. Didn't want to think about what he'd been missing.

The image changed to an open field, a red pup leaping at him. It nipped at his ear, knocking him over. He nipped back, growling softly, as he got to his feet to retaliate.

He pushed the image away. That time was gone. He'd forgotten the path back to them, didn't want to remember how to get there.

She spoke again, more in his head than out loud. "You remember. You'll find it. You know where that is. Now go, my lost one. And be lost no more."

Eric opened his eyes. She was gone. He looked around and sniffed the air, but there was no trace of her. He lay down and put his head on his paws, trying to make sense of what had just happened.

But he knew, even if he didn't want to accept it. He knew what he needed to do. He just didn't know if he could make himself do it.

"Go," she whispered in his mind, and with a sigh, Eric stood and made his way hesitantly down the mountain.

HE LAY on the hill, overlooking the waterfall and stream, trying not to think about what he should do. A strange-smelling shifter sat on the deck attached to the back of the house, doing something on a laptop. What he could see of the man wasn't familiar to Eric visually either.

While he debated, a big blue SUV pulled up in front of the house and parked. Eric lost sight of the person when they got out of the car, but the scent, carried on the breeze up to him, was one he'd never forget. He sat up a little, his heart pounding at the thought of crossing the ridiculously small distance.

He wondered briefly if Tanner could smell him too. *Does he even miss me? Does he wonder about me?* The questions came unbidden, some of his deeper fears surfacing, but before he could try to answer them for himself, he got an answer from somewhere—someone?—else.

Yes, very much so.

Eric's heart went into triple time. He stood but couldn't seem to force himself to move. Then a feeling, almost like a poke, came to the back of his mind, and without realizing what he was doing, he was following the narrow trail down the side of the hill and into the valley.

As he emerged from the trees and stopped at the edge of the stream, the shifter on the balcony sat up and peered at him. Eric squirmed, not sure, now that he was there, what to do. Should he just shift? Should he approach the house?

Yet again, before he could answer the question for himself, a door off to the left opened.

And there, standing with a look of pure shock on his face, was Eric's best friend in the world.

"Eric?" It came out on a whisper, as if Tanner was afraid to believe his eyes.

Eric whined softly, dropping his head.

"Holy shit, it is you!"

The words had barely registered when Eric had a pair of human arms around his neck.

"I thought you were…. I was sure you'd been…. Shit." Tanner's words sounded a little shaky, but he cleared his throat and let go. "Can you… will you shift? Talk to me?"

Eric took a breath that wasn't nearly deep enough, then stepped back. Tanner's face fell, but when Eric didn't move farther away, a hopeful smile spread. With one more breath, heart still thumping, Eric nudged his wolf back.

It took longer than he remembered it taking, but perhaps that was just because it'd been so long since he'd shifted. Even though it took longer, it felt as natural as ever. His bones moved, muscles reformed; then his fur and claws receded. His paws turned into hands and feet, and finally his teeth retracted and his vision turned from gray to color.

He couldn't seem to bring himself to look up, though. He panted hard, swallowing around a very dry throat, heart trying to burst out of his chest. He stared at the grass under him, working to make himself move, but nothing seemed to be obeying his commands. He wasn't sure he could stand just yet either, even though his now human-shaped legs did not like the position he was in.

Apparently the actual act of standing wasn't required of him. Because a moment later, Tanner yanked him up and hugged him harder than he'd ever been hugged before.

"Oh my gods, you're back. Please tell me you're back. I've missed you so fucking much." Tanner nearly mumbled this last part, but of course Eric heard it.

He managed to get his arms around Tanner and return the hug for a moment. Then he pulled back—though kept his hands on Tanner's arms to steady himself—and looked his best friend in the eyes.

He had to clear his throat twice before he could speak, because his human vocal cords didn't want to work. "Uh, well, yes. If… if you want me to be."

Tanner blinked at him several times, then, with a crooked smile, said, "Duh?"

Relief flooded Eric. "Then, yeah, I guess I am."

At that moment the strange shifter from the deck stepped through the door, grinning from ear to ear. Eric's nose twitched as he sniffed the man, then Tanner, then the man again. He blinked and turned a confused look at Tanner. "He's your… mate?"

Tanner let go of Eric, though he kept a hand on Eric's elbow when he swayed. Once he was steady, Tanner released Eric's elbow and held out a hand to the other man. "Yes. This is Finley. My *destined* mate."

Eric's eyes widened, and he stared at Finley. "Destined? There are same-sex destined mates?"

Tanner and Finley both nodded, and Finley smiled. "Yes, there are. It's great to finally get to meet you, Eric." He stepped forward, holding his arms as if he wanted to hug Eric, but hesitated, obviously letting Eric decide.

Though slightly bemused to be hugging someone's mate, Eric nonetheless accepted and couldn't resist savoring the warm, welcoming feeling he got from it.

Finley pulled back. "Would you like to come in? Maybe put some pants on? Perhaps have some coffee?"

Eric blinked. "How long have I been gone?" he asked in lieu of an answer. He couldn't quite assimilate the idea that Tanner was not only mated but to his destined *male* mate, and he even had a house! He shoved aside the pang that Tanner *was* mated, said goodbye to his ancient crush, and focused on being happy for his best friend.

Tanner and Finley exchanged looks. Tanner cleared his throat. "Just over nine years."

Eric's mouth fell open, and his eyes nearly bugged out of his head. "Nine years? I've been wolf for *nine years*?" He was aware time didn't pass the same for him in wolf form as in human, but he hadn't realized just *how* different it was.

"Yeah. Uh…."

Eric shook his head hard, trying to make his brain work. It seemed to have disappeared somewhere. "Yeah, uh, perhaps this would be better inside."

Finley turned and stepped back into the house. Tanner held his hand toward the door, and Eric followed Finley, his mind in a whirlwind. As he stepped into what was obviously a mudroom, Finley held out a pair of gray sweatpants.

Eric took them but fumbled with the waistband for a moment. He couldn't seem to get his hands to work right. "Nine years," he muttered, opening and closing one fist. "No wonder I can't even pull on a pair of pants."

Tanner chuckled. "Dude, I'd be surprised if you could do much of anything right away. That's a *long* time to stay in wolf form. I was a little worried there for a minute that you *couldn't* shift back."

Eric turned to Tanner. "*I* was worried for a moment that I couldn't. But… I knew, deep down, I could. I…. Um…. Hey, why do you smell different? I mean, besides smelling like him." Eric tilted his head toward Finley. He finally managed to get his hands to work well enough to open the sweatpants. But when he tried to step into them, he nearly lost his balance. If Finley hadn't caught him, he'd have toppled over like a pile of children's blocks. When the pants were in place, Eric suppressed the urge to make a face at the scratchy fabric against his apparently oversensitive skin.

Tanner blinked. "Ah, yeah. A lot has changed since you've been gone. I'm the alpha now."

Eric was sure his eyes were going to pop out of his skull at the rate things were going. He dropped his head to the side, showing his neck in respect. "The alpha? Holy… uh…."

Tanner grinned as he put a hand on Eric's shoulder in recognition. "Nah, not holy. Just alpha."

Eric found himself laughing. "That's good. I'd hate to have to call you a god…."

This laugh came from Tanner. "Damn, I've missed you. Let's head upstairs. I think I need that coffee."

WHEN FINLEY spoke, Eric turned back to him. "Would you like a T-shirt too? Maybe some socks? I don't think underwear from either of us would fit you." Finley frowned, looking Eric up and down. Both Finley and Tanner were bigger than he was, probably by a good fifty pounds of pure muscle, so he didn't think too many of their clothes would fit, but he didn't have much choice.

"Uh, T-shirt and socks would be great." Eric wrinkled his nose. "I guess I don't have much of anything anymore."

"Doubt you'd fit your old clothes, anyway," Tanner said, chuckling. "You've put on muscle. You're not that skinny brat anymore."

Eric scowled without heat. "I was never a skinny brat."

Tanner smirked, and Eric rolled his eyes as he followed Tanner into the dining area of the house.

Windows filled two walls, showing the surrounding forest and waterfall valley behind the house. A long table that could probably seat nearly twelve people took up most of the space. The rest of the house invited him to feel at home as well. Rustic and comfortable with overstuffed furniture, it was offset by plenty of technology—some of which Eric wasn't even sure he could identify. The enormity of all he'd missed was starting to make itself known, and Eric pushed the thought away, not ready to face it.

The dining room opened into a kitchen full of brickwork and wood, complemented by copper pans and stainless-steel appliances. Tanner busied himself with coffee as Finley disappeared up another set of stairs.

Eric had trouble taking his eyes off Tanner. He *had* missed his best friend. They'd run and played often as wolves before he'd gotten involved with Kim. He pushed thoughts of her *far* away and instead tried to focus on the now.

"So, uh, why are you the alpha? Did something happen to your dad?"

Tanner came back, holding two coffee cups. He set one in front of Eric and the other at the chair opposite. "Well," Tanner said, going back to the kitchen. "My dad kind of had to step down because…." He picked up another mug of coffee and turned around, pausing when Eric fumbled to pick up the mug.

He scowled down at the cup. Something as simple as holding a damned coffee mug shouldn't be this hard. He flexed his hand again, then forced himself to go slow, wrapping one hand around the main part and deliberately working two fingers around the handle. "You'd think I was a newborn pup, for fuck's sake," he grumbled.

"In a lot of ways, you are. You haven't had opposable thumbs in too long. It's going to take time to get used to it again. I'd bet a lot of your senses are amplified right now as well. You may even have to relearn how to filter things."

Eric frowned as he took a sip of the coffee. The bitter brew hit him hard. "Whoa." He looked down into the cup, then up at Tanner. "Is this brewed strong, or is that my messed-up taste buds?"

Tanner laughed. "Finley does tend to brew it a bit strong, but I suspect it's more your taste buds right now. You haven't had coffee in nine years, man."

"True." Eric shook his head. He set the cup down and rubbed his face, then looked up at Tanner. "So, uh, your dad?"

"Oh, yeah." Tanner chuckled. "He's the alpha prime now."

Eric blinked at him several times, mouth falling open in shock. "*Your* dad is the alpha prime? But… what happened to the old one? And how did your dad end up prime? What… oh my fucking gods, I've been gone way too long." He dropped his face into his hands again.

"Okay, one question at a time—"

"Here you go," Finley said, and Eric looked up. Finley held out a plain blue T-shirt and basic white sport socks.

Eric took them and tugged the shirt on gratefully. Despite his naturally higher body temperature, he was *cold*. He suspected not being covered in fur had something to do with that.

Once he'd put the socks on, Tanner took the seat next to Finley and spoke again. "It's a *long* story and should involve you meeting a couple of people before we tell it, because I'm not sure you'll believe me without seeing or smelling them first."

Eric raised an eyebrow. "Okay…."

"Really," Finley said, nodding.

"Suffice it to say, yes, my dad is the alpha prime now, which means I had to take over." Tanner shrugged. "Earlier than I would have liked, but…."

Eric nodded. "Right. You wouldn't walk away from it." He sipped his coffee in silence for a moment, not sure what to say. He couldn't seem to wrestle his scattered thoughts into place. "Um…."

"Do you want to go see your parents?" Tanner asked.

Eric didn't look up right away, instead staring into the coffee cup like it'd give him the answer he needed. Finally he shook his head. "I'm not ready to see them yet. I saw them a couple of times, while I was in wolf form. My mom… I know she recognized me." He swallowed and looked up at Tanner. "She turned around and walked away. Didn't even try to approach me."

Finley scowled. "That's no way to treat your kid."

Eric gave a half smile. "My mother was never the most… maternal of women."

"Doesn't matter. Not cool." Finley shook his head, still scowling, and Eric decided then and there that he liked Tanner's mate.

"He's a good match for you," Eric said, grinning at Tanner.

"I'd like to think Diana knows what she's doing," Tanner said, chuckling. "But yeah, he is." He leaned over and kissed Finley's temple.

A spike of jealousy he didn't like went through Eric, and he dropped his gaze to his cup again. It was true he'd harbored a crush on his best friend years ago. It was the main reason he'd never told Tanner he was bisexual. He didn't want things to get awkward, and he'd known back then Tanner was hoping to meet his destined mate—if same-sex destined mates even existed. So when they both matured and nothing happened between them, Eric had put the crush away, as much as he could.

As he dug through the feeling, though, part of him was more jealous about the fact that they had each other and that it *did* seem so good between them. Were all destined mates like that? Not that Eric expected to ever meet his, and even if he did, he wasn't sure he could take the chance on him or her walking away like Kim had. He pushed the thought away.

"So, uh...."

"What made you come back?" Tanner asked.

Eric frowned, not sure if he could really explain it. He *was* certain neither would believe him if he told them he thought he'd met their goddess. "I... something just pushed me—instinct, I guess—that it was time to come back. Not that I really know what I'm going to do or where to go. I'm sure my apartment's long gone, as is my stuff."

"I think your parents collected some of it. Pictures, personal things, that stuff." Tanner frowned. "The rest, though, I'm pretty sure they donated. They were convinced you'd never come back."

"That doesn't surprise me," Eric said, swallowing around the lump that thought caused. "I'm pretty sure everyone was."

"I kept hoping," Tanner said, pulling Eric's gaze to him. Tanner nodded. "Yeah. I saw you a few times, up in the mountains. I kept wanting to go up there, but I really didn't think you wanted me to get too close."

"Early on... I didn't. When was the last time you saw me?" Eric tried not to let it hurt that Tanner hadn't approached him either.

"God... five years? Six? Something like that. I kept looking for you after, of course, but I couldn't find you. Maybe sheer dumb luck that you were somewhere else."

Eric let out a breath. "Back then I wouldn't have wanted to see you, no. I... well, anyway. Here I am. But... now what?"

"You'll stay here, of course, learn how to be human again, and decide when you're ready, that's what," Finley said, reaching out and taking his hand.

Eric blinked at him, then looked at Tanner and back to Finley. "Stay here?"

Finley wrinkled his forehead in consternation. "Well, I'm not about to let you try to relearn how to be human on your own. What kind of alpha mate would I be if I did that?"

"I… didn't think about it like that."

Finley beamed at him. "Then it's settled. You can pick whichever bedroom you'd like, except ours, of course. You might be most comfortable in the one down here."

Eric most definitely did *not* want to hear them having sex. "That's… probably true."

Tanner got up and disappeared. When he came back a few minutes later, he held something out.

Eric stared at it for a long moment before reaching out to take it. "You still have this?"

Tanner nodded. "Yeah. I held on to it, just in case."

Eric lifted the cover on his old sketchbook, then flipped slowly through the pages. One design after another that he'd worked into leather over the years filled the book. He'd loved his job, once upon a time, loved drawing those images, then hand-tooling them into the leather to make the bags and purses and other items they'd sold in the shop.

"And when you're feeling better, more able to handle things, your job will be waiting for you, if you want it."

Shaking his head, Eric looked up. "I don't know if I can even do that anymore."

Tanner just smiled. "We'll see. Don't make any decisions yet, okay?"

Eric nodded. "Okay, uh, yeah."

"Cool. I think it's about time we think about dinner. How about some burgers?" Finley asked, standing up.

Chapter 2

BEN DIDN'T need his preternatural senses to know she was there. Despite how quiet she was trying to be—or, at least, he assumed she was trying—he still heard her crying. He was pretty sure their human neighbors heard her.

He focused on packing the few things he had left into the last box. He closed it up, ignoring the sniffling, and picked up his overnight bag. After checking the toiletries bag, he turned around to go back to the bathroom.

"Jesus—"

"Ben, Mamá. Why can you not at least call me by the name I prefer?" he asked, deliberately speaking in English.

"I named you Jesus for a reason!"

Ben sent up a prayer to Diana for patience, though he wasn't entirely convinced she was there. He wasn't convinced *any* god was there. "You also named me Benjamin—Ben—for a reason. You've told me more than once what *mi abuelo* meant to you."

She scowled at him. "Of course he meant a lot. But—"

"Mamá, I don't believe in that. Just... never mind. Excuse me." He slipped by her into the hall, then down to the bathroom and retrieved his toothbrush as she followed him. After stowing it in his toiletries bag and tucking the bag back in the overnight case, he turned to her one more time.

"I still do not know why you have to go so far away. *Somos familia!*" She took off in a long string of rapid-fire Spanish that he tuned out—the same arguments she'd been giving him for months, since he'd made the decision to move to another part of the country.

"Mamá, this is exactly why! You could never accept me. Nothing I do makes you happy! Every time I even *mention* my wolf—"

She crossed herself, making him roll his eyes.

"—you cross yourself and tell me I'm going to hell for not exorcising him."

"It is a demon in you, Jesus!"

"Ben."

She ignored that.

He sighed. "It's not a demon. He is part of me. We've been over this more times than I can count. If it's not my wolf—"

She crossed herself. Again.

"—it's because I did not go to medical school. Or I did not marry the girl you picked out for me. Not that I'm even *ready* to get married, Mamá."

"You could have been a doctor!"

"I *wanted* to play my guitar! That was not good enough. I did go to school, but even accounting was not good enough!"

"I do not know why—"

"Never mind. I'm not going to keep fighting with you, Mamá. This is why I have to go. I cannot keep doing this. I need to go somewhere that I can be myself. Even the pack here is not as welcoming as I would like."

"Jesus Benjamin Arellano!" she shouted.

"Alicia! That is *enough*."

Ben took a breath and sent a grateful look at his papá. "Papá. I cannot—" He spread his hands and shook his head.

"Let me take the last box. Do you have everything?" Papá asked.

"Yes, this is it."

Mamá started crying again. Ben ignored her—again—and picked up his overnight bag, then followed Papá through the house to the driveway. He stowed the bag on the floor of the passenger seat next to his backpack, then shut the door and turned back to Mamá. "*Te quiero*, Mamá. You know that. But I need space to be me."

"But… so far."

"The pack in Pennsylvania needs an accountant. They'll welcome me—all of me." He shrugged a shoulder. "Maybe I'll meet my destined mate there."

"Je—Benjamin…."

"Let him go, Alicia," Papá said.

She shook her head. "I do not understand how you can hurt me like this!"

Ben sent up another bid for patience, but apparently, if Diana was there, she was busy. He took a deep breath, but his tolerance was getting shorter and shorter the longer she fought. "This is not about hurting you, Mamá! I am an adult! I need to do what is right for me. This is right."

"There are plenty of good Catholic girls here. You can work—"

"Alicia—" Papá tried, but she ignored him and opened her mouth to speak again. But Ben held his hand up, stopping her.

"No, Mamá. Just stop, please, before we say something we'll regret."

She scowled this time and actually stamped her foot. "You listen to me! I am your *mamá*! I know what is best for you."

"No," Ben said, his own expression turning thunderous. "You have not done what is best for me in years. *Years*, Mamá! You have done nothing but make me feel bad for how I was *born*. You've told me all my life I am a half demon." He shook his head and turned toward his car.

"If you walk away from me, Jesus Benjamin Arellano—"

He swung back around. "You will what? You will not talk to me? *You* are the one that will lose out! I do not have to come back here ever again. I do not have to bring my mate—whoever they turn out to be—back here to meet you. I do not have to do *anything*!"

"*Alicia!*"

Yet again she ignored his papá, stilling. "They? You mean, she, do you not, Jesus?" she asked in barely a whisper.

He cursed himself silently. He hadn't meant to let that slip. He took a breath. "No, Mamá, I do not. I mean they. I do not know who—or what—my mate will be. It could be a nice girl. Or a nice boy."

She blinked at him, her color draining. "What are you saying, Jesus?"

He ignored the name and sighed. "I'm saying I'm bisexual, Mamá. It's the *other* reason I cannot stay here. You're not the only one that would not accept that side of me. The pack will not either."

She crossed herself again, though Ben wasn't sure if it was the mention of the pack or his sexuality that sparked it. "Jesus, you must stay here and go to church with me! You cannot give in to the—"

"No." He sent a look at his papá, who sighed. "Please, Papá, help me?"

"Alicia, no more. You have to let him go. His sexuality is none of your—or my—business. Come on." He put an arm around her shoulders, but she shrugged it off, turning an accusing look at him.

"Did you know this?"

Papá looked distinctly uncomfortable for a few seconds, but then his expression firmed and he nodded. "Yes. It's why I helped him find the Forbes Pack. They'll accept him there."

"He should not *be* accepted! He must exorcise these unholy—"

"Alicia!"

"Goodbye, Mamá," Ben said, shaking his head. He rounded the car and pulled open the driver's door. He gave her one more long look. Despite her insistence on ignoring what he was, on arguing with what he wanted, he *did* love her. "*Te quiero*, Mamá. Adiós." He slipped into the car and pulled the door shut. Without looking in the rearview mirror, he started the car and took off.

He got out of his neighborhood on autopilot. Half a mile down the main road, he pulled into a Taco Bueno and parked, then dropped his head onto the steering wheel, bouncing it a few times, his heart *hurting*. His phone went off, and he contemplated ignoring it, sure it was his mother, but picked it up anyway. He'd never been able to truly ignore her.

Thankfully, it was Papá. *Call or text me when you stop for the night.*

He sent back a quick *I will*, then turned his notifications off. He rubbed his face hard. Even with her... problems with his nature, he would miss her.

He sighed, wishing, not for the first—or thousandth—time, that she could just accept him. He knew growing up Catholic would have made it difficult, but he would have thought after all those years of seeing him, his papá, and his younger sister shift and *not* turn into monsters, she would have accepted it. But apparently not. He couldn't remember exactly when they'd stopped shifting at home, but he hadn't been all that old. Even so, he'd never so much as growled at her when he'd been in wolf form. So he didn't understand why she wouldn't accept it.

It still boggled his mind that she and his father were destined. He didn't understand—entirely aside from her humanity—how Diana could pair them—if that was, in fact, how it worked. But he guessed there was a reason for it. Still, it made life very difficult on all of them. No wonder his younger sister went all the way to California to go to school. He wished he'd left that early too.

Instead, he'd done his schooling there, only delaying the inevitable fight, which turned out to be just as bad as he'd been afraid of. With another sigh, he connected his phone to his car's Bluetooth and set it in the holder on the dash. He picked his playlist, set the navigation up, then pulled out of the spot.

Glancing at the clock, he decided to go through the drive-through and get something for the road. He hadn't intended to leave already, had meant to have dinner with them before leaving in the morning, but he wouldn't, couldn't go back there. Maybe someday.

Shoving the fight to the back of his mind, he turned down Carlos Santana and approached the menu board.

BEN SAT heavily on the side of the bed as he hit the speed dial for his papá's number.

"Bueno!"

"*Hola*, Papá. I'm in Texarkana. Found a Hampton."

"You stopped so soon?"

Ben sighed. "Yeah. I could not concentrate much anymore. My wolf was getting too pushy, distracting me."

"When was the last time you shifted?"

Ben frowned as he tried to figure it out. "The last full moon."

"No wonder you're distracted. You cannot go that long."

"I know. With Mamá, though, it's hard to run."

"Well, you will not have to worry about that anymore." Papá didn't sound too happy.

"Are you regretting sending me away?" Ben asked, frowning.

"I'll miss you, of course. But you're not happy here. And if you did end up with a man?"

Ben didn't answer, because they both knew how that would go. East Texas was *not* the place to be openly bisexual. "I think I'm going to spend the night in my fur. It'll be inside, but still."

"It'll help," Papá said. "Just giving him time, even if you can't run."

Ben kept silent for a long moment, trying to decide if he wanted to ask, then forced the words out. "How is she?"

"Eh," Papá said, chuckling. "She's your mamá. She is brooding now, but she'll come around. Give her some time to really miss you."

"Is that really going to work?" Ben picked at a loose thread on the hotel bedspread.

Papá sighed. "I think so."

"She'll never accept my wolf, Papá. She still thinks he's a demon. How… how did she ever accept you?"

"Destined, *mijo*. And she did fall in love with me. I regret claiming her without her knowing what I was, but it happened and could not be undone. I do not regret claiming her completely, just not talking to her before. I think that is a bigger part of why she is the way she is."

"That *was* kind of a rotten thing to do, Papá." Ben was unable to repress a small laugh.

"Yeah, it was." Papá chuckled. "She forgave me for the most part, but I think there's still some of that holdover. I'm sorry for that—that you have had to take the worst of her attitude about it."

Ben let the silence sit for a moment, not knowing what to say to that. "I… it's not your fault she took it out on us—me and Tina."

"You took most of it. Always trying to shield your little sister. Christina could have handled it."

"But I did not want her to have to. Is that not what big brothers are for?"

"Maybe." There was a smile in his papá's voice at that. "Do you think you'll find your mate there?"

"I do not know. I hope so. I mean… it seems pretty coincidental that you were told about them when you were."

"True. Well, be safe on the road, please. We may heal fast, but that does not mean I want you hurt."

Ben snorted. "I'm not a fan of pain, you know. I do not plan to get into an accident."

Papá laughed. "Good. How far will you get tomorrow?"

"Uh, I had originally planned to stop in Nashville, but probably will go on to Louisville instead. Then Pittsburgh the next day."

"Well, text, okay? Let me know where you are. I'll worry."

"Of course, Papá." Ben paused to take a breath as his wolf pushed on his consciousness. "I should go. He's getting more antsy."

"All right. Good night, Ben."

"Night."

Ben turned the phone off and set it on the nightstand. He stopped to plug it in, then kicked his shoes off and pulled his shirt over his head at the same time. A moment later, he was naked and greeted his wolf.

It felt good to let him take over. He'd spent so much time ignoring him, trying *not* to be the shifter he was, all for Mamá. It had affected him as a wolf, though he tried not to let it show. He had always shifted slower than his papá and sister, had always struggled with hunting, though they couldn't do much of that in their small running area, anyway.

Still, giving over had always seemed *right*. Seeing his vision change, savoring the sensations of his bones realigning and muscles reforming… it felt good. He hoped to spend a good deal more time in his fur when he got to the new pack lands. If they accepted him. He still worried more than a little that they wouldn't want a Mexican, or that their acceptance of other sexualities was exaggerated.

When he landed on four paws, he shook himself hard, then jumped up on the bed. He settled on top of the bedspread and sighed. He wanted to go hunting, wanted to spend time running, but he didn't dare, as unfamiliar with the local area as he was. Besides, he was fairly certain there was a local pack that would *not* appreciate him hunting on their lands without warning.

Even without running, simply giving time over to his other half offered him a peace that had eluded him for a long time. He hadn't shifted outside the full moon in months. It was no wonder he was starting to have attention issues.

One of the advantages of his wolf was that he couldn't hold on to the supercomplicated human worries. His wolf liked things much simpler, more basic. Eat, sleep, hunt, fuck. He couldn't do some of that, but he could sleep, giving his other half time to simply have more control.

His mind settling into more peace than he'd had in a long time, Ben fell asleep.

BEN WASN'T entirely impressed with Pittsburgh yet. He *did* appreciate all the green foliage, but the city itself wasn't quite what he expected. The whole trip on the interstate to the west of the city looked… rather boring. Much the same as any other city: shopping centers, office buildings, and suburbia.

The hills and sheer amount of green made it better than Dallas, without even seeing anything else, though. And he had seen pictures of the city itself, so he knew it was there somewhere, but thus far, at—he checked the GPS—only two miles out from the center of the city, he hadn't seen even a hint of the tall office buildings of downtown.

He took one curve, then another, then found himself at the top of a rather impressive hill. At the bottom, the opening of a tunnel through the mountain waited, and just before there were an almost ridiculous number of bright green signs. The traffic leading up to the entrance seemed a little much for the time of day—midafternoon. Still, he glanced at the GPS, found the lane he was supposed to be in, and tapped the steering wheel to the music while he crawled along the road.

It went faster than he'd expected. As he approached the tunnel, he was surprised he could barely see the other end. Traffic sped up, however, and a moment later, he was coming out the other side.

His eyes widened and his breath caught. *Right* in front of him, barely the width of a river away, rose the huge buildings of downtown. It took a loud honk for him to realize he'd slowed down and was staring. He hurried to move over to the lane he needed, then took the exit he wanted.

He couldn't stop himself from looking over at the city several times as he drove along the river. It wasn't until it more or less disappeared behind the hills again that he was able to focus on the road. He hit the Bluetooth button and told his phone to call Tanner Pearce. It only rang twice before it was answered.

"Hello?"

"Hi, Mr. Pearce, this is Ben Arellano, from Texas?"

"Oh, ugh. Tanner, please. Or alpha, if you must. Mr. Pearce is my father."

Ben found himself laughing. "All right, alpha. I just passed downtown Pittsburgh. I understand I still have a bit before I'll get out there, but I wanted to ask if you'd like me to meet you first before I did anything else."

"It's not necessary. Hey, your dad said you were just moving into the area. I meant to ask if you have an apartment already lined up?"

"Oh, no. I was going to find an Extended Stay and look. I left a day before I expected to."

"In that case, yes, come see me first."

Ben wasn't sure what that had to do with anything, but he wasn't about to argue with his new alpha. "All right. Could you, um, send directions? The GPS thinks I'm driving into a river."

Tanner laughed. "Yeah, it's not so great out here. I'll text them as soon as we hang up."

"Thank you. I'll see you soon."

"See ya."

Tanner was as good as his word, and directions that seemed almost too easy arrived within a couple of minutes. Ben managed to focus on them rather than the scenery—except for the second tunnel he went through—and before too long, he was off the interstate and following the state roads, then a small paved road, and finally what could only be called a dirt path.

He found himself intensely grateful he'd gone with an SUV. The CR-V handled itself and the bumps well, and a moment later, he pulled up next to a deep blue Outlander. He turned off the engine, his heart pounding. Despite the friendly tone of the voice on the phone, there was still so much that could go wrong here. He'd pinned a lot of hopes for his future on working with and being a part of this pack.

He closed his eyes. Despite his argument with his mother, he hadn't necessarily embraced the gods the way he probably should. She'd done her best to instill her Catholic faith in him. And while he *didn't* believe in her god, he still wasn't 100 percent sure of those his father followed. He accepted something was up there, but he wasn't entirely positive *what* yet. He took a deep breath, though, and spoke. "Diana, if you are up there, please… I… I do not know. Just let them accept me? Please?"

With one more breath, he climbed out of the car.

Before he could even knock, the door opened. A tall, somewhat muscular man with thick black hair and green eyes full of good humor opened the door. He smelled of *welcome,* and Ben immediately liked him.

"You must be Ben!"

Ben nodded, a little stunned. "Um. Yes. Hi. Are you… Tanner?" He didn't *sound* like the man on the phone, but phones *could* do weird things to voices.

The man laughed. "Oh, no, that's my mate. I'm Finley. Come in, please."

Mate? So the rumor is true. At least the fact that the alpha was mated to a man.

Letting go of some of his nervousness, Ben followed Finley into the house.

He immediately loved the rustic, warm feeling. The focal point of the main room they stopped in was a huge river-rock fireplace. Overstuffed couches and chairs invited him to sink in and get comfortable. Before he could absorb more, the most amazing scent hit him. Leather, something sweet, and a smell that he could only call *home.*

"Fin, where can I put these?"

Ben spun around to face a *gorgeous* man. Longish black hair parted to frame a round face. Bright hazel eyes and a beautiful smile filled it. And all this topped a long, lean body that made Ben's mouth water.

It also caused his eyesight to go gray, his teeth to drop, his claws to sprout, and his dick to stiffen.

Mate.

He stared at the man, who stared back at him, looking as if he'd just been shot. His eyes bled black, teeth dropped, and the scent of arousal hit Ben with the rest.

"Oh, fuck no," the man said, dropping the bundle of clothes he held. Then a moment later, he'd shifted, shredding the jeans and T-shirt he wore, and bolted for a set of stairs that went down.

Ben blinked after him, his heart twisting. His mate was here. He had a destined mate. A *male* destined mate.

Who didn't want him.

He couldn't breathe all of a sudden, and the twisting in his heart spread to knot his stomach as well. He tried to suck in air, but his lungs refused to cooperate.

"I'm sorry, Ben," Finley murmured, putting a hand on his shoulder. "He'll be back."

"He sure as hell will. I'm not letting him do this a second time," another man said, coming around the corner from the other direction. Ben was so messed up, he couldn't take in more than a muscular body much like Finley's and a head full of thick auburn hair. "Especially not *now*. Hi, Ben. I'm Tanner. It's nice to meet you. My mate will take care of you for a few."

"Come sit down, Ben," Finley murmured as Tanner went down the same steps Ben's mate had just disappeared down.

Ben followed Finley to one of the couches and took a seat. He stared into space, trying to make sense of what had just happened. He turned to look at Finley, finally finding his voice. "Is... is it me? That I'm a guy?"

Finley frowned. "I don't know? I didn't know he was bisexual, but he might just have been in the closet. Diana doesn't make mistakes, though, with destined mates. He'll come around."

Ben wondered, then, if it wasn't something else about him. Was it his appearance? He didn't think he looked *that* Latino that one look could tell someone his family's origin. But what else could it be?

As if reading his mind, Finley spoke again. "I'm sure it's not you. He's been through a lot recently—and not so recently. It's not my place to tell you. But trust me, he'll be back. Can I get you some coffee?"

Ben nodded absently and took another breath. *Diana, what do I do now?*

Chapter 3

ERIC RAN. He paid no attention to where he went, paid no mind to what he passed. He simply ran.

He couldn't do it, couldn't go through that again. He didn't care if it was destined or chosen; he could *not* deal with another mate.

He was forced to slow as he ran out of breath. He kept going until he found a stream, then flopped down on the side of it. He knew his peace would be disturbed, and that there was no way Tanner wouldn't come after him. But he needed some time to get a grip on himself.

He put his paws over his eyes as memories he did *not* want tried to surface. He'd gotten good at putting them away over the years.

But they refused to behave, refused to stay away.

ERIC HAD only been one of several guys going after her. He had no idea why she chose *him*; he'd just counted himself lucky. They'd dated, spent a huge amount of their time together, fallen in love. They hadn't done a lot of talking—they'd been teenagers, after all, full of hormones. They hadn't bonded early, both aware of what it meant, but they'd done plenty of other stuff together—kissing hadn't been an issue, and they'd certainly done everything *else* they could think of that wouldn't form a bond.

Eric had built dreams of a life with her. He'd imagined a small house in the woods, pups with her, a fairly quiet life in the pack. It seemed a forgone conclusion that they'd mate.

So, he'd asked. And she'd accepted.

He'd been over the moon. His parents had been thrilled when they announced it. Alpha Noah had cautioned him, however. Tried to tell him Kim hadn't been as invested in the mating as he was. But Kim swore she loved him and wanted to be with him.

So the night after their senior prom, they'd taken that last step: he'd claimed her and they'd bonded.

He didn't want to admit things had started going wrong right away. But now, years later, he had to concede they had. In fact, the night after they'd mated, they'd had their first full-blown fight when Kim found out he wasn't going to college.

He'd discovered his talent for leatherworking while doing his summer work in the pack leather business. He'd loved designing pictures to be worked into the leather and, when he'd talked to Alpha Noah, decided he'd wanted to make a living at it. Alpha Noah had been thrilled, as had Eric, and offered him a permanent position on the spot.

Kim… not so much. Eric hadn't understood it. He had a good job and certainly made enough for that small house, a good car, and so on. Sure, it wasn't going to pay what a doctor or engineer would make, which was what his mother had wanted him to do, but it paid well enough. His dad had been the one pushing him to go for medicine. Eric wanted nothing to do with either. He'd considered going for computers, but the truth was, other than using them when he had to, he wasn't all *that* interested. So discovering his talent and going into leatherworking had been easy for him.

They fought most of the summer over his decision. She kept telling him it wasn't too late to sign up for classes, and he kept saying he didn't want them. Why go into debt for a degree he wasn't going to use? He didn't know why it was so important to her that he go, when he knew what he wanted to do.

In the meantime she insisted she was happy just being his mate, which only confused him further. If college was so important, why wasn't she going? That sparked another rather epic fight, especially when the truth finally came out: she didn't really want to work at all.

Eric would admit he'd never been the swiftest person when it came to understanding people, but he'd put two and two together and finally understood she wanted him to go to college, which would mean he could make more money and take care of her so she wouldn't have to work.

It didn't help that his parents had been telling her they were going to get him to go. That they'd even find a way to pay for it, just until he could get a good engineering job or start his residency. All behind his back. They'd assured her they'd get him to "come around."

That had been the biggest explosion he and his parents had ever had. He had, for the most part, gotten along with them. He hadn't always agreed with them, and because of them, he'd ignored a part of himself— the part that was attracted to men. They'd claimed they had accepted the alpha's son—though Eric wasn't completely convinced of that—and as such, he'd kept both his attraction to guys and his crush on Tanner to himself.

All these years later, he could finally truly see they'd been pushing him and Kim together. And while he'd loved Kim, if they hadn't been so encouraging, he wasn't entirely sure he'd have mated her as soon as he had either. It was easy: she was female, she wanted to be his mate, and he could keep the rest of his private wants just that—private.

He wished he'd listened more to Alpha Noah. That summer he'd mentioned a couple of times that if Eric had anything he wanted to talk about—and even then Eric had known Alpha Noah was referring to Kim—he could talk. Eric hadn't taken him up on it. Instead, he'd kept it to himself and continued to fight with Kim.

But when the beginning of September came and went and Eric refused to go to college, she had apparently realized she wasn't going to get what she wanted. He'd hinted that they start trying for pups. She'd *completely* lost it on him, packed a suitcase, and walked out.

He'd told himself she just needed a break, needed time to understand he was happy. And he was—if not about them fighting, then about everything else.

So, he'd waited. September bled into October, which blew coldly into November. And still she hadn't come back. Hadn't so much as called him in all that time. He had no idea where she'd gone, just that she wasn't in Pittsburgh anymore—Alpha Noah had told him he knew that for sure, but not where she'd gone.

He'd lost himself in his work and focused on spending time with his friends. But one Monday night, during football, his life changed forever.

The Steelers were close, on the ten-yard line, looking good for a touchdown. Halfway through the play, a pain hit that was so sharp, it stole Eric's breath and forced him to lose control of his wolf, something he hadn't done since he was a pup. He'd shifted on the spot, howling. It'd taken the alpha, using his alpha power, to get him to shift back.

His chest physically *hurt*. He'd known, in that second, what had happened. He couldn't breathe, the pain was so sharp. He managed to get back to human form and stared at his best friend, trying to figure out how to handle this, but his wolf was too much in the forefront, too close to the surface because of the pain. He'd managed to tell Tanner he was sorry, then shifted again and bolted.

Eric had torn through the screen door of Alpha Noah's house and run as fast as he could. Away from the pain, away from the heartache. Away from the understanding of what had just happened.

Kim had cheated on him. Cheated on him and allowed another wolf to claim her. She hadn't just left him to figure things out.

She was gone.

With another howl, he'd run. Run as far and as fast as he could. And he hadn't looked back for a very, *very* long time.

ERIC WHINED, trying yet again to forget. There was no way he could go through that again, no *way* he could open himself up to the possibility. *Diana, why?*

He smelled his alpha only a few moments later. But Eric wasn't ready to face being human again. Life as a wolf was so much easier. He didn't have these things to deal with. He could focus on a few basic things—fighting, feeding, running. He didn't need to think about emotion, didn't need to worry about something he should have had but didn't.

"Come on, Eric. You can't do this again," Tanner said.

Eric tried to ignore him. He'd recognized Tanner as his alpha, so if Tanner wanted to push the issue, he could. Eric really hoped he wouldn't.

"Dude, really. Come on. I know it was hard on you. I saw it happen, remember? I didn't feel it, but I know. You can't do this again, though. You can't do it to your mate."

The whine got louder, and Eric shook his head. *I don't have a mate! I can't!*

"Eric, shift, man. Let's talk about this at least."

Eric sighed but shook his head again.

"Uh-uh. I'm not letting you do this a second time. Are you going to make me go alpha on you?"

He couldn't answer, because he really didn't want to piss his friend—or alpha—off.

"Godsdammit," Tanner grumbled. "Eric, *shift*."

The alpha power went through him, and a few seconds later, Eric squatted opposite Tanner, looking at him in full color. "Did you have to do that?"

"Were you going to shift?" Tanner countered.

Eric kept his mouth shut.

"That's what I thought." Tanner shook his head. "I'm not letting you do this again. Especially not now."

"I can't, Tanner. I can't go through the pain again."

To Eric's surprise, Tanner nodded. "I get that." He sat back, leaning on one hand and tilting his head. "Have a seat. I didn't get a chance to tell you much about what happened with Finley and me, did I?"

Eric scowled. "What does that have to do with me?"

"Sit and I'll tell you."

"I'm not a dog," Eric grumbled, earning himself a snort from Tanner. But he sat, getting more comfortable.

"I didn't claim Finley for two years after we met. To a large degree, that was because of you."

Eric blinked at him, mouth dropping open. "Me? Because of me?"

Tanner nodded. "Finley was sixteen when we met. I had just finished college and was twenty-two. I will never, for as long as I live, forget the tormented look on your face before you shifted the second time and took off—right through my dad's screen door. The whole scene had been kind of surreal. The Steelers were scoring a touchdown, everyone in my dad's living room was completely stunned and silent, and you had just run off. I knew, without a doubt, I *knew* what had happened, even without you telling me."

"You knew it was Kim?"

"Yeah." Tanner sighed. "Unlike you, I had a feeling she wasn't coming back. But I honestly never imagined she'd break the bond. And when I saw she did—that she *could*—I knew I couldn't go through that. So, when I met Finley, I was scared to death of claiming him."

Eric blinked again, looking confused. "But… why?"

"I thought it was your age."

"My age?"

With a nod Tanner frowned. "I thought it was because you guys were too young, that Kim wanted to experience more and wasn't ready to be tied down."

"I don't know about that. I think part of it was just that I wasn't what she thought I was going to be."

"Oh, I know that's the case. My dad's talked to me quite a bit since about it, and I understand much more about what was going on. It was my mom, though, who really got through." He laughed. "I thought I'd stepped into *The Twilight Zone* or something. She dropped the C-word."

Eric's eyes widened. "Your mom cussed?"

"Yeah. I thought my dad was going to blow a gasket or something. Right there, at the dinner table. She called Kim a cunt."

"Whoa."

"You can say that again."

"Whoa."

Tanner laughed, punching Eric in the arm. "Asshole. But yeah, so… they finally got me to understand part of the problem was that you two were chosen. And part was…. Kim didn't love you. Not the way you needed her to, not the way the bond needed her to."

Eric frowned, dropping his gaze to the forest floor. "I didn't know mates could break a bond like that. I thought… I thought she had to come back, you know? That if nothing else, the bond would make her want to."

"It doesn't work that way."

"Obviously. She let someone else fuck her." Eric winced at the bitterness in his voice but couldn't pull it back.

"Yeah, she did. And that's on her. She had serious issues—probably still does. I don't know. I have no idea where she is."

Eric nodded. "So… you didn't claim Finley because of me?"

"Yeah, well, at first. He kind of gave me the ass-kicking I needed. He left me."

Eric's head snapped up. "He *what*?"

"He took a train out to Oregon and told me in no uncertain terms that if I didn't get my head out of my ass, he was going to find another mate."

"Holy shit."

"Yeah, you—never mind. Yeah, he did. And to make matters worse, he met someone out there. Another young, single gay guy."

"Oh hell." Eric stared, then shook his head. "Finley doesn't seem the type."

"Because he's not. He's an amazing man. He's loyal and caring and was more devoted to me than he should have been, truth be told." Tanner sighed. "He could have fucked the guy he met. He'd given me every indication that if I'd even *hinted* that I was coming to claim him, he'd have even met me halfway somewhere. But no, I was too stuck on the idea that he was too young to mate. I couldn't even get through my head the idea that all the things I kept telling myself he needed to experience… he wanted to do *with me*."

"Did he fuck the guy?"

Tanner smiled. "No. Not for lack of trying, but no. They kissed. That was it. He couldn't do it in the end. And, truthfully? I deserved that." He shrugged. "I called him, the morning after a full moon, not long after he'd gone out there. His new friend had answered his phone—apparently Finley had come back covered in mud and was showering. His friend—Jamie, by the way—told me Finley didn't have a mate and that *he* was Finley's boyfriend. I don't know what sound I made, but apparently Finley's wolf thought I was hurt and tried to run to me."

Eric blinked. "But… wasn't he in Oregon?"

"Yeah. His wolf tried to run to me in PA from Oregon."

"Whoa."

"No kidding, right? He got all the way into Idaho before I caught up to him. I flew out to Oregon the next morning and managed to run from his grandparents' place. I never want to do that again." Tanner shook his head, chuckling.

"Geez."

"In the end I figured out that Finley would never do to me what Kim had done to you. In part because we were destined. Diana doesn't fuck things up like that. She has a reason people are put together. Finley makes me a stronger person, gets me out of stuck thought processes… makes me a better alpha. If she gave you a destined mate, it's for a reason—not the least of which might just be she wants to see you happy. Also… how did I not know you were bi?"

Eric blushed, clearing his throat. He picked up a tiny stick and started playing with it. "A couple of reasons. Um… for one, my parents wouldn't have accepted it. They, uh, well, you were the alpha's son, so you were… if not okay, they couldn't say anything about it, right?"

Tanner nodded.

"Right. But their own son, I knew without asking that they'd never accept me."

"And the other reason?" Tanner prompted.

With a sigh Eric looked up at Tanner through his eyelashes. "I had a crush on you for the longest time."

Tanner stared, his mouth hanging open. "You did?" He blinked, still obviously in shock. "How did I not see that?"

"I did my damnedest to make sure you didn't. Even mating the alpha's son—not saying we would have, mind you—but even if I *had* managed to mate the alpha's son, it wouldn't have been enough for my parents. And I knew you didn't like me that way, so… I put it aside. And I did. I let that go a long time ago. But I thought if I'd told you I was bi, with my crush, things would have been awkward at best."

Tanner dropped his gaze. "I don't know if it would have. I did always think you were cute but knew you to be straight so never let it go any further. The thing is, though… I have to admit I'm glad I didn't know. I might have chosen you." He gave a crooked smile. "Which would have been *really* awkward when I met Finley."

"No shit."

"Yeah, so… anyway. I finally claimed Finley. It was what I needed to understand what he was trying to tell me all that time. And I'm glad I did."

"He does seem like a great guy." Eric paused, not sure what to do next, when something occurred to him. "What happened to the friend?"

"Jamie? Oh, he's my beta now."

Eric blinked. "He's… I don't think I can even figure that one out."

Tanner laughed. "It's another story for another day." He sobered. "You need to talk to him." Eric didn't even pretend not to know who Tanner was talking about. "His name is Ben, and he needs to understand what has happened to you. Be open and honest about your past. I made that mistake with Finley—I never told him my fears, just made excuses. Not talking really *does not work*. So… talk to him and tell him all about it. Just… let me make a suggestion. I won't make it an order, but consider it carefully, okay?"

Eric hesitated, sure he knew what Tanner was going to ask him to do, but nodded anyway. "Okay."

"Don't outright reject him. You don't have to accept him right away, but don't outright reject him."

Eric blew out a breath, looking around at the forest. He had no doubt now this was why Diana sent him back. He didn't know if he could give Ben what he needed, but at the same time, Eric didn't think he *could* outright reject Ben either.

Ben. His destined mate. His absolutely *gorgeous* destined mate. His gorgeous *male* destined mate.

"I won't. I… I don't know if I can accept him—or, if I can, when— but I won't reject him, either."

"Good boy."

Eric flipped him off, making Tanner laugh.

"All right. Let's go back. You owe your mate a conversation."

"Shit. I have a destined mate." Eric looked at Tanner, eyes wide as it hit him again.

Tanner grinned. "Yup. I think it's also about time you met some of our other friends. Come on."

A moment later Tanner stood in front of him, covered in auburn fur and managing to look like he was raising an eyebrow even in wolf form. With an eye roll, Eric shifted and followed him.

WHEN THEY got back to the house, Eric's heart pounded. He wasn't entirely sure he could do this, but he'd promised Tanner—his best friend, his *alpha*—that he'd at least talk to Ben. The memory of Kim breaking their bond poked him, but he could admit it wasn't *quite* as sharp as it'd been when he left earlier. Was that because of Ben?

The fear was still there, though. The idea of bonding like that to someone else, giving them the ability to hurt him so badly, made him more than a little scared. Terrified might be a better word. He didn't think he could recover from that a second time.

He shook the thoughts off as he shifted back to human form. That, at least, was getting easier the more he did it. He took the sweatpants Tanner handed him and pulled them on, glad his hands were working better. They were still clumsy; he was still dealing with some of that, more than forty-eight hours after becoming human again for the first time in so long.

"Hmm. Actually, you might want to get dressed before you talk to him," Tanner pointed out. "In more than sweatpants."

Eric blushed. "Uh, I kind of shredded the last set."

"Yeah, I saw the pile. I've still got plenty, so does Finley. I'll get you something. Hang on."

He disappeared up the stairs and returned a few moments later with a green T-shirt, flannel button-down, fresh socks, and another pair of jeans. "We need to get you out shopping for clothes. If for no other reason than so you stop going commando."

Eric laughed. "Thanks. Yeah, I guess so." He frowned. "I don't have any money, though."

"Yeah, you do. We'll talk about that later too. Now, you have a mate to talk to."

Eric ignored his pounding heart and concentrated on getting dressed again. Once he was more covered, he took a deep breath and went up the stairs. He stopped a few feet from the sofa his… mate… was sitting on.

Eric took a long inhale, focusing on his mate's scent this time. He had to use all his effort to keep from partially shifting, but he managed. Instead, he savored the smell—fresh pine mixed with something spicy.

Ben must have heard, because he lifted his head, then stood and turned toward Eric.

With a steadying breath, Eric gave a wobbly smile. "Uh, hi. I'm… I'm Eric, apparently your destined mate." He swallowed, then had to clear his throat. "Um… I think we need to talk."

Ben's Adam's apple bobbed as he swallowed, and there was nothing but pure fear in his gorgeous light brown eyes. "O-okay."

Eric stepped forward, holding out a hand, but not touching. He shoved it in his pocket to resist temptation, not sure he was ready for that yet. "I'm not rejecting you."

The relief in Ben's eyes would have been obvious to a blind man. "You're… not?"

Eric shook his head. "No, I'm not. I don't know how things will go and… I don't know when… or how long things might take, but I'm not going to reject you. You, uh, need to understand some things, though, okay?"

Ben nodded. "Yeah, okay."

"Want to get some coffee and sit on the deck?" Eric asked.

Ben swallowed again, then nodded one more time, a slight smile similar to Eric's touching his lips. "I'd like that."

Eric's smile steadied. "Okay."

"You guys go out. I'll bring out the coffee," Finley said, making shooing motions toward the dining room.

Eric threw a grateful smile at Finley and held his hand toward the door. Ben stepped forward and Eric followed him. He opened the french door leading to the deck for Ben, who gave him another small smile. "Oh, and Ben?"

Ben paused, raising an eyebrow.

"It's… really nice to meet you."

Ben's smile was downright blinding. And made Eric feel like about a million bucks.

Chapter 4

HE'S NOT rejecting me. He's not rejecting me. He's not rejecting me!

The words repeated in Ben's head as he stepped onto the deck and walked with Eric to the round glass-topped patio table in the center. Ben managed to look around a little, and his breath caught. "It's gorgeous out here," he whispered, pointing at the waterfall at the end of the little valley the house sat in.

"Yeah," Eric agreed, and Ben turned to look at Eric, but Eric's gaze wasn't on the waterfall. It was on Ben.

Ben blushed bright red. "Uh…."

"Sorry," Eric mumbled, his own cheeks coloring, and waved a hand at the table.

Ben took a seat, ignoring Eric's cheeks to give him a chance to recover a little. Happiness filled Ben when Eric sat next to him, rather than across from him. Ben felt calmer than he had since he'd stepped into Tanner and Finley's house. He wondered if it was simply being close to his mate that did it. He cursed himself for not asking Papá more about destined mates.

"So, uh—" Eric started, but paused when the door opened.

Finley came out, holding two cups of coffee, and set them on the table. "If you guys need anything, let me know. I'll be right inside—I promise not to eavesdrop." He grinned when they both chuckled, then gave them a wave before disappearing back into the house.

Eric blew out a breath. "Okay, so, uh… ten years ago, I had a chosen mate."

Ben winced before he could stop himself. His wolf growled inside him, but he managed to suppress that reaction. He swallowed instead and picked up his coffee, knowing his reaction was ridiculous. He hadn't even been old enough to mate ten years ago.

"I'm sorry. I never expected to even *have* a destined mate then."

Ben shook his head. "No, you do not need to apologize." He set the cup down and frowned. "It's certainly not fair of me to be upset by anything you did before you met me." He shrugged a shoulder. "I had a girlfriend through most of high school and college."

If Ben hadn't been watching Eric, he might have missed the tightening around Eric's lips. Then he gave a crooked smile. "My wolf didn't like hearing that."

Ben chuckled. "Yeah, I guess neither of them like hearing about our befores."

Eric's smile widened. "Guess not. Look, she is long gone, and I have zero interest in her—even without you in the picture. She…." His smile faded and he swallowed. "She cheated on me. Broke our bond and let someone else claim her."

"*Mierda*!" Ben stared at Eric with wide eyes. "*Esa cabrona*!" Despite the fact that she was his mate's former chosen mate, Ben found himself indignant on behalf of Eric.

Eric's lips twitched and he nodded. "I don't know exactly what that means, but I can guess. And… yeah, that about sums it up. I… I didn't take it well."

Ben blushed at the use of the Spanish. He still wasn't sure what Eric—and the rest—thought of that, but he had a hard time *not* slipping into Spanish when he got emotional. It seemed Eric let it pass, so he focused on just moving on with the conversation. "I cannot imagine anyone would. I did not think mates ever separated."

"I don't know about that. I'm sure it happens. I can't be the only one it's happened to." Eric shrugged a shoulder. "I'd guess it's pretty rare, though."

"Yeah," Ben whispered, staring down into his cup. "I'm sorry. That had to be horrible."

"It was," Eric said, nodding again. "I won't lie about that. I shifted on the spot, like, uncontrollably shifted. My wolf took over. It took my alpha to get me back to human form, but I couldn't stay human. I apologized to my best friend—Tanner—then went wolf." He took a deep breath and let it out. "I stayed wolf for nine years. I just came back yesterday."

Ben blinked at him, trying to absorb what he was hearing. "You were a wolf for nine years?"

Eric swallowed and looked up at him. "Yeah. I… I was prodded, I guess you could say, to come back. I think maybe because of you."

Ben wasn't sure how to take that. "I did not really expect to find my destined mate. I'd hoped, you know. I guess like everyone does. But… I did not really expect to. And even being bi, I did not *expect* my mate to be male." He shook his head. "My mamá is going to freak."

"She's not open about that?" Eric asked.

Ben shook his head. "No. But that is, at least in part, because my mamá is human, was raised Catholic."

Eric winced. "Ouch."

"Yeah. She, uh, she thinks my wolf is a demon."

"Eww." Eric wrinkled his nose. "That must have been a seriously shitty thing to live through."

Ben found himself laughing. "Yeah, well, that's one way of putting it."

"You have a beautiful smile," Eric blurted, then turned red.

But it just made Ben feel good, and his smile spread even wider. "Thank you. I'm glad my mate thinks so."

"That's still weird to hear… to think about. I have a destined mate." Eric shook his head, then sighed. "I have to be honest, Ben. I don't know what to do with it. The idea of a mate scares the ever-loving fuck out of me."

Ben's smile faded, and he reached out but stopped just shy of touching. Eric looked at Ben's hand, then took it with his own slightly shaky one. Despite the shake, a warmth, a sense of acceptance Ben had never felt before filled him.

"Oh wow," Eric murmured, and Ben looked up. "That… I've never felt anything like that before."

Ben raised his eyebrows. "No?"

Eric shook his head. "No. Chosen… she never felt like that."

"Is it terrible of me if I am glad?"

Yet again, Eric shook his head. "I don't think so. I can actually kind of understand. Did your g-girlfriend feel like that?"

"Oh hell no. But… I did not love her either. We were good friends. We had fun together and we *did* date, but I did not love her, not like I should have if I was going to mate her. I was sort of hoping to find my destined mate too, so it was another reason we did not mate."

"Is it terrible of me if I'm glad?" Eric asked.

Ben laughed at the echo of his own words. "No, I do not think so." He cleared his throat. "I cannot exactly understand. I have never been through what you've been through, but I can be patient, Eric. I have wanted my mate for so long, and I *will* wait. You are worth it."

"I hope you can. It could take a long time for me to get past some of this."

"I'm sure it will. But I will help you if I can."

Eric considered him for a long moment. "I think it might. What has you scared?"

Ben blinked. "You can feel that?"

Eric nodded. "Yeah. The first connection—you felt it, didn't you?"

"I thought maybe I was imagining it."

"From what I understand—what Tanner has told me and what our pack elders taught us—when we meet, the first portion of the bond is formed. I can feel strong emotions from you, and you can feel mine. Only the strong ones, though. Until we bond more. Which tells me your fear is pretty bad."

Ben let that comment pass. "I wish I'd asked my papá more about destined mates. We did not… um, we did not spend a lot of time with the pack."

Eric raised an eyebrow. "Why not?"

"My alpha was a good Texas boy, and my papá and I are Mexican—both he and my mamá were born in Mexico and came over the border later on. There is still a lot of prejudice against Mexicans there, at least there was in my area—and with my alpha."

"Former alpha. Tanner won't do that." Eric squeezed Ben's hand gently. "And neither will I."

Ben swallowed. "I'm… really glad to hear that." He took a breath. "It was something I… w-worried about."

"I can understand why, but I don't see anyone in this pack having a problem with it. Tanner's father didn't put up with that kind of bigotry, and I don't see Tanner putting up with it either."

Ben fell silent for a long moment, contemplating that and savoring the feel of touching his mate. "I really hope so."

Eric squeezed his hand again, then let go and sighed. "So… it's not just my former mate," he said, frowning. When Ben looked up, raising his eyebrows, Eric clarified. "The things I have to work through…."

"Oh?"

Eric frowned. "I've… I've forgotten what it's like to be human."

"You seem pretty human to me," Ben said, confused.

Eric chuckled. "I'm glad you think so." He turned serious again and reached out toward his coffee cup. His fingers seemed stiff, like they didn't want to curl at first. Eric stopped moving, then very slowly wrapped one hand around the main part of the mug and carefully curled two fingers around the handle. "Yeah… I'm still having trouble holding things—coffee mugs, eating utensils." He blushed, and Ben laid a hand on his arm, squeezing. The blush faded a little. "Everything seems ridiculously loud and smelly. Even touch is weird still—you seem to be the only thing that *doesn't* bother me. Clothes irritate me. Food even tastes very strong. I don't… I have no idea how to filter things like I once did. I have no idea how I'll react to being around people—especially humans. I don't have a job, not that I think I could handle it yet. Don't even have a place to live yet."

"I can help you with some of that, maybe. I mean… mates can help calm and soothe, right?"

Eric frowned but nodded, letting go of the cup and taking Ben's hand again. "I guess? She didn't, but maybe that was a chosen versus destined thing. Or maybe that was just her. I don't know. But… I just…. It's not very fair to you to have a mate who can't even do basic things." He looked away and started to pull his hand out of Ben's, but Ben tightened his a little, hoping Eric would take it for the comfort he meant it to be. He didn't want to let go.

Eric stopped trying to pull his hand out and looked up at Ben again, who shrugged, then said, "I don't care. Isn't part of being mated accepting the problems your mate has?"

Eric swallowed. "Yeah…. You don't have them, though."

"I have plenty of my own fears, as you can feel. I heard what you said about prejudice, but it is not easy to set it aside. For one thing I have a tendency to slip into Spanish when I am stressed." He smiled ruefully. "As you heard before. How well will the locals take that? My mamá did not accept my wolf. I still worry I will not control him well after all these years trying to ignore him. And *I* still do not have a place to live either. Though I do plan to do something about that."

"I have a suggestion," Finley said, stepping through the door.

Eric looked up, raising his eyebrows. "Eavesdropping?"

Finley snorted. "Hardly. I can filter better than you, but I still hear."

Ben blushed, thinking about the thinly veiled accusations he'd made.

Finley crossed the deck and put a hand on Ben's shoulder. "It's okay," he said, almost as if he'd read Ben's mind. "Tanner isn't going to allow people in the pack, at least, to give you shit for where you—or your family—are from. As for where to live… I think you should both stay here."

Eric raised an eyebrow. "I'm not going to leech off you and Tanner."

Finley snickered. "Who said anything about leeching? You can pay rent."

Eric scowled. "That's not funny."

"It's not meant to be." Finley shook his head. "Tanner will talk to you about it. But putting that aside for the moment... you two should be physically close. If you don't claim and you're not bonding and sleeping together, then you should at least be in the same house."

Eric's scowl faded. "Tanner told me what happened. I'm sorry."

Finley waved that away, glancing at Ben. "Nothing for you to be sorry for. That mess was on Tanner and me. But... yeah. Um, you can tell Ben about us, if you like. But... I know what it's like to be apart from a destined mate. It sucks," he said succinctly. "And I have no wish to see anyone go through what we did."

Eric tightened his hand around Ben's and met Ben's gaze. "I don't know how long it might take for me to be comfortable with the idea of a mate again. It could be a really long time. Maybe... maybe he's got a point."

Ben frowned and looked up at Finley. "Will you allow me to pay you for the room?"

Finley rolled his eyes. "Stubborn men," he grumbled, but sighed. "Yes, if you must."

Eric and Ben exchanged looks, both smiling. Eric raised his eyebrows, and after a brief hesitation—how hard was it going to be to be so close but not bond? How much harder would it be to be physically apart?—Ben took a breath and nodded. Eric looked up at Finley. "I think we'll stay."

"Good! Now. Tanner wants you to meet a few people. He's called them and they should be here in a little while."

BEN FINISHED his coffee quickly, and they went inside and left their cups in the sink. He found Finley at the dining room table in front of an open laptop. "If you would tell me which room I should take, I can get some things from my car and be out of the way of your company."

Finley scrunched his eyebrows. "Why ever would you do that? I mean, if you want to unload, that's cool, but you should be meeting them too."

Ben blinked. "I should? But I'm—"

"A member of the pack and Eric's mate. Both good reasons to meet them. Besides, one of the guys coming is Tanner's beta, who you really *should* meet."

"Oh, I… okay, um…."

"Why don't you talk to Eric about the rooms? He is on the first floor here, but we've only got one bedroom on this floor. He hasn't really settled in yet, though. Maybe you two would like the other bedrooms upstairs? Tanner and I can be quiet or wait until you're not around to have sex."

Ben turned bright red, and Finley laughed. "Uh…."

"Sorry, I'm teasing. Seriously, though, I know how sensitive hearing is. We can be courteous."

"It's okay. I do not want to cause problems for you and your mate."

Finley waved that away. "Really. Don't worry about it. We're happy to have you. This place gets lonely with just the two of us. We had a couple of other guys here for a while—Tanner's beta and his mate—but they went back to their own place, so it's been too quiet." He leaned to the side, looking around Ben. "Hey, Eric!"

Eric came over from talking to Tanner and stopped next to Ben. "What's up?"

"I know we gave you the first-floor bedroom, but what about taking the other one upstairs, so Ben is close?"

Eric looked thoughtful, then shrugged. "That would probably be better, I think. I mean, being close to me should help at least until he gets used to you guys. You're not going to fuck where we can hear you, are you?"

Finley threw back his head and laughed. Despite being somewhat embarrassed, Ben found himself smiling too. "I thought we'd fuck in front of you instead. Just make it as bad as possible."

Eric rolled his eyes. "You're hilarious. How does Tanner put up with you?"

"He keeps me sane," Tanner said, joining them. "And seriously, dude, I have *no* wish to be near you when I'm fucking my mate."

Eric flipped him off, and Ben watched the whole thing in bemusement. "We're freaking out my mate." Eric shook his head, glancing at Ben. "Sorry, that word's going to mess with me for a while."

Ben held up a hand. "It's okay. You can just call me Ben if it will make things easier."

"I think using the word would actually help," Finley offered.

Eric tilted his head. "He's got a point. I need to get used to it. Mate." He turned to Tanner. "You can be a real ass sometimes."

"Only around you."

Finley snorted at this. Tanner turned and raised an eyebrow at him. Finley looked uncomfortable for a moment, then rolled his eyes. "Anyway…. There are two other bedrooms besides ours upstairs. You guys can pick which ones you want. They share a bathroom, but there's another, separate bathroom in the hallway too."

"Thank you," Ben said, glancing at Eric. "I will take whichever one you do not want."

Eric shrugged. "I don't care either. Let's go take a look. We can leave them to their childish ways."

"I'm not childish. And don't forget, I'm your alpha."

Eric snorted as he walked away.

Tanner rolled his eyes. "He's like a pup all over again."

"I heard that!" Eric said from the stairs.

Ben couldn't resist chuckling as he followed his mate.

"You were supposed to!" Tanner called.

THE TWO bedrooms were pretty similar in size and makeup. They both had fireplaces, double beds and other simple furnishings, and decent closets. Eric took the one closer to Tanner and Finley's room. "I figure if they *do* start something, I won't care as much." He considered Ben for a long moment, and Ben was sure he didn't want to hear what was coming. "I should tell you… I've been in the closet my entire life. I never told anyone—including Tanner—that I was bi. He knows now, of course, but he didn't before. My parents wouldn't have accepted it. And I didn't tell Tanner… because I once had a crush on him."

Ben swallowed the growl that wanted to come out and resisted the urge to tell Eric they could get their own place… on the other side of the state. Instead, he took a breath and said, "Had?"

Eric nodded. "Had. A long time ago. I got over it back before things with Kim, even. I figured you should hear about it from me, rather than risk it coming out in jokes with Tanner. I don't want you to think I'm keeping anything from you. I've never believed in that. I think it only leads to a lot of shit."

"Yeah. Mamá used to hold on to everything, then sort of… blow up at us… when it got to be too much. I always wished she'd just tell us when she was mad and what about."

"Yeah, see? Just causes messes. Tanner and Finley didn't talk about everything for a long time and that caused all *sorts* of problems." Eric shook his head. "Anyway. I don't mind having to be a little closer to them. Besides, this one has a balcony. If I start feeling closed in…."

"You can get air. Uh… let me know if I can do anything, though, for you?"

Eric smiled. "I'll try. It's still weird to know I… that someone's… there for me, you know?"

"It's okay. You were alone a long time."

Eric nodded, then froze, tilted his head, and scrunched up his eyebrows. "I guess the people Tanner called are here."

Ben raised his eyebrows. "They are?" He closed his eyes to listen, and if he focused, he could hear a car approaching, but it was still a distance away. He opened his eyes again. "You heard that?"

Eric frowned. "Yeah. Filters still suck, probably will for a while yet." He sighed. "Let's go meet people." He wrinkled his nose as he turned toward the stairs, and Ben laughed.

"I'll be there, for what it's worth."

Eric paused at the top step and turned toward him, looking at him for a long moment. "It's worth quite a bit."

Ben felt ridiculously good at that little line as he followed Eric down the stairs.

Chapter 5

"YOUR COMPANY is here," Eric said as he joined Tanner and Finley in the living room.

Tanner raised an eyebrow. "I don't hear them."

"They are. Or, will be in a minute," Ben said, stepping up next to Eric. "They're on the road." He tilted his head toward Eric. "His filters still are not working well yet."

Tanner winced, but before he could say anything, two cars approached and shut their engines off. "And there they'd be."

Finley went out to the front door and, a moment later, led four men into the living area. Eric tried not to tense, but either he failed or Ben picked up on his nervousness through their link, because he moved a bit closer. That thought still freaked Eric out more than a little. He couldn't help but wonder how much they were bonded already. If Ben left now, would it hurt like it had when Kim broke their bond?

Despite the not-so-minor freak-out, he found himself glad Ben was there. Despite his fears of Ben leaving, the calm from his mate helped as Eric was faced with four men he didn't know. Other *people*. He'd been away from them so long, including shifters, he was afraid he was going to do something completely stupid, even though they were all… wolves? Except they weren't. Eric blinked at them, especially the one with black hair.

"I know what you're thinking," Tanner said, turning to Eric. "Give me a moment and we'll explain everything."

Eric blinked at him. "Um… okay."

The guy with the black hair gave him a small smile. Eric tried not to sniff—he really did—but couldn't seem to stop himself. The guy smelled *really weird*. Not human, but not wolf. Eric tilted his head unconsciously as he tried to figure it out.

"Gods, you're all alike like that," the black-haired guy said, chuckling.

Another of the guys sighed. "Really, Q. Give him a break."

"You're one to talk. You're the worst of them."

The other guy flipped Q off.

"All right, all right. As you've guessed, this is Eric. The other guy is Ben—" Tanner turned to Ben. "How do you pronounce your last name again?"

Ben blushed but cleared his throat. "Arellano."

Eric scowled, not liking the nervousness he could feel from Ben. "It's not that hard to pronounce. Ah-day-yah-noh."

Tanner smirked at him. "I didn't know you were so good with languages."

Eric rolled his eyes and muttered "asshole" under his breath.

"It's okay, Eric," Ben murmured.

Eric turned to him. "No, it's not." He didn't even think about it as he reached out and took Ben's hand to squeeze it in comfort. Eric turned back to the others. "Ben's family is from Mexico and he grew up in Texas, where they faced a lot of prejudice—even from their alpha."

Tanner winced. "Sorry, man. Didn't mean to make you uncomfortable."

Ben shook his head. "Really, it's okay."

Eric considered him, but the jumble of emotions that had been so strong a moment before eased. He nodded and turned back. "He's my mate," he said, swallowing but relaxing a bit when he was greeted with nothing but smiles.

"Let's get the rest of the introductions out of the way, and then we can talk more," Tanner said. He pointed to the blond guy on the far left. "That's Jamie Sutton, my beta and Fin's best friend."

Finley and Jamie both grinned.

Eric raised his eyebrows. "Wait, Jamie, the friend—?"

"Yes, the one who almost won me over Tanner." Finley's grin widened, and Jamie laughed.

"Hardly. I didn't stand a chance," Jamie said, shaking his head. "Besides, it worked out. I have my own destined mate, which is *way* better than chosen."

Eric wondered if Tanner had told them about him, then figured he probably had. He shook the thought off.

"Definitely," Tanner said, and Eric *knew* that was deliberate. "That's his mate and husband, Chad Sutton," Tanner said, pointing next at the guy who'd spoken to Q earlier.

"Wait, husband? You can get married now?"

"Oh yeah, I guess you didn't know about that. Marriage equality went through earlier this year. Supreme court voted in favor in… June, I think." Tanner grinned. "Finley and I are married, in fact."

Eric blinked. "Shit. I've missed so much," he mumbled. Ben squeezed his hand, and Eric took a deep breath, then let it out.

"Anyway, next to Chad is Miles Grant, the pack doctor, and next to him is Quincy Archer, our newest pack member. And… a jaguar shifter."

Eric's eyes widened. "That's why you smell different." Eric's cheeks colored as he realized he'd said that out loud.

Quincy just laughed, though, and waved it away. "It's okay. I still get that quite a bit."

"I didn't even know they existed," Eric said, shaking his head.

"Neither did I," Ben said, and Eric glanced over to see him staring. He looked at Eric and blushed. Eric squeezed his hand again.

"It's okay, really. I know I'm unusual. There aren't many of us left."

"Sorry. Uh… why?"

"We nearly wiped them out. More than once," Miles said, scowling, but at an elbow poke from Quincy, the scowl faded. "It's nice to meet you both. How are you feeling, Eric? Anything causing problems?"

"Only everything," Eric said, sighing. "But I'm okay."

"Everything?" Miles asked.

"Don't get him started if you don't want him poking at you," Chad said, and Miles snorted.

Eric turned to Chad. "You have problems lately?"

"Um… that's another thing you don't know," Tanner said. "Chad… used to be human. He's a newly made wolf."

Eric swung around to stare at Tanner. "Newly made? You can *make* wolves?"

"You can?" Ben asked, and Eric looked back at his mate to see wide eyes.

"Yeah, uh, how about we all take a seat and we can talk more?" Finley asked.

As they moved over to the couches, Jamie approached Ben, holding his hand out. "It's good to meet you, Ben."

Eric's wolf did *not* like the man so close to their mate. Apparently his wolf wasn't nearly as bogged down by fear as he was, because before he could stop himself, he was growling. He slapped a hand over his mouth when he realized it, and Jamie stepped back quickly.

"Oops."

Eric closed his eyes and turned around, wishing he could slide through the floor. "Ugh," he muttered, shaking his head. "I'm sorry."

"Hey. It's okay, *cariño*," Ben murmured, putting a hand on Eric's shoulder.

Eric opened his eyes and looked at Ben.

"Really." Ben's gaze bounced behind Eric, then back. "I'm sure he understands."

"I totally do," Jamie said.

"I'm being ridiculous. I mean, we just met. And… I'm resisting us, and that's totally not fair." Eric frowned. "But… he doesn't like other guys near you."

Ben actually smiled. "I really do not mind that. In fact, cariño, it makes me feel good to know he wants me."

"Oh, he does…. Wait, cariño?"

Ben blushed. "Sorry, uh, habit. It's a term of endearment where I'm from in—"

"I like it," Eric said softly.

The hopeful look in Ben's eyes made Eric ache for him. "Really? Even though it's Spanish?"

Eric nodded. "Yeah, really. Maybe especially. It's beautiful. What… what does it mean?"

"Um… loosely, it means something like "my darling," but I promise, down there it's not so lame."

Eric found himself chuckling. "It doesn't sound lame." On impulse he pulled Ben against him and hugged him.

Ben wrapped his arms around Eric, and he let out a breath.

"Oh, this feels good," Eric murmured, eyes closing. "Please, call me that?" He got hit with a blast of happiness he couldn't resist savoring.

"I would like that."

Tanner cleared his throat, and Eric reluctantly let Ben go to turn back around. "Sorry. Uh… can't seem to help it."

All six of them were grinning. Chad put his hands up. "We *totally* get it. I was *horrible* about it when Jamie and I first got together. Well, after he turned human again, anyway."

Eric raised an eyebrow at Jamie, who laughed.

"Yeah, we met when I was stuck in wolf form. In the city—Oakland."

"Oh shit, that must have been…." Eric shook his head.

"Frustrating, but… funny in a way." Jamie nodded.

"Should have seen my face when he shifted in front of me the first time. I had *no* idea shifters even existed."

"I bet that was hilarious."

"Confusing, but… yes, very," Chad said. "I had no idea what to do with it."

"Should have seen me when I reacted to him the first time," Miles said, tilting his head at Quincy.

"Yeah, he ran away," Quincy said, smirking.

Miles scowled without heat. "I didn't run away…."

Quincy simply stared at him, lips twitching.

Miles rolled his eyes. "Okay, I ran away. But really, my world had just turned upside down."

Eric found himself smiling. "You guys are funny."

"Glad you think so," Tanner said, finally herding them all to seats.

Ben sat close to Eric, who put his arm around Ben's shoulders. Ben looked a little surprised, but smiled and settled against Eric's side.

"Is this okay?" Eric murmured.

"Very much so, cariño." Ben smiled.

"So," Jamie said, drawing their attention. "I hope we'll all be friends."

"I don't have many anymore. I kind of alienated most of mine when I took off." Eric frowned.

Ben put a hand on his knee and squeezed. "And I've only met a few people here."

"Most of the guys worried about you," Tanner said. "Jake is up in Erie with his mate, so we can see him sometime. He'll be glad to hear you're okay. The others only left because they found jobs other places. I'm sure they'd want to know what's up too."

Eric frowned. "You think so?"

"Oh yeah. They were just worried… and pissed for you." Tanner grinned. "Should have heard the language. Damned near sent my dad into a serious fit."

"Oh shit!" Eric said, eyes widening. "I, uh, need to call your dad."

Tanner blinked. "What?"

"I need to call him."

Tanner raised an eyebrow but pulled out his phone. The rest of the guys seemed as perplexed, but no one said anything. Tanner swiped his finger over the front of his phone, and a moment later, put it to his ear.

The room sat in silence as they waited. Eric's heart pounded hard. Finally Tanner spoke. "Hey, Dad. How's everything?"

"Busy," Alpha Noah said through the phone.

Tanner chuckled. "Is it ever not?"

Alpha Noah snorted. "No. Not here, anyway. What's going on?"

"Uh, well, I have some news. Eric is back."

"Is he?" Alpha Noah asked, sounding pleased and easing Eric a little.

"Yes. He just came back yesterday. He's staying with us for now. Him and his destined mate."

"Oh, that's good to hear. Who's his mate?"

"The accountant from Texas." Tanner chuckled.

Alpha Noah laughed. "Well, then. Somehow I don't think that was coincidence."

"Me either. Anyway, Eric wanted me to call you. Said he needed to talk to you," Tanner said.

"Well, give him the phone," Alpha Noah said.

Tanner handed the phone out to Eric, whose heart went into triple time. Ben's hand tightened on Eric's knee, and Eric calmed down just a little.

He took the phone, drew a deep breath, and glanced at Ben as he spoke. "Uh, hello, sir."

"Just call me Alpha as always, Eric. How are you?"

"I am so, so, *so* sorry," Eric blurted.

Alpha Noah hesitated for a moment. "Uh… whatever for?"

"Your screen door."

Tanner blinked at him, and there was silence on the phone for a few seconds, and then both Tanner and his dad started laughing.

"That's what's got you worried?" Alpha Noah asked.

"Uh… I tore right through it. I didn't mean to. I'm so sorry I did."

"Calm down, son. It's all right. I needed to replace it anyway."

"You did?" Eric asked, blinking.

"Yeah. Carol had been on me for almost a decade to replace that thing. I'd repaired the screen more times than I could count. It's all right, really."

Eric's heart slowed finally. "Oh. Uh, okay, then. Sorry to bother you."

"I'm glad you had Tanner call. It's good to hear you're back, son. Are you going to work in the shop again?"

Eric hesitated. "I don't know yet? I... I haven't had opposable thumbs in too long...."

Alpha Noah laughed, and most of the guys in the living room chuckled, making Eric smile. "Well, yeah, that could cause problems. Kind of hard to use tools if you can't use your thumb too well. I do hope you'll think about it, though. We missed having you there."

"I will, Alpha." Eric took a breath. "Thank you."

"You're welcome, son. Take care. Tanner, I'll talk to you later."

"Bye, Dad!"

Eric pulled the phone away from his ear and, when he saw Call Ended on the screen, handed it back to Tanner. "Well."

"Yes, well. So.... Q, think you could show him your cat?" Tanner asked.

Quincy nodded, kissed Miles on the cheek, then stood and kicked his shoes off. When he pulled his shirt off, Eric got hit with a blast of jealousy and glanced at Ben. "Not interested, baby," he whispered.

Ben blushed. "I cannot seem to help it."

"I know. It's okay." Eric took a chance and kissed Ben on the cheek.

Ben's eyes widened, but he smiled at the same time.

The sound of a throat clearing caught his attention, and Eric looked back at Quincy in just enough time to catch the human form turn into a huge black cat. A long tail twitched as Quincy moved around the coffee table and approached them.

"Wow," Ben muttered.

"Seriously," Eric said, shaking his head. He glanced up at Miles. "May I touch your mate?"

Miles hesitated briefly, then grinned. "He says *he* doesn't mind, and if I do, I can sleep on the couch."

Eric and Ben both laughed. Eric turned to Ben. "Are you okay if I do?"

Ben's smile bloomed brightly. "Thank you for asking, but yes. Will you be okay?"

Eric nodded, and they both reached out together to touch Quincy's head. "Wow, soft," Eric murmured.

"Yeah, no one seems to expect that," Miles said, shrugging. "Not sure why, except I guess they figure jaguar fur is usually coarse."

"Is their fur the same as their hair, like us?" Ben asked.

Miles shook his head. "No. They come in two flavors: black and spotted."

Quincy's tail twitched, and Miles snorted.

"He says I'm not supposed to refer to him as a flavor, but—"

"I do *not* want to hear where you were going with that," Chad said, holding a hand up.

Miles laughed. "Anyway, there's an in-between too, where the spots are a little more visible under the black, but they're not common. The *most* common is the spotted. Quincy's black is a genetic thing."

"Huh. That's... cool." Eric turned back to Quincy. "Thank you."

Quincy dipped his head, twitched his tail, then went back to where he'd left his clothes.

In deference to Ben, Eric looked away, to Chad. "So... you were human?"

Chad nodded. "Yeah. Used to be. Up until about five months ago. Hurt like hell to change," he said, shaking his head. "But... so totally worth it." He nodded, completely serious, and said, "I can lick my own balls now."

Eric snorted, and Ben started laughing. "Not all it's cracked up to be, is it?"

Chad grinned and shook his head. "Nah. Still better if he does it," he said, tilting his head toward Jamie.

Jamie rolled his eyes and elbowed Chad. "They do not need to hear about that."

"So, these are the crazies we call friends," Tanner said, earning himself not one but *four* separate middle fingers. Eric and Ben both laughed at this. "And... I'm thinking that's probably as much as we should subject Eric to for now."

Eric scowled. "I'm not some invalid."

Tanner raised an eyebrow. "Are you going to tell me you want to hang around people a lot yet?"

The scowl deepened because Eric couldn't really argue. He sighed, sending an apologetic look around the room.

Before he could speak, though, Ben spoke up. "He has not been around many people yet. Me, Tanner, and Finley, and that's all."

Miles and Chad both winced. "Totally get that, then," Chad said. "I was kind of freaked out by humans for a while. Weird, right, 'cause I was human?"

Eric frowned but nodded.

"But the problem was, my wolf was *really* close to the surface for a long time. I'm guessing yours is?"

"Yeah. He's not too sure about this human-form thing yet."

Chad laughed. "Exactly. We also have a tendency to sniff at people…. It takes a while to learn how to appear normal. I totally get it, even if they don't."

"No, it makes sense," Quincy said, nodding. "Jaguars are solitary—sometimes too solitary—but I get not necessarily wanting to be around people."

"And I saw enough of Chad's problems. So… we'll take off." Jamie smiled.

"Actually…," Miles said, standing. "Can I look you over quickly?"

Eric scrunched his eyebrows. "Okay?"

"We're not meant to be in wolf form for so long," Miles explained. "I just want to make sure you're okay."

"Oh." Eric glanced at Ben, who nodded.

"I think it's a good idea, cariño."

Eric nodded, then turned to Jamie, hoping he was as devout as Tanner said he was, as should be of their religious leader. "Okay. Um… Jamie, can I talk to you when we're done?" He tried not to wince at the jealousy from Ben, but he didn't think he managed when his mate gave a muttered sorry. He leaned in and kissed Ben's temple. "I'd like it if you were there."

Ben looked up, cheeks red. "It's okay. I—"

"No, I mean it. Please?"

Ben considered him for a moment, then nodded. "Okay."

"Good."

ERIC KEPT Ben with him during the exam as well. He'd figured it'd be a better idea if he was getting naked around another shifter—even a doctor. The expression on Ben's face told him he'd made the right choice.

"You'll need to be sure to eat things besides meat," Miles said as he tucked his stethoscope into his bag.

"Uh… okay?" Eric squinched his eyes up at Miles.

"As wolves, we're carnivores, so the meat we eat as wolves is enough. However, humans are omnivores, and we need vitamins and minerals we can't get from meat. Now, yeah, you heal. But it'd be better for your system in general if you remember to eat like an omnivore while you're in human form. You can actually end up feeling really run-down."

"Oh, huh." Eric shook his head. "I'd have never thought of that."

"Which is why I said something."

Eric wrinkled his nose. "Vegetables are not my favorite thing."

"You can make sure he eats his broccoli." Miles smirked at Ben.

Ben grinned. "I can get a few vegetables into him."

"Some mate you are." Eric scowled up at Ben.

Ben's grin just widened. "Yeah, one that cares for you."

Eric rolled his eyes, but it felt good nonetheless. He tried not to let the thought intrude that it wouldn't feel good if Ben left, but the whole idea was still too close to the surface. Annoyed with his thoughts, he looked back at Miles. "I'll eat them," he grumbled, but his lips twitched, making Miles laugh.

"If you have any problems with anything, let me know. If there's any way I can help, I will."

"I will. Thank you."

Miles patted him on the shoulder. "Happy to do it. Take care."

"Vegetables." Eric sighed and glanced over at Ben, wrinkling his nose again.

Ben laughed. "You are like a pup."

Eric rolled his eyes. "Come on. Let's go talk to the beta."

THEY TOOK the table out on the deck, all three with fresh cups of coffee.

"So… first… I mentioned this to Tanner and he told me he knew what you'd say, but I am going to say it anyway." Jamie cleared his throat. "You weren't here when he chose me as his beta. I know you were best friends—"

Eric held his hand up. "I'm in absolutely zero position to watch anyone's back right now. Besides, he chose you for a reason. He trusts you and believes you're right for it. I would have taken it, way back when, if I'd never disappeared like I had. But I'm not the same guy I was then. So… no, I think you ought to keep it."

Jamie blew out a breath. "He said you'd say something like that."

Eric flashed a grin. "Yeah, we were best friends most of our lives. He knows me pretty well."

"We're still best friends. But I'm glad I still know you," Tanner said, coming out onto the deck. "You up for them sticking around for dinner?"

Eric glanced at Ben, who shrugged.

"Fine with me, cariño. Only if you're okay with them."

After kissing Ben on the temple, Eric turned back to Tanner. "That's fine. Don't let Miles tell you I need broccoli, though." He scowled without heat.

Tanner laughed. "Fin's already got plans. No worries." He waved and went back into the house.

Eric turned to Jamie again. "Anyway…."

Jamie grinned. "I'm not big on veggies either. When I was stuck in wolf form, Chad offered me his salad as a joke and I refused to eat it."

Eric laughed. "No kidding."

"I do eat vegetables, but they are usually cooked a certain way," Ben said. "And almost always with a sauce of some sort."

Eric glanced at his mate. "Mexican food?"

Ben nodded. "Yes. I'll make some for you. You can get the veggies Miles wants without them being horrible."

With another laugh Eric nodded. "All right. So…." He took a breath, then looked at Jamie. Ben slipped his hand into Eric's, and Eric felt a little better. "I think… I think I met Diana."

Jamie blinked at him. "You… our goddess?"

Eric nodded. "Yeah." He described the woman in the forest and recounted to the best he could remember what she'd said to him and even the prodding when he'd gotten to the house but couldn't seem to get down the last hill yet. When he finished, Jamie's eyes were huge.

"I am *so* jealous!" he said, shaking his head.

Eric laughed. "I'm not entirely sure it was her—"

"Oh yeah, that was her. I wish I could meet her." Jamie sighed. "She did help me, when Chad was being changed. I had a few really scary moments, but I could have sworn I *felt* her making me feel better, if you know what I mean."

"Yeah, I do." Eric glanced up. "You don't think I'm nuts?"

Jamie shook his head. "No. I think it's what you needed. I'm glad for you, that you had that help."

Eric swallowed. "I was wondering if I was just… imagining things or something."

"I really don't think so." Jamie reached out and touched Eric's arm gently, shooting a glance at Ben, who nodded. "You'd been gone so long. I bet you probably would never have come back without help. He—" Jamie nodded toward Ben. "—needs you."

Eric glanced at Ben. "I'm… well, truth be told, I'm still scared to death of having a mate."

"I'd think you were nuts if you weren't," Jamie said.

"Oh?" Eric raised his eyebrows.

"After what you went through… anyone who dealt with that would be afraid. You trust Diana and that will help. You trust your wolf and *that* will help. But it's going to take time and faith."

Ben squirmed at that, and Eric looked at him. "What's wrong?"

"I… faith is hard for me." Ben frowned, but Jamie nodded encouragement. "Uh, my mamá is Catholic and tried to raise me Catholic. I do not believe in that, but with all of that there, it was hard to accept the gods my papá followed too."

"It would be," Jamie agreed, turning back to Eric. "All the more reason to keep yours. He will need your faith too. Just remember what a lucky bastard you are that Diana visited *you*."

Eric laughed. "Yeah, okay. Thanks. I feel a little less crazy."

Jamie shrugged a shoulder. "It's what I'm here for. Well, the faith part, at least. I'm afraid we're all a little crazy…."

Chapter 6

BEN HAD enjoyed meeting the jaguar, the former human, and their mates a lot more than he'd expected to. He was grateful to find none of them had seemed even remotely put off by his accent or background.

He was going to have to get over that. Hopefully he'd be able to once he'd met more of the pack, though that carried its own terror. He was comfortable enough with Tanner to know his new alpha didn't put up with bigotry. But there was only so much an alpha could really do. He'd just have to wait and see and face it when the time came, which was hopefully not until the full moon, some three weeks away.

It'd also helped Ben to see all of the alpha's friends were men with male mates. He'd never have imagined there were that many same-sex destined mates in the world. Then again, he'd never known jaguar shifters existed, and the idea of changing a human to a wolf was just as foreign. He *had* known human destined mates existed—his own parents were proof of that—but the idea of them being same-sex and the changing were altogether different and something he'd have to talk to his papá about.

In the meantime he had work to do with his mate and to simply get settled. Eric would take a lot of care and patience until he was ready to even think about bonding, much less claiming. Not that Ben blamed him. The things Eric had been through… well, Ben didn't know if he could be as together as Eric was after all that—even after spending so much time as a wolf.

Eric had offered to help him carry his things in from the car. Ben had hesitated initially, but it hadn't taken him long to figure out Eric needed to feel useful for something, so Ben had taken him up on it. He'd set Eric to bringing in the boxes and figuring out where to stack them in the limited space he had. He'd been expecting to find an apartment when he got to Pittsburgh, not a room in a house, so he wasn't sure where he was going to put everything. The CR-V held more than he'd realized.

He had handled some of the other things, like his backpack with his computer, his guitar case, and so on.

"Oh, do you play?" Eric asked, setting a box down.

Ben looked up at him, then back at his guitar. "Not in a while. My mamá liked music, but she was so insistent I focus on school and learning that I could not spend as much time with it as I wanted to. It got to be such a fight that I had just set it aside, but I could not leave it behind completely."

"I can understand, at least to a point. I'm sorry to hear how your mom was, though. Not cool."

Ben shrugged a shoulder. "I'll get back to it eventually, though I once thought it was what I'd do—play the guitar, rather than with numbers."

Eric laughed. "Playing with numbers is important. And it's what brought you here."

Ben considered him for a moment before nodding. "That is very true, cariño."

"Which, despite my hesitation, I'm very glad for," Eric whispered before disappearing out of the room.

With a huge grin, Ben set his guitar carefully in the corner, then went on the hunt for power outlets while Eric carried the last of the boxes in. He was happy to find an outlet behind the bedside table. Just as he did, his phone beeped at him, reminding him it hadn't been plugged in for a while. "Cariño, could you get the phone charger out of my backpack there?" Ben asked, pointing at the bag he'd left on the desk.

"Sure." Eric picked up the backpack but had trouble getting it open. At first he couldn't grasp the pull, and then he seemed to get ahold of the pull but couldn't get it to move.

Ben had to struggle to keep from laughing, until frustration hit him that wasn't his own. If it was coming across their fledgling bond, it was *bad*. Ben was annoyed with himself for not thinking about the trouble his mate would have with it. He hurried over to Eric. "I am sorry, cariño. I wasn't thinking."

"I can open a damned bag," Eric grumbled. "I feel like a fucking invalid. Or a brand-new pup. Or something." He struggled with it another moment, then *finally* had it opened. With a sigh he handed the cable over. "Sorry." His cheeks were red, and he wouldn't look directly at Ben.

"No, the fault is mine. I know you're having trouble. I am sorry for—"

"No. Really."

Ben swallowed but nodded, understanding Eric needed to let it go. He dropped his gaze, but then he realized Eric was wearing jeans. "Uh, if

you are still having trouble with zippers, how did you close your jeans?"
The question was out before he'd meant to ask it, and he slapped a hand
over his mouth.

Eric just smirked at this, though, and pulled up his T-shirt, showing
a belt holding the pants up, with the button open and zipper down.

And Ben got a clear view of part of Eric's dick. His own responded,
thickening quickly, and he blurted, "We *definitely* need to get you some
clothes."

Eric blinked at him, then looked down and yanked at his T-shirt to
cover his open zipper. "Uh…."

"I did not mind the view one bit, cariño." Ben looked up at Eric.
"Though I can't say I'd want others to have the same view."

Eric's red cheeks darkened a little, but his lips spread into a small
smile. "As much as having a mate still freaks me out… I like hearing that."

Ben crossed the short distance between them and reached up to
brush a thumb over one red cheek. "Please… do not worry so about
needing to work through this. I can be patient. Really."

Eric hesitated, then nodded. "Okay." He tilted his head. "Can I do
anything else for you?"

Ben considered it. "I still have clothes to unpack and such."

"I can help. Even if it's got a zipper." Eric managed to smirk, and
Ben smiled.

"Most of it is in boxes."

Eric laughed. "Even better. Where?"

Ben directed him to the boxes that had his clothes. "I do not care
how they get put in the dresser. Just… let me know so I can find them, or
I'm afraid I'll be running around the house naked until I find you to tell
me where they are."

Eric raised an eyebrow. "I'd prefer you don't spend a lot of time
naked around Tanner and Finley, thank you. Unless you're, like, shifting.
Or something." His cheeks were once more red when he finished.

Ben gave in to his wolf a little and pulled Eric into his arms, needing
the touch. "Is this okay?"

Eric looked up, meeting Ben's gaze. "Yeah," he whispered. "This
is okay."

"I do not want anyone else, cariño. Until you tell me you do not want
me at all—and even then, I do not think I will do anything. Even if you
outright reject me, I do not see myself wanting anyone else. I already care

about you. I hurt for all you've been through." He closed his eyes when Eric slid his arms around him and held him tight.

"I won't. I mean it, Ben. I'm not going to reject you. I... I don't think I have it in me. My wolf wants you. I am sure you were given to me by Diana herself. I can be a bit of an idiot, but not *that* much."

Ben chuckled. "Well, then. We just give it time." He couldn't resist nuzzling Eric's face a little. Then, so he didn't give in to temptation and actually kiss Eric before they were ready, he pulled away. "So, the simple solution is... make sure I know where my clothes are."

Eric laughed. "All right." He gave a shy smile, then kissed Ben on the cheek before stepping back. "Let's see what I can do."

He was slow, but Ben wouldn't have said a word about it in a million years. Eric kept at it, even though it took time for him to organize things and fold the articles that invariably became unfolded as they were unpacked. Ben was—probably absurdly—proud of his mate for trying so hard.

Instead of making a big deal about any of it, Ben focused on taking care of the things that Eric would have really struggled with. Like unpacking his computer and cables, connecting everything, and emptying the overnight and toiletries bags—which *did* have zippers to them.

In an amazingly short time, he was more or less unpacked. The boxes that held the books and other things he'd brought along were still stacked in the bottom of the closet and along one wall, but there were quite a few less after Eric finished.

"Thank you," Ben said, when they had the empty boxes stashed and everything pretty much put away. "Is there anything I can do for you?"

Eric looked up at him for a long moment, then took a breath. "Could... would you be willing to go shopping with me?" He dropped his gaze.

"I would be very happy to, cariño."

Eric met his gaze, raising his eyebrows. "Really?"

Ben nodded. "I had intended to offer. I didn't want to push but hoped...." He let out a breath. "Hoped that, as your mate, I could help in some way."

"It's what you are, Ben. You don't have to hesitate over the word. I think Finley's right. The more we say it, the easier it'll get." Eric smiled. "And I think you will help. It'll help calm me to have you near."

"Then we will go. Tomorrow, if you think you can handle it."

Eric nodded. "Okay." He turned toward the door but paused. "Good night, my mate."

Ben's smile was a mile wide. "Good night, cariño."

"BUENO!"

"Hola, Papá."

"Mijo! How are you? Are you in Pittsburgh?"

"Yes." Ben let out a breath. "I found my destined mate, Papá."

"Really? Oh, that's wonderful, mijo! Who is it?"

Ben appreciated the fact that his papá didn't automatically ask who *she* was. "It is a he. His name is Eric. He is the alpha's best friend. He's been through a lot, but he's a wonderful man."

"I'm so glad we found that pack for you. How did you meet him?"

"He was just walking into the room when I showed up. He was not expecting to meet me… or a destined mate at all, actually." Ben picked at a spot on his jeans. "He was hurt, Papá, badly. It may be a long time before he could be ready to claim."

"There's nothing wrong with being patient, mijo. You have learned that lesson."

"I know, Papá." He sighed. "I just… I am frustrated."

"That is understandable. Do you want to tell me what happened? Can you?"

"I… it's not up to me to tell everything, but…."

BEN FELT a lot better after spending some time talking with his papá. He learned more about destined mates, though he still had a lot of questions. Unfortunately, they were things his papá didn't even know, so he was still in the dark about a lot of it.

When the phone rang that night right before bed, he thought at first it was his papá. But instead of his papá's name, he saw *Tina* and smiled. "Bueno!"

"*Oh. My. Gods! You met your destined mate!*" The screeched words had him yanking the phone away from his ear. He held it out for another moment while Tina kept it up, until finally, her voice quieted and all he heard was "Ben? Ben? *Ben!*"

Ben chuckled and brought the phone back. "Hi. Are you done screaming in my ear?"

"Ugh. Here I am, *so* happy for you, and you're going to complain about me screaming?" She huffed but then laughed. "Yeah, I'm done. Holy crap, what happened?"

"Who would I be if I did not tease you?"

"A good brother?" Tina asked.

Ben snorted.

"Right. And that didn't answer my question! So… tell me!"

"Fine, fine. But then you must tell me about your new boyfriend."

"Hey! How'd you find out?" Tina actually sounded a little embarrassed.

"Papá told me."

Tina grumbled under her breath something Ben couldn't understand, then sighed. "This is why I didn't want to tell Papá, but *no*, Annie *had* to say something while Papá was on the phone. Well, at least you're on the other end of the country and can't beat him up."

"Do I have reason to?" Ben asked, though they both knew he wasn't about to actually get violent. He *could* look threatening, though, and had on a few occasions when one of Tina's boyfriends seemed like they were getting too close.

"Ugh. No. And you didn't tell me about your mate! Fine. I'll talk, but you first."

Ben laughed. "Okay, okay."

By the time he hung up almost an hour later, he couldn't help but feel even better about everything. Tina was as confident as his papá had been that eventually Eric would come around. She'd been ridiculously happy about it for him, and it did a lot to lift his mood. He'd felt even better when he could spend a good while teasing her about the new wolf in the pack out where she was going to school.

Even with the positive note the day ended on, Ben had a lot of trouble falling asleep. He couldn't believe it'd been less than twenty-four hours since he'd arrived in Pittsburgh. He was trying to absorb the simple fact that he had a *mate*. A destined mate. Despite talking to him, touching him, it seemed impossible. Maybe Ben would wake up and find himself still in the hotel room in Louisville.

Gods, he hoped not. Eric had problems, that was true, but who didn't? Ben had plenty of his own issues to work through.

Like his set of beliefs. He *had* long since recognized he didn't believe in his mamá's god. It was going to be awfully difficult to question his papá's gods, though, after what he'd heard from his mate. If he believed what Eric saw, he had to accept it, and there was no reason for Ben to think Eric lied. He hadn't heard anything in Eric's voice and there'd been nothing in his scent, no indication of it in any way. So Eric, at least, believed wholeheartedly in what he'd seen.

And Ben couldn't deny a goddess his own mate had seen, could he?

There were other species, so many things he'd learned, and Ben's head spun with all of it. It wasn't until he took a deep breath, focusing on the remnants of his mate's scent still in the room, that he managed to settle down enough to go to sleep.

"SO, BEN'S agreed to go with me to do some clothes shopping. I still don't, uh, know what to pay for it with, but if you guys could lend me enough to buy a set of clothes and maybe some underwear—" Eric smirked at Ben, who grinned. "—I'll find a way to pay it back."

Finley rolled his eyes but didn't say anything at first, simply took a sip of his coffee.

Eric frowned, and Ben wished he could do something to take a lot of this burden off his mate. If they *were* mated, there would be no issue with money. What was Ben's would be Eric's.

Ben was sure, however, that Eric wasn't ready for anything like that. He *did* understand Eric's need to earn his own money. He'd been insistent on the same thing with his parents for the last few years. But with the current state he was in, Eric was in no place to work yet.

A moment later Tanner came into the dining room and set a piece of paper in front of Eric. Ben guessed Finley had said something over their telepathic link.

"What's this?" Eric asked, looking down at the paper.

"When you left, Dad immediately went in and locked your money up. I guess he didn't trust Kim *or* your parents with it."

"But, uh, when I left, I had, like… maybe $5K saved up. This is… a hell of a lot more."

Tanner grinned. "Dad knew what he was about when it came to money. The pack isn't just financially sound because of the shop."

Eric blinked at Tanner, then back down at the paper. "Are you telling me he invested it?"

"That's exactly what I'm saying. He was mostly safe with it, but he was also insistent that you have something to work from if you ever came back."

"Well, shit," Eric whispered. He looked over at Ben, then slid the paper to him.

"You do not have to show me, cariño."

"You're my mate. You should know." Eric shrugged a shoulder. "Besides, you're an accountant, right?"

Ben nodded. "Yes."

"Well, then. You can figure out how to handle all that." Eric nodded toward the paper.

That's when Ben looked down at it. He shouldn't have taken a sip of his coffee, because he nearly choked on it. As it was, he barely managed to keep from spraying it all over the paper. "Whoa." Not very eloquent, maybe, but he thought it appropriate.

Eric laughed. "That's about the size of it."

"And then some, cariño."

"You'll, uh, help me with it, right?"

"Of course," Ben said immediately. "I am not an investment broker, but I can at least take care of it as far as taxes and the like are concerned."

"Good. I sucked at numbers even back then. Of course… I never went to college. Everything I knew was what I learned in high school." When Eric finished, his cheeks were red.

"Cariño, college is not for everyone. I did not want to go. But my mamá simply would not take any argument. She wanted me to be a doctor." Ben shook his head, wrinkling his nose. "I talked her out of that. I do *not* like the sight of blood, but…."

"Yeah. Kim…." Eric sighed. "I think the fact that I didn't want to go—because I enjoyed what I did—was the final straw for her."

Ben blinked at him. "She left because you did not want to go to college?"

"That b—" Tanner cut himself off and growled. "She thought he was going to be a doctor—because Eric's parents said he would be, without asking him, even. When she found out he wasn't going to be swimming in money…." He scowled.

Eric squirmed. "Something like that. Anyway."

"She really did not deserve you." Ben shook his head.

Eric looked at Ben, and the expression on his face made Ben ache. And wish he knew where Kim was, just so he could go… he didn't know what. He wasn't a violent person. But to see his mate hurting so much because of her filled him with an anger he rarely felt. He took Eric's hand and kissed it softly.

"So… where is the closest store for clothing?"

THERE WAS both a Walmart and a Target reasonably close to Tanner and Finley's house. Ben thought a Target might be a little less overwhelming, since Target *usually* wasn't as busy, so they went there. The drive itself didn't seem to cause Eric too many problems, but they were inside the car, with muted sound, tinted windows, and nothing stronger in scent than an old air freshener.

When they got out of the car, though, Eric immediately covered his nose. "Oh my gods, how does anyone deal with this?"

Ben, who'd long since learned how to filter smells, had to force himself to *un*filter them to understand what Eric was having trouble with. He was immediately hit with an overabundance of exhaust, restaurant odors, and even garbage. No wonder Eric was having such a hard time.

"Um… get back in the car a moment, cariño."

Eric raised his eyebrows. "Why?"

"I'm going to see if I can find out how to help you. The car is not as bad."

Eric didn't ask anything further, simply slid back into the passenger seat and closed the door.

Ben pulled out his phone and hit Tanner's contact.

"Ben? Is something wrong?"

"Aside from Eric nearly being knocked over by exhaust smell?"

"Eww," Tanner replied. "Yeah. What can I do?"

"Do you have the phone number for… um… the former human. That's a horrible way to say it, but—"

"Chad would just laugh at it. Don't worry about it. Yeah, good idea. I'll text it to you."

"Thank you."

"Of course. Good luck."

A moment later Ben saved Chad's number as a new contact, then dialed.

"Hello?"

"Hello, this is Ben Arellano. Eric's mate? The new pack member?"

"Oh! Hi! How's it going?"

"Um…. Eric is making his first trip away from the house."

"Eww."

Ben chuckled. "That's what Tanner said. Is there any way I can help him? I do not… I have no idea how I learned how to filter."

"Yeah, actually. It's hard as an adult, no doubt. First, make sure he doesn't breathe deeply. Seriously *shallow* breaths for a while. Then tell him to focus only on what he *wants* to smell. We can't filter it completely, you know."

"Right."

"But if he picks *one* thing he either wants to smell or doesn't mind smelling and focuses on that, it can help. Same with sound, though sometimes all you can do there is earplugs. Those foam ones work well."

"Thank you very much. It's… difficult to be so helpless."

"I know what you mean!" Jaime said.

Ben chuckled. "Hello."

"Hi."

"So, yeah. Try that. I can come out in the next day or two and work with him, if you think it'll help."

"It might. I'll say something to him. Thank you again, uh, Chad." Ben cleared his throat.

"Uh, you okay?"

"Yes. Alpha said you'd laugh, but… I could not remember your name when I asked him for your number. I called you the 'former human.'"

Ben was relieved when Chad actually did laugh. "Oh, I like that. Maybe I'll have to adopt it as a nickname."

"Gods, you're bad enough to live with now," Jamie said. "Maybe we should call you skunk instead." He snickered.

"I think I'll stick with pup, thanks."

"Skunk?"

Jamie snickered again. "He couldn't tell the difference between skunks and squirrels for a long time."

Chad sighed. "It took time for me to trust my other instincts. So, uh, yeah. Kept thinking they were just big squirrels."

Ben laughed. "I did that when I was young. My mamá used to have a fit when I came home with it in my hair."

"Yes! And it does *not* like to come out of hair."

Ben chuckled. "Yes. Well, thank you for the advice."

"No worries. Good luck, Ben. It'll get better, I promise. It'll just take a while. If he has other things to focus on—like, something to occupy his mind instead of *just* filtering—and works on sticking with the things he wants to smell and hear, it can help. As for his vision… sunglasses are the only thing that can help that."

"Thank you. I'll tell him about you coming to help."

"Good. Later."

Ben opened Eric's door and squatted next to it. "I called Chad." When Eric raised an eyebrow, Ben said, "The former human."

Eric laughed. "Right. I forgot a lot of their names."

"Me too. He thought that was funny. Anyway, he gave me a few suggestions for you that might help." Ben outlined what Chad had said, and Eric nodded as he finished.

"That *might* help. Thank you."

"I am your mate. If I can help… I have to. I do not like seeing you go through so much of this." Ben shrugged a shoulder.

Eric swallowed but nodded. "I can understand that. So…." He closed his eyes, took several shallow breaths in a row, then opened them again. "Well. It's not quite as bad, but… I think I might take him up on the help."

"Good. Now, let's get you some underwear so I do not go so nuts when you're around gay men."

Eric laughed as he climbed out of the car. "Come on."

Stepping into the store was its own challenge, but Eric seemed to be fighting hard to keep going. Ben leaned in and said softly, "Any time you want to go, tell me. We do not have to do much today."

"I'm not sure I'm going to want to do this again anytime soon," Eric muttered, then blew out a breath. "Let's get a cart."

As they stood in front of the underwear shelves, Ben kept an eye on Eric, looking for any signs they needed to end the trip. He seemed to be doing well enough for the moment, so Ben turned to the shelves. "What did you wear before?"

Eric wrinkled his nose. "Tighty-whities."

Ben chuckled. "And I take it they do not appeal now? Perhaps boxers?"

Eric shook his head. "No. The thought of the tighty-whities that snug against my skin right now...." He shuddered. "And boxers always felt like I was just going commando, with everything just kind of flopping everywhere."

Ben laughed. "Perhaps you could try boxer briefs, then. And we can go online and find you more appealing underwear."

Eric grinned at this. "And I can avoid people all at the same time."

"Indeed," Ben said, grinning. "What size?"

"Uh... well, before I was still, like, small. I don't think that's going to work now."

After examining the back of the package, they bought two different sizes, just in case.

Trying jeans on turned out to be almost a nightmare. The rough denim seemed to make him more and more uncomfortable, no matter which ones they tried.

"I guess it's just because Tanner's and Finley's jeans are worn?" Eric suggested.

Ben frowned. "That might be. We can wash them a few times. That might help."

Eric nodded. "Yeah. Well, I can't keep wearing their clothes, so...." He turned around, looking at his butt in the mirror. "What do you think? Not too tight?"

"They look very good on you," Ben said, trying not to stare at Eric's ass.

Eric looked at him, raising an eyebrow, but then sniffed, and based on the grin, Ben knew he'd failed—both with where he was looking *and* not getting aroused. "Yeah, I think these will do."

Ben cleared his throat. "I'll, uh, go... um... find socks." *And adjust myself.*

Eric reached out and caught Ben's wrist. "It does me good to know. You know... she didn't even want me toward the end."

Ben took a carefully filtered deep breath. "She was—is—the biggest fool on the planet for not recognizing what she had. If things were different, cariño, I would have bonded with you last night."

Eric smiled. "Thanks. I... ugh. It sucks that I'm not ready for it, but it still helps to hear."

Ben kissed his temple. "Stop worrying about that. Now... you should change before I go too crazy."

Eric's laughter followed Ben out of the dressing room.

They ended up only getting the one pair of jeans, a couple of T-shirts, a pair of sweats, and the underwear and socks. By the time they'd picked that stuff out, it was clear the store was getting to Eric. He pushed through long enough to try on and pick out a pair of sneakers. But by that time, he was clearly only holding on by sheer force of will.

That got infinitely worse when someone made a particularly loud and long announcement over the intercom. Even *Ben* winced over the volume. With a kiss to Eric's temple, Ben gave him the keys and nearly pushed him toward the door. "I'll pay for it and you can pay me when I come back out or something. Now, go, cariño. I will be out shortly."

It was a testament to how bad it was that Eric didn't even argue over the money. Instead, he took the keys and went out, barely not running.

Ben grabbed a simple pair of sunglasses to go with the clothes, then took a little bit of time to find Eric a sweatshirt for the colder evenings, which Ben had noticed the night before while they'd been out on the deck, and a jacket to go with it. He also stopped to pick up a package of earplugs as well.

When he made it out to the car, Eric was looking quite a bit less bothered. Ben pulled the sunglasses out of the bag and handed them over. "You look better. Do you feel better?"

Eric nodded. "Yeah. Just… too much, you know?"

"Yeah. Even I was getting a little nuts from the noise. Especially that announcement." Ben made a face.

Eric gave a weak smile and put the sunglasses on. "Thank you for thinking of them."

"I had no idea if that was a style you like or not. I figured right now, blocking the sun was the most important thing."

"Yeah. I'm not really picky. I'm just glad to have them." Eric took a breath and let it out, then shifted in the seat to face Ben more fully. "Thank you. I… I know you're my mate and you're happy to help, but still. You didn't have to. You didn't have to put up with all my crap. Thank you for helping, for understanding. Just… for being here." He dropped his gaze briefly, then met Ben's eyes again. "I think I'd have been a *lot* more nuts if you hadn't been there, if I'd gone with Tanner and Finley. They'd have given me the same advice—about filters and stuff—but I wouldn't have felt as good as I did. My wolf was calmer than he's been in a long time. Because you were there."

Ben took Eric's hand for a moment and kissed it, thrilling in just what that showed. Warmth filled him when Eric didn't let go right away. "You're welcome. I *wanted* to do this. I would have helped even if you were not my mate. Being my mate just made it that much more important to me. I'm glad I could be that help for you."

Eric nodded. "Uh, so… hey, could we get some food? I'm starving."

Ben smiled, letting the conversation go. "Sure. Is there anything you'd like? Since you have not eaten it in nine years…."

Chapter 7

"Taco Bell," Eric said, staring at the big pink and purple sign across the street.

"Um...."

Eric turned and blinked at Ben over his hesitation. "What's wr— oh!" He dropped his face into his palm. "Wow, that was good, Eric. Let's ask your Mexican mate to take you to the most fake Mexican restaurant on the planet."

Ben threw his head back and laughed. "It's okay, cariño. If that's what you really want, I will take you. Just so you recognize it is not *really* Mexican food."

Eric grinned. "Nah, I know that. And it's okay. I'd be just as happy with, like, a Big Mac or something. I mean, none of it's real food, anyway, you know."

Ben nodded. "True." He started the car and backed out. "Do you truly want McDonald's?"

"Really, I'm fine with that. I don't mind *not* having Taco Bell. Besides, as much as we'll probably stick together, there will be times we're apart. I can save my heretical eating for then." Eric winked.

Ben laughed again. "Very well."

Neither spoke as Ben navigated traffic through the parking lot and busy streets. As they approached the drive-through menu, though, he turned to Eric. "You should probably cover your nose."

Eric raised his eyebrows. "You think so?"

Ben nodded. "Yeah. It's going to be *strong* here. Trust me."

Eric shrugged a shoulder but did as Ben suggested. The second the window was down, he was glad he had. The exhaust and overabundance of restaurant smells hit him hard, even with his hand over his face.

"Did you really want a Big Mac?"

Eric nodded. "Fries too."

"Got it." Ben turned to the menu board, and Eric did his best to simply ignore the smells and sounds around him, focusing instead on Ben's scent and voice. Ben put in the order—for two of the same of everything—and Eric worked on filters again.

He supposed he should have more patience with himself, but it was really getting to him that the reminders of Ben as his mate still bothered him. The simple idea that Ben's scent, voice, and touch were the only things that *didn't* make him nuts shouldn't get to him so. He wanted to forget all that, wanted to just be happy that Ben was there, that he had a destined mate at all. But the fear that it'd end just like it had with Kim still lurked inside him.

Shaking his head at himself, Eric pulled his wallet out and removed some of the money Tanner had given him that morning, a minuscule part of the balance he'd learned about.

When they got to the payment window, Eric handed the money to Ben, glad when he didn't even say a word, simply passed it over to the clerk. She made the change, and they moved on.

Ben rolled his window up, and Eric breathed a sigh of relief. "How are you?"

"Annoyed," Eric said, sighing. "I'm done with the lack of filters already."

Ben chuckled. "I can imagine. I can *only* imagine, but I forced myself to *un*filter earlier, so I have a small idea." He shook his head. "I do not envy you, cariño."

Eric smiled, leaned in, and kissed Ben on the cheek. He paused to take a deep inhale of Ben's scent. "Gods, I could smell that all day," he whispered.

Ben kissed his temple, and Eric sat back. "What do I smell like to you, cariño?"

"Spice carried on a fresh breeze," Eric said, then blushed.

Ben just grinned. "So you're a poet."

Eric's color got worse. "Hardly. I don't know where that came from." He shrugged.

Ben kissed his cheek. "I like it, cariño."

"What do I smell like to you?" Eric asked, tilting his head.

"Leather. Something sweet, and… home."

That did all sorts of crazy—but good—things to Eric's insides. "I've never been someone's home before." He dropped his gaze to his hand. "None of this feels even remotely familiar," he confessed. "Before… I mean… I have to admit." He looked up and met Ben's gaze. Ben nodded and Eric sighed. "I did love her. I don't... I don't think it was what it should have been, not to be together like we were supposed to be."

Ben didn't speak for a long time. "My wolf might not understand. But I do. What happened before... you cannot help that. And I understand you cared for her. I hope, someday, you can love me."

Eric swallowed. "I... I think I will. I don't... *fuck.*" He took a deep breath. "I am frustrated with myself that I can't just let go and let it happen, you know?"

Ben nodded. "I know, cariño." He reached up and brushed a thumb over Eric's cheek. "Give it time. I have only been here a day."

Eric blew out a breath. "I know. This is only my third day back. I've never been the most patient person on the planet." He chuckled. "Especially when it comes to my own shortcomings. I'm impatient with my impatience."

Ben laughed as he pulled up to the second window. "That's not so bad, really."

Eric focused on covering his nose and working through the smells, putting his frustration with himself aside. He tried to concentrate on *not* smelling the wrong things and felt better when he could take his hand away from his nose and not be overwhelmed. He was going to have to thank Chad for that advice.

ERIC MANAGED to be mostly responsible for getting his clothes de-tagged and into the washer. Ben had offered to help, and Eric recognized he was being stubborn, but he needed to be able to do at least *some* of this himself. And he was sure the more he did, the better he'd be able to handle the fine motor control tasks he was still having trouble with.

So when Finley approached him, asking about dinner, he forced away his reticence and smiled. "I'd love to have steak." He hesitated—he really didn't want to piss Finley off—but he didn't like not paying for his keep, either. "Hey, uh, I know you and Tanner are a little annoyed that I want to, but, um, can I help buy groceries or something?"

He gave Finley credit for not rolling his eyes. Instead, Finley tilted his head. "If it's important to you, then, yes. How about you give me the money, though, and let me shop? At least until you have your filters in better shape."

Eric would never in a million years admit he was grateful for Finley's perception. "Thanks. Yeah, I think that'll work."

Finley nodded. "Good. All right, then, I'll get started. Tanner's meeting a client." He wrinkled his nose.

Eric laughed. "Can I do anything?"

Finley shook his head. "Not right now. Maybe I'll have you scrub potatoes or something later. Or maybe I'll just stick with something easier rather than baking them." He waved a hand. "I'll figure that part out later. I'll let you know when dinner's ready."

ERIC WANDERED out to the living room, flopped onto the couch, and laid his head back. He was more than a little tired after the day he'd had. He was already incredibly frustrated with his lack of filters, his fumbling, and everything else. He could handle zippers better and fasten his own jeans buttons. So that was something. But there were still a lot of things he struggled with. He'd never imagined going wolf for a time like that would lead to him regressing to puppyhood.

It made him wonder what he was going to do for a job. Alpha Noah had done well with the savings he'd put together, but it wouldn't last forever, even sharing a house with Tanner and Finley. And he couldn't do that forever either. He had his own mate who, eventually, would want a separate place. Hell, *he'd* want a separate place when they finally got to the point that they could bond and claim.

And while he had no doubt Ben could take care of basic living expenses, Eric had zero interest in living off Ben. *His* former mate might have wanted that, but that wasn't how he worked.

So he'd need a job. But could he get his hands back to working well enough to do his leatherworking? And if not, what *could* he do?

He sighed, annoyed with his cyclical thinking. Before he could get up, though, and find something to do, Ben sat next to him.

"Are you okay, cariño?"

Eric frowned. "I don't know?" He shook his head. "I almost said, 'I'm fine,' but I know you'll see through that."

Ben smiled. "I'd hope so. There *are* advantages to being your mate."

Eric couldn't resist smiling at that. "True. I just... I mean...." He shook his head in frustration. "It didn't work that way with her, and I don't *get* it. Are destined mates *that* different from chosen? I thought… I thought chosen still had good matings, good relationships."

Ben frowned. "My parents were destined. They have troubles, but I think Mamá's humanity causes a lot of that. I have known a number of chosen couples, though, and they seemed to have… if not quite the same closeness my parents do, it was similar. I think…." He frowned, reaching up and touching Eric's cheek. "I'm sorry to say I think it is because she was not very… uh… invested in the mating."

Eric sighed. "I guess I knew that. I just… it's hard to accept because it means I was a bigger fool than I had even realized."

Ben shook his head. "No, cariño. You are only guilty of loving her."

"Doesn't make me less foolish. I should have seen the signs." He waved a hand. "Anyway."

"Yes, anyway. I believe the wash is finished. Would you like help moving it over?"

"Yeah. I'll take that." Eric stood and held his hand out toward Ben. "Come on, mate. Let's do something domestic."

ERIC SAT, staring at the plate in front of him, cursing himself for not giving more thought to what would be required to eat *steak*. The steak knife mocked him, as did the fork on the other side of the plate. Huffing to himself, he picked them up and forced himself to go slow.

His knife grip was still horribly awkward, but he managed to stab the meat with the fork and work the knife across the piece. He more tore than cut a chunk off the steak and stuffed the bite in his mouth.

He refused to look at anyone else at the table. He knew he looked ridiculous and just couldn't take whatever look they'd give him. Pity? Amusement? Neither appealed.

Eric hadn't expected the clatter of silverware next to him, so before he could stop himself, he looked up at Ben—

—who'd put down his silverware and was eating his steak with his hands. Eric blinked at him, uncomprehending, until two *more* sets of utensils hit the table. Eric turned to look at Tanner and Finley to see they'd done the same thing. They were eating the steak with their hands.

Eric was torn between embarrassment and gratitude. He decided to take the gratitude and put his own silverware down, then picked up his steak with his hands. He tore off a piece, unable to stop the smile at the grin Ben gave him.

"You know, cariño, there is a lot of Mexican food that does not require silverware."

Eric finished his bite and laughed. "You'll have to show me."

Ben's smile widened. "I can cook. So I will make it for you."

Eric raised his eyebrows. "Oh yeah, you said you could, didn't you?"

"Yes." Ben nodded. "My mamá taught me."

Eric frowned. Ben was leaving something out, he could feel it, but he didn't know what. Clearly it wasn't something he wanted to discuss in front of Tanner and Finley, though, so Eric let it go. "Well, perhaps you can teach me."

"You can't cook?"

Eric shook his head. "No. My mom wasn't the most… domestic person on the planet."

Tanner snorted. "Dude. You ate with us more often than not. And when you didn't, you ate out."

Eric grinned. "Hey, I couldn't help it. Your mom is such a good cook."

"Well, she certainly didn't mind feeding you. I'm not sure anyone else would have gotten vegetables into you."

Eric wrinkled his nose. "What is everyone's fascination with vegetables?" he grumbled, poking the broccoli on his plate.

"We're half human, remember?" Tanner asked. "We kinda need a bit more than meat as humans."

Eric stuck his tongue out. "Maybe I'll just do all my eating in wolf form."

"Nope," Ben said, shaking his head.

Eric looked over at him, raising his eyebrows. "Oh?"

"Yes, no. I promised the doctor I would make sure you ate vegetables."

Eric rolled his eyes. "Maybe I *don't* want a mate."

Tanner scowled. "You don't have a choice."

Eric held up a hand. "Joking!" He turned to Ben and leaned in. "I'm sorry. I didn't really mean it."

"It's okay, cariño. I actually knew that." Ben smiled and kissed Eric's cheek.

Eric sighed. "I'll eat my vegetables," he mumbled, picked up a piece of broccoli, and put it in his mouth.

Ben grinned at him and ate one of his own—with his fingers, just like the steak. "That was not so bad, was it?"

Eric rolled his eyes but was grinning as he ate another piece of broccoli.

THE STEAK dinner made Eric even more determined to get *past* this bullshit with his hands and at least be able to do basic things with them. At the same time, he wanted to get his filters in place again. He was tired of feeling like a pup, tired of fighting with that. He wanted to feel *normal* again.

He was more than a little grateful when Chad showed up only a couple of days later. Jamie came with him, and to Eric's surprise, they both hugged him. To his *annoyance*, it still felt… off… for anyone but his mate to touch him. So he had to force himself to return the hug and relax after he stiffened from the contact.

"I'm sorry," he mumbled when he stepped back.

"Hey, it's okay," Jamie assured him. "I can't begin to imagine how this feels."

"Fucking ridiculous," Eric blurted.

Jamie laughed. "Well, that I can certainly understand."

"I do get it, at least to a point," Chad said. "Let's go outside. There are stronger smells out there."

"I thought I might talk to Ben a little about how to help you. Will you be okay if we're in here without you guys?"

Eric actually had to think about it but nodded. "Yeah. I'm sorry it's even—"

Chad held up a hand. "You should have seen us when we first got together. I growled at people—and I didn't even have a wolf yet."

Eric laughed. "Wow. I don't feel so bad, then."

"Do not feel bad, cariño." Ben kissed his cheek. "I'm glad you are possessive of me. I like the reminder of our bond."

Eric turned to Ben and pulled him close, wrapping both arms around him. He savored the feel of Ben's arms around him too. "I am definitely possessive of you. And sometime soon, I'll be able to do more with it."

"I am a patient man, cariño."

With a kiss to Ben's cheek, Eric turned to Chad. "Let's get my damned filters fixed."

Chad laughed. "Not sure it'll work that fast, but...."

Eric waved a hand. "Then I want to get to working on it."

They spent the better part of a whole day outside, with Eric working through the same type of exercises he'd used at the store.

"Remember, first, to take *shallow* breaths until you can filter. That's the first thing I had to remember to do. Every damned *semi*deep breath just about did me in. Way too many smells at once."

Eric nodded. "Yeah. I think that's the worst part. Just... so many different ones."

"Exactly. So. Shallow breaths."

Eric closed his eyes and worked on taking several smaller breaths. Already the sheer number of things to smell seemed to diminish. "Oh, yeah, that's better."

"Now, you can't keep doing that, though."

Eric laughed. "Yeah, I'd look like a nutjob doing that every time I went out in public."

Chad threw his head back and laughed. "Yeah, no doubt. So, for me, I found that if I separated the different smells, cataloged them, I could let them go and more or less forget about them."

"Okay. So, look for specific ones."

Chad nodded. "Yeah. When you take a breath, think about what you're smelling, identify them, and your brain will let you ignore them better."

Eric nodded and once again closed his eyes. He took a—slightly— longer breath. Instead of just wincing and trying immediately not to breathe, he forced himself to think about what he smelled. When he found the pine and spruce, he separated them and was able to ignore them. Next, he recognized the rabbit, squirrel, and deer nearby. It took a moment to ignore his wolf's urging to chase and instead work to recognize and catalog them. A moment later he felt like he could ignore those too. He opened his eyes and grinned at Chad. "Holy shit, it works."

Chad grinned back. "Yeah! Let's work on sounds next."

By the time Finley was serving hamburgers from the grill, Eric felt like he could, at least, handle smells and most sounds quite a bit better.

And he was feeling a lot closer to normal.

WHILE HIS filters were getting better, Eric was still having problems with fine motor control, but practice with his zippers helped. And he forced himself to eat things for breakfast that required silverware. It wasn't nearly what it took to do things like cut steak or draw or handle leatherworking tools, but he was better and was starting to feel a lot less useless. He wasn't sure he could do the steak-cutting or leatherworking yet, but in the end, he was making progress, and that went a long way toward making him feel better about a lot of his limitations.

The next day, Ben had to go into Pittsburgh, apparently to see about transferring his CPA license, so Eric used that time to work on his filters. When Ben came back, Eric didn't actually hear him until the car was almost at the house. And he didn't even remotely smell Ben until his mate was in the same room. In a weird sort of way, he was proud of himself for it.

He was surprised, though, when Ben set a bunch of plastic bags down in front of him. "What's this?"

Ben opened one and Eric peered in.

"Clothes?"

Ben nodded. "After I left the office I went to in Pittsburgh, I passed a Target and thought you might not mind if I picked up a few more shirts and things for you. I figured you would not mind just paying me back, and if I did not get the right colors or sizes or whatever, I could return them later."

"My filters are a lot better, but… yes, thank you. I'm still not sure I want to be around that many people yet."

Ben grinned. "Good."

Eric pulled the clothes out one by one, more than a little surprised that Ben had apparently remembered all of his sizes and color preferences. At the bottom of one bag, though, he found something he wasn't expecting.

A sketch pad.

"Ben…?"

Ben sat down next to him on the couch. "I found the other one. Tanner said it was yours. You used to do such amazing work, cariño. I thought, perhaps, instead of looking at all the ones that remind you of before… maybe you could start new. I'm sure it's still there, your art."

Eric held the sketch pad a little tighter and stared at it, not seeing it. He swallowed. "I… I don't know."

"Would it hurt for you to try?"

Eric blew out a breath. "I don't know. Maybe? But… maybe I should, even if it does."

"I would love to see you draw."

Eric looked up at him and tilted his head. "If I do, will you play your guitar for me?"

Ben smiled. "I think I can manage that."

Eric grinned and looked back at the sketch pad, running his hand over the cover. "I'm not sure I even know where to begin."

"Perhaps you could draw your favorite place in the forest. I'm sure you have one."

Eric nodded, the picture of the place Diana had appeared to him popping into his head. "Yeah, I do."

Ben kissed his temple. "Then you should draw it."

"I... I don't know if I'll be able to go back to the leatherworking, though. And if—"

"You will."

Eric shook his head. "Such confidence in me."

"I'm learning about you, cariño. I believe I'm getting a feel for what you can do. How strong you are."

Eric fought the immediate urge to shake his head, denying his strength. Ben would only argue with it. Instead, he took a breath and said simply, "Thank you."

"Thank me by drawing for me." Ben kissed his temple again. "But first... we have laundry to do."

"Yay," Eric said, standing and making Ben laugh. But as he set the sketch pad aside to focus on the other things he needed to do, he found himself anxious to pick up a pencil. He was sure it would be crap, at least at first. But maybe... just maybe... he could do some of this again.

Chapter 8

"I KNOW it might seem strange that the first movie I want to show you is fairly recent. I promise, though, you'll appreciate it." Ben set the big bowl of popcorn onto the coffee table before taking his seat.

Eric smiled. "Whatever you think. I've got *so* much to catch up on."

Ben nodded. "That much is true, cariño. We have our whole lives to get you caught up. There is no rush."

"Well, most of our lives. Another, oh, two hundred seventy years or so...."

Ben grinned. "I do not know if that will be enough time with you."

Eric's smile spread into a grin. He leaned over and left a soft kiss on Ben's cheek. "I suspect, when I finally get my head out of my ass, no amount of years will be enough."

Ben's heart skipped a beat, and he couldn't seem to breathe for a moment. "That does me good to hear, cariño."

With another kiss to Ben's cheek, Eric sat back. "So, let's see what's in?"

Ben picked up the remote and hit Play, waiting impatiently for the piracy warnings and other stuff to pass by. He wished he'd have thought to set it to right before the crawl, but there was nothing for it.

As soon as the menu came up, Eric gasped. "There's... that's... is that... Star Wars?"

Ben grinned. "There is a whole new trilogy coming out. This is the first."

"Oh my gods, fuck yes!"

Ben laughed.

"Wait." Eric held a hand out. "Is it any good? I mean, I remember when *The Phantom Menace* came out and it was good, but two and three...." He shuddered.

Ben waved a hand. "No, this is much—*much*—better than *Attack of the Clones* or *Revenge of the Sith*."

Eric narrowed his eyes and considered Ben. "Well, the bond—such as it is—says you're telling the truth." He made a great show of sniffing Ben. "And you don't smell like you're lying."

Ben laughed. "No, cariño, I really did enjoy this one. I did not exactly *hate* the other two, but…."

Eric nodded. "All right, then. Let's go."

Ben was surprised, despite the touching they'd done in the week since they'd met, when Eric put his arm around Ben's shoulders. Ben settled in against Eric's side, then took a handful of popcorn and focused on the words passing by on the screen. He decided he liked watching movies with Eric. He reacted, cheering and booing, laughing out loud, and Ben even caught him clearing his throat once, clearly in an attempt to keep from tearing up. Ben had a hard time deciding between watching the movie and watching his mate. Star Wars, of course, won out, but not by much.

"They are so totally gay for each other," Eric said, nodding at Finn and Poe hugging each other.

Ben laughed. "I can only imagine all the stories written about them."

"Oh yeah. Seriously, though, does that look like a 'bro' hug to you?"

Ben shook his head. "No, it does not."

"It'd be really nice if they'd put a decent gay or bi character in one of these movies. You know, that isn't the comic relief or—"

"Tragic death, yeah." Ben nodded. "Well, I think you're right and those two are definitely more than just friends."

Eric flashed him a grin. "I'm glad you acknowledge my brilliance."

Ben laughed. "Indeed, cariño." He leaned in with the intention of kissing Eric's cheek, but Eric turned his head at *exactly* the wrong time, and instead of getting a five-o'clock shadow, Ben got smooth lips. He couldn't have fought his wolf for anything in the world. His hands came up and cradled Eric's face in his palms. Eric moaned softly, tilted his head, and ran his tongue over Ben's lips.

Ben didn't even hesitate to open to him. Their tongues touched, then slid, and Ben let a moan out this time. Eric just tasted *so good.*

Just as he was getting lost in the kiss, however, the bond between them, that something tying them together, thickened. As that was happening, something invisible wrapped around them and pulled them together.

They broke apart, and Eric stared at Ben with wide eyes. "Was that… did we just…? What the fuck just happened?"

Ben winced before he could stop himself. He let go of Eric, his heart pounding and aching at the same time. "I think we strengthened our bond," he whispered.

"We *what?*"

Ben managed to keep from wincing again, though he definitely cringed on the inside.

Before he could speak, Finley came out from the kitchen. "Is everything all right?"

"Hell no," Eric said, then paused. He took a deep breath, then let it out. "Sorry. I… no. I think we just… I think we just bonded."

Finley raised his eyebrows, looking from one to the other. "Uh… you're both still dressed. If you've found a way to fuck without moving your clothes even a little, I'd love to know how. That'd come in *really* handy."

Eric blinked. "This isn't a joke."

Finley shook his head. "I'm not joking. What do you mean, bonded?"

"Uh, our bond is stronger than it was before we kissed."

"Ah." Finley nodded. "Yes, to a small degree, your bond will strengthen through kissing, but *only* a little. It'll fade and be almost as if you never kissed." He shrugged. "The only difference might be your wolves pushing a little harder to continue the bond."

"So… it'll mostly go away?" Eric asked.

Ben tried not to let the hopeful tone of voice hurt. He knew Eric was scared, and if Ben wasn't also messed up over the partial bond, he wouldn't be as upset as he was. Ben recognized that, after only a week, Eric wasn't going to be ready to bond, wasn't going to be able to trust like that yet.

Ben tried not to think about the fact that it could be *years* before that could happen.

"Yes. It will fade." Finley shook his head. "It's one of the differences between destined and chosen. Destined mates bond more and earlier. But," he said, staring right at Eric, "destined don't leave either."

Before Eric could respond, Finley went back out to the kitchen, leaving them alone.

Eric blew out a breath. "Well, fuck. I didn't know this could even happen."

"Me either, cariño. If I'd known, I would have been more careful about kissing. I'm sorry." Ben swallowed around the lump in his throat.

"Hey, I know you didn't do it on purpose. It's okay."

Ben nodded, then took a breath—though it was too shallow—in an effort to keep his voice steady. "Listen, we can just let it fade. I doubt it would take long, and then I think you'll feel better."

Eric growled as he jumped up off the couch. "How can you be so patient with me? How does this not bother you?" The last ended on a shout, Eric's hands clenched into fists.

"I did not say it didn't bother me. But I told you the first day we met: I can be patient. And I will be. You are worth it."

"But *how*? How are you not ready to climb the fucking walls?"

Ben sighed. "I told you my mamá hated our wolves. We did everything we could to suppress them outside the full moon. I had to learn to be patient, because if I did not, I would have said many things I would regret with her. I still did, when I left, but…." Ben shook his head. "Mamá is one of those who can be very, very stubborn when she believes firmly in something, and hiding our wolves—ridding ourselves of our demons—was one of them. It took a long time before she could accept we were not going camping on every full moon."

Eric blinked. "Wow. Seriously?"

Ben nodded. "Yes." He let out a breath. "I *will* wait, cariño."

"I hope you can," Eric whispered. He cleared his throat. "I need some air." He turned toward the stairs leading down to the mudroom but paused on the top step. He looked over his shoulder. "I'll be back. I will. I just…."

Ben nodded, at a loss for what else to do or say. When Eric was out of sight, he laid his head back on the couch, doing his best to hold in any emotion. Even though they hadn't fully bonded, Eric would feel it—at least in part—and Ben did *not* want to risk that.

He'd heard Eric's words, knew they were the truth to a point, at least—Eric would be back; he had nowhere else to go unless he stayed wolf—but the look on his mate's face hadn't been reassuring. Was Eric reconsidering mating after all?

Was Ben going to lose his destined mate before he ever really got one?

"Finley, I am going to shift for a bit."

Finley came out of the kitchen again, tilting his head. "What's wrong? Where's Eric?" He frowned. "Did he take off again?"

"He said he needed some air and would be back. I… I could use some too. I have not shifted since I've been here. Are there places I should not go?"

Finley shook his head. "Watch the road north, but there's plenty of forest to the south of the house."

Ben nodded. "Thank you." He got up and turned toward the stairs.

"Hey, Ben?"

Ben hesitated, turning back to Finley.

"He'll be back. He won't reject you completely."

Ben shook his head. "I'm not so sure of that, Finley."

Finley nodded and gave a small smile. "I am. You'll see. Go, run. It always helps me clear my head."

"Thank you," Ben said, then hurried to the stairs before Finley could say any more.

BEN TOOK a long drink out of the stream, then flopped down on the bank. He closed his eyes, resting his head on his paws, trying to block out the memory of the look on Eric's face earlier, trying not to think. He'd run, focusing on the feel of the wind in his fur and the forest under his paws. He hadn't gotten to do that much back in Texas, and in fact, it had been very rare altogether. Even as an adult, his mother had made it clear she didn't want him shifting any more than he absolutely had to, which meant getting away to run had been difficult at best.

Ben glanced up at the sky, noting it had gotten quite a bit darker since he'd left. He had no idea how long he'd been gone—time didn't pass the same for him in wolf form as it did as a human—but he didn't believe he'd really be missed, so he didn't worry too much about it.

With a soft whine, he put his paws over his head, even though he was well aware that the pain was inside, rather than out. He didn't want to let his brain keep going over the fact that it was starting to feel like no one wanted him.

If he was thinking clearly and not out of hurt, he'd know that wasn't true. He knew Eric's problem wasn't that he didn't want Ben. Eric's problem was simple fear. But right then, it felt too much like *he* wasn't wanted—much like it felt that his mamá didn't want him.

That, too, wasn't accurate. She didn't want his *wolf*, but since his wolf was such an integral part of him, it sometimes felt like she didn't want *him*.

He needed to stop thinking, not remember. Yet despite his best efforts, he did. The memories cropped up of the times when he'd been a pup, too young to control the shift, and his mother spanking him when he turned human again, scolding him, even at four and five years old, about controlling his "demon." He winced, even now, when it was only a memory. He'd hidden in his room after that, so confused, because he couldn't understand why he was getting spanked for something he couldn't help. What was worse was that his mamá couldn't seem to explain it either, just that it was "wrong."

There'd been more Sunday mornings than he could count over the years that he sat on hard, uncomfortable church pews, his mother giving him looks he didn't need to interpret. He was to listen to the messages and use them to rid himself of his demon.

He'd never forget the guilt and fear when he never succeeded. It took him too many years to understand he couldn't get rid of his demon. When his papá had realized what was going on, he'd put his foot down and kept Ben home, but by then the damage was done. Ben knew he was *wrong*, and there was nothing he could do to fix it.

The one good thing he could say that came out of the situation was he spared his little sister the church pew, at least. She'd been too little to understand the church's message, so Papá had kept them home. It was before she could be put through the same thing.

It was, in fact, one of the few big arguments he'd heard his parents have. They normally didn't fight, but the shouted rapid-fire Spanish had been hard to miss. He'd kept Tina occupied on the PlayStation, though, of course, she heard as well as he did. Their preternatural hearing didn't allow them to ignore it completely. They'd both winced over the shatter of pottery, then exchanged looks when things went silent. That had been more ominous than the shouting.

Eventually his mother had apparently given in, because neither he— nor Tina—had ever gone back to the Catholic church. With patience and understanding, his papá had helped him get over some of his fears. He and his sister learned more and more about their species, and their history and lore, and could put away a lot of the things his mamá had insisted on.

But Ben had never completely gotten over the idea that his mamá didn't love a huge part of him.

He sighed, looking up at the now setting sun. Was Eric second-guessing him? Was his destined mate going to not want him either? Just like his mamá? His former alpha?

Before he could think it through, he lifted his head and let loose a howl of worry and frustration.

"See? I knew it bothered you," Eric said from beside him.

Ben jumped and dropped his head, shaking it slightly, annoyed with himself for not hearing Eric approach.

"Hey, baby. It's okay, really." Eric ran his hand over Ben's head and neck, and having his mate's hands on him, even petting him, felt ridiculously good. "You are a beautiful wolf, but can I see my human mate?"

Ben took a breath, then pulled his wolf back. Like the shift to wolf earlier, the return to human form took longer than it should have. He'd have to get better at it, but he'd worry about that later.

Before he could say or do anything when he was once more human, Eric lifted Ben's face, then slid his hands up to cup Ben's cheeks. A second later... Eric kissed him. The full, thorough kiss went through him as Eric's lips moved over his, brushing, then nipping, then deepening the kiss.

Stunned, Ben could do nothing but sit there for a moment. Finally he pulled himself together and returned it. Their tongues slid, the taste as incredible as it had been earlier and maybe even more so somehow because *Eric* started the kiss. Ben couldn't stop his body from reacting, feeling his very naked mate against him, though at least he wasn't embarrassed, because Eric was reacting too. His hard cock brushed Ben's, and it took all Ben had to simply moan at the feel and not do more.

Even so, when they broke apart, he scrunched his eyebrows together while looking at Eric, who was now in shades of gray. "What... but...."

"I hurt you," Eric said. Ben opened his mouth to argue, but Eric simply raised his eyebrows, and Ben sighed but closed his mouth again. "You can't lie to me, baby."

Ben frowned, slightly relieved as his arousal faded enough for his vision to go back to full color. "But... I mean.... Okay, I cannot lie, but you do not have to kiss me because I am... unhappy."

Eric shook his head. "That was more than being unhappy. I hurt you. My fears, while yeah, I have reason to be afraid... they're not a good reason to *hurt* you the way I did."

"Cariño, I will be—"

"Don't. I know it's not true." Eric ran a thumb over Ben's cheek as Ben dropped his gaze to Eric's throat. "You're still worried I'll reject you. The only thing I can do is tell you I won't... and not let the portion of our bond that is there now fade."

Ben looked up again. "The portion of our bond?"

Eric nodded. "Yes. The bit that we strengthened with our first kiss. I'm so sorry, baby, that I ruined it."

Ben was having trouble breathing. "You mean it? You do not want it to fade?"

"Yeah, I mean it. And no, I don't." Eric pulled him closer, wrapping both arms around him. "Gods, you feel so fucking good here. I *want* to bond with you, Ben. I *want* to do more. But I'm not there yet. However, I'm not going to do this to you. It might not have been all *that* long, but it's time I start facing these fears. If I trust my wolf and our goddess, then I have to face them. They aren't going to go away on their own."

Ben took a deep breath. "Thank you, cariño. I—" He cut himself off, burying his face in Eric's neck instead to keep the words he'd almost blurted contained. He was sure Eric wasn't ready to hear them yet. He put his own arms around Eric and held tight, taking a deep inhale and letting his mate's scent help calm him.

"I'm sorry, baby," Eric murmured.

Ben pulled back. "You do not have to be sorry."

"No, I do. I hurt you and I ruined our first kiss. It should have been something we celebrated. Instead, I freaked out. So, yeah, I do have to be sorry, and I am."

Ben didn't know what to say to that. "Well. Uh…. It's okay." He frowned. "How did you find me? And, uh, why did you go looking? Did Finley or Tanner go after you?"

Eric shook his head. "So sure you're not wanted," he murmured and Ben blushed. "I was worried about you. You were gone so long. I know we lose track of time as wolves—I lost track of years. Almost a decade." Ben chuckled and Eric smiled. "But even so, it seemed too long. And I followed your scent."

Ben blinked. "You can do that?"

Eric raised his eyebrows but nodded.

Ben drooped. "I did not hear you approach. I didn't even know I could find your scent like that. I am a terrible wolf."

Eric flashed him a smile. "Well, as it so happens, I'm an *excellent* wolf. I can help you be a better wolf, just like you're helping me be a better human."

Ben blushed but looked up. "You'd do that? Teach me to be a better wolf?"

Eric nodded. "Happily, baby."

"I like that," Ben whispered.

"Baby?"

Ben nodded.

"Then that's what I'll call you." Eric kissed him softly on the lips, and Ben savored the feel of his mate's lips on his, even as light as the kiss was. "I have something to ask you."

"Oh?" Ben blinked.

Eric nodded. "Would you like to go out on a date with me?"

Apparently Ben wasn't done being surprised. "You… want to go on a date?"

Eric grinned. "Yup." He chuckled. "I gotta show off those silverware skills you helped me get back, don't I?"

Ben couldn't resist laughing, but he sobered again. "But… what about people?"

Eric's grin faded a little. "I've been letting myself hide. Like getting past my fears about bonding, I'm never going to get better about being around other people if I'm not… around other people. I can't think of a better way to deal with it than spending time with you, my mate."

Ben's smile was huge. "I'd like that very much."

"I'm not sure I'm up to driving yet. In fact, I don't even know if I have a driver's license anymore." Eric shrugged. "You'll have to drive us for now. But—"

"I do not care even a little, cariño. I will be happy to drive us."

Eric flashed his smile again. "Good. Now… I think we should get back to the house before I do something I'm not ready for. You are way too hot to be around naked right now."

Ben blushed to the roots of his hair. "Uh…."

Eric grinned. "And that just makes you cute."

Ben scowled. "I am not cute."

Eric chuckled. "Yes, you are. So, mate… how about we finish Star Wars?" He stood and held his hand out.

Ben stood with him and nodded. "That sounds good to me."

"Let's shift and run. We'll get there faster. And I won't have to look at your hot naked body."

Ben laughed. "Race you?"

"You're on!"

Eric waited for Ben to shift but then took off. Ben followed, feeling more hopeful than he'd been in a long time.

Chapter 9

ERIC FLEXED his hand a couple of times, then clicked the pencil until he had a decent point and took a deep breath. He closed his eyes, brought the image to mind he wanted, and put the pencil onto the sketchbook.

Then froze. He couldn't seem to make himself move the pencil, even to draw a straight line—not that he wanted one. That didn't matter, though. His hand did *not* want to move.

He took another breath and closed his eyes again. "Diana, I could use a little help here. I need to be useful to the mate you've given me," he whispered, grateful Ben wasn't in the house at the moment. In fact, no one else was. He was alone, which was one reason he'd decided to try drawing right then. He just couldn't seem to speak louder. "It's all I know how to do, Goddess. Please help me."

With one more deep breath, he focused again on the pencil. This time he forced himself to move it. Lines, rough circles, vague shapes emerged on the page. Within a short time, he turned to a fresh sheet and started over.

It took several of those pages before he even remotely liked what formed. It was still rougher than he wanted it to be, but he had to admit, he'd been without a pencil for nine years. It was *going* to take time for him to like what he did.

Still, he didn't stop. While the house was quiet and the light was good, he put the picture of the two wolves—one very dark, one lighter— aside and tried something different. Trees formed, rough ground cover joined them, and Eric was pleased to see the picture actually resembled something vaguely forestlike.

He lost track of time; the only thing indicating its passage was the change in sunlight through the windows. He was, in fact, so absorbed in what he was doing, it wasn't until the door opened that he was even aware another person was around.

He scrambled to close the sketchbook, not ready to show anyone what was inside yet, not even his mate. Even so, when Ben walked in, he didn't try to hide what he'd been doing. "Took a while?"

Ben nodded. "Yeah, I had to get fingerprinted and set up for a background check apparently. And there was a line for that."

Eric stepped up to Ben and leaned in, pressing his lips against Ben's. Ben wrapped his arms around Eric, who reciprocated with his free one. They got lost for a few moments, simply kissing. When they broke apart, he rested his forehead against Ben's. "I like being free to do that. I like feeling like I can."

"So do I, cariño. I'm very glad you can." Ben pulled back and tilted his head. "Did I see you with your sketchbook?"

Eric nodded. "I'm not ready to show it, but yeah. I've been drawing."

Ben's face split into a wide grin. "I better make sure my guitar is tuned, then."

Eric grinned. "Yep. Though…." He glanced at the clock. "Maybe tomorrow night? If I recall, we've got plans."

"Yes, we do. Are you sure you're ready for this?"

Eric took a breath but nodded again. "Yes."

Ben raised an eyebrow. "Really?"

With a laugh Eric nodded once more. "Yeah, I am. If you're there."

"I would hope you do not intend to take someone else out on a date meant for me."

This brought another laugh from Eric. "Right. Well, we should get ready, right?"

"Yes." Ben wrinkled his nose. "The downtown offices were very stuffy and hot, especially for a fall day. I need to shower."

Eric made a show of sniffing him. "Yeah, you do."

Ben snorted, dropped a kiss on Eric's cheek, then stepped back. "You are lucky we are fated."

Eric flashed a grin. "You'll keep me around."

With an eye roll and another kiss to Eric's cheek, Ben turned toward the stairs. "I'll be done shortly."

Eric checked the clock. "We have a bit of time. I'll want a shower too."

"All right." With a wave, Ben started up the stairs.

Eric watched Ben's ass wiggle as he took the steps, then forced himself to turn around and sit back down. He had a few more moments to draw.

ERIC ENDED up having to scramble to get ready. He'd gotten completely lost in a drawing, surprising himself when Tanner tapped him on the shoulder. He'd blinked at the piece in front of him, not sure where it'd come from. A very beautiful wolfy-version of his mate stared up at him, mouth open, tongue lolling.

"Glad to see you're drawing, but I think your mate's ready to go."

"Shit!" Eric jumped up, slamming the sketchbook closed, and spun around. "Um... fuck. Tell him I'll be ready shortly." With that he dashed for the stairs.

"Yeah, just don't forget to actually get clean!" Tanner called to him.

Eric replied by waving his middle finger over his shoulder.

He jumped in the shower and scrubbed off—making sure he did, in fact, get clean—then hurried into his bedroom. He grabbed the hanger he'd put aside earlier and almost scrambled to pull on his clothes. He had to unbutton and rebutton his shirt when he realized they were off by one. He blew out a breath and slowed down, finally getting *that* right, at least. He was annoyed with himself for not leaving enough time to shave, but he'd just have to apologize profusely for that one. Instead, he made sure his hair didn't look like a train wreck, then stuffed his feet in his new dress shoes.

When he got downstairs, he was happy to hear Ben in the kitchen with Finley, so he snuck through the front door, ignoring Tanner's raised eyebrow. Checking himself in the window glass one more time, he rang the doorbell.

He grinned when Tanner called, "I think it's for you, Ben!"

A moment later Ben came to the door, a puzzled expression on his face, then laughed when he looked through the glass. He pulled the door open. "Hello, cariño."

Eric grinned. "Hi. I'm here to pick you up for our date."

Ben grinned back at him. "Well, I am ready." He paused, his gaze traveling down Eric's body, eyebrows going up as he did so. "You look really good. When did you get those clothes?"

Eric cleared his throat. "Tanner picked them up for me earlier today so I could surprise you. So... I pass, then, huh?"

Ben nodded. "You most definitely do, cariño." He smiled. "I especially like the blue on you."

Eric glanced down at the blue silk button-down shirt he'd picked out, then to the black twill pants. "Well, it's not much, not exactly a suit or anything, but... where we're going, one would be a little too much anyway." He grinned and winked. "Also, sorry I didn't shave." He rubbed his cheek.

Ben laughed. "It is okay. I like it a little rough. Should we go, then?"

Eric held a hand out toward the car. He let his gaze travel over his mate's body, taking in the lean, muscular frame that made something as simple as the khaki pants and basic dress shirt look good. Eric was very glad he'd gone with the pants and shirt he'd had Tanner get for him.

When they got to the car, he went to the driver's side and opened Ben's door for him. Ben raised his eyebrows and Eric grinned. "I asked you on the date. I can't drive, but I can still open your door for you."

"Thank you," Ben said, then kissed Eric before getting in the car.

"You're welcome." Eric shut his door, then ran around to the other side, pulling out the piece of paper he'd printed earlier. "All right. I want to give you directions, but not tell you where we're going right away. Is that okay? It's a little ways away, but I think you'll appreciate it."

Ben nodded. "That is fine with me." He looked sideways at Eric. "I'm just happy to be going out with you."

Eric couldn't resist leaning over and turning Ben's head. He cupped one cheek, then brushed his lips over Ben's. Ben responded, putting pressure behind the kiss, and Eric opened, deepening it. When they broke apart, Eric brushed his thumb over Ben's cheek, smiling at the look on Ben's face.

"I haven't gotten used to those yet," Ben whispered.

"Well, I hope to fix that." Eric's smile widened when Ben grinned. "Now…. How about that date?"

They didn't speak much as Ben drove. Once they were on the smooth streets, he held Eric's hand, following the directions he gave. It took them the better part of an hour, especially since they ran into traffic first outside Latrobe, then in New Alexandria, then on the approach into Monroeville. Ben introduced Eric to some of his favorite Spanish singers, and Eric was surprised he knew of a couple of them. Ricky Martin was singing something about goodbye—adiós, actually, since it was in Spanish—as they pulled into the parking lot of the shopping center.

Eric tensed when they pulled into a spot in front of the Mexican restaurant. He'd done a *lot* of research to find the place. Even so, he didn't know if Ben would appreciate it. He took a breath, braced himself, and looked over. But Ben had a huge grin on his face, and Eric relaxed.

Ben leaned over and kissed Eric's cheek. "Thank you, cariño."

"It's supposed to be the most authentic for the Western Pennsylvania region. I'm not sure how much that says, but…."

"I am sure it will be good." Ben kissed him again. "Stay. I will open your door this time."

Eric shook his head, but before he could protest, Ben was out of the car and around to his side. "I asked you on the date, silly."

Ben shrugged. "So? I can open a door for my mate too."

With a thank-you, Eric climbed out of the car. When he drew in a breath, he was thrilled to realize he wasn't immediately overwhelmed by the smells. Sure, the exhaust was still there, the strong restaurant smells still filled the air, but it wasn't any worse than it would have been before he'd gone wolf.

"Are you okay, cariño?"

"Yes, actually. I'm *really* good. It seems my filters are finally back in place." Eric's face split into a wide grin.

"That is wonderful!"

Eric took Ben's hand as they crossed the parking lot. Ben tensed when they got close to the door, and Eric looked over at him. "What's wrong?"

"Sorry, it is just that back in Texas, I would not have held a man's hand going into a restaurant like this."

"Ah." Eric nodded. "We're quite a bit more tolerant up here. Even those of other cultures, I think. If you're uncomfortable with it...."

Ben studied him for a long moment, then let out a breath and shook his head. "No. I will not hide you."

Eric considered him, then nodded and opened the door. Ben stepped through and, to Eric's happiness, took his hand again when they were both inside. The bright yellow walls, colorful murals, and red tile floors showed the effort the restaurant owners put into making the place *look* authentic. Eric hoped that extended to the food, which was much more important in his opinion.

It was a bit busier than Eric expected for a weeknight, but the host greeted them before too long. The man didn't even bat an eyelash at their hands, simply led them to their table. Eric wasn't sure if the guy was that tolerant or if he just had a really good poker face. Eric decided he didn't care and turned his attention to taking a seat at the table. It sat along the back wall, with high booths on either side, giving them a nice bit of privacy. After leaving their menus on the table, the host left.

Eric looked the menu over, a little taken aback that he didn't even recognize some of the names of the dishes. He was so lost in reading the descriptions, he didn't know the waiter was there until the bowl of tortilla chips landed on the table. When he looked up, he was surprised to see a very Mexican-looking man next to them, especially since the host hadn't been of any obvious ethnic origin. He didn't know why that would throw him off at all, except despite it being a Mexican restaurant, he hadn't really expected to find the waitstaff to be as well.

Before Eric could speak, Ben greeted the waiter in Spanish, and then the two of them went into a rapid string of it that Eric couldn't hope to follow, not that he understood *any* Spanish. Finally he heard, "Corona, Corona Light, Dos Equis, Modelo—"

"I heard Corona. I'll take that," Eric cut in.

Ben looked at him and blushed. "For me too." He looked back up to the waiter, who nodded and left.

"I am going to have to learn that."

Ben blushed bright red, and fear and panic hit Eric *hard* across their bond. "I am so, so, *so* sorry, cariño! I did not even think about it!"

Eric reached out and laid his hand over Ben's. "Hey, hey! I'm not upset. Really, it's okay. I just realized I *should* learn your native language. If my mate speaks something, I should know it too."

"But—"

Eric got up and stepped around the table. Ben looked puzzled but scooted over, and Eric sat next to him. He turned on the bench a little and took Ben's hand again. "I can't imagine what it must be like to *always* speak in a language other than the one I learned to talk in. If I were in another country—say, Mexico—outside the cities, where English is less common, I would need to speak Spanish most of the time, right?"

Ben nodded, looking puzzled, but Eric just continued.

"If I ran across someone who spoke English, I'd slip into it without even thinking about it, because that's where my ability to talk began. I understand it's the same for you with Spanish. I'm assuming that's what your parents spoke when you were little?"

"Yes. In fact, I did not learn English until I was in school, and even then, it took a while." Ben frowned. "You should not have to learn, though."

"I don't have to." Eric shrugged a shoulder.

Ben blinked at him. "But, I thought you said—"

"I did phrase it that way, but what I meant was that I want to be able to speak to you in your native language, so I am going to have to learn it if I want to do that."

The fear and panic eased, and Eric mentally patted himself on the back.

Ben peered up through his eyelashes at Eric. "If... if you really want to learn, I will help you."

Eric beamed at him. "Good. I sort of slept through French in high school, so I have no basis for learning a language."

"Perhaps we can find you a program on the computer or something."

"Good idea." Eric squeezed his hand. "Now, would you order for me?"

"Really?"

"Yes." Eric nodded. "Besides... I don't know what half of those dishes are."

Ben laughed. "Okay, cariño."

"Hey, you know what I like." Eric glanced around, and when he was sure no one was watching, he kissed Ben on the temple, then moved back to the other side of the table. "I figure we're doing enough by being here together," he said at Ben's puzzled look.

"I understand. More tolerant, perhaps, but we could still get bad reactions if we're too outward with affection."

"Yeah, and I don't really want to get into a fight on our date."

Ben smiled. "No, that would be messy."

"Exactly. There are much more pleasant ways to get messy on a date." Eric winked.

"Yes, yes there are," Ben said softly.

The heat in Ben's eyes went straight to Eric's cock. He was going to have to adjust himself. He wished, in that moment, with everything he was, that he didn't have the hang-ups he did about bonding, because he wanted nothing more than to drag Ben home and fuck him into the mattress.

Eric cleared his throat and looked at the menu again. "So, uh, what do you suggest?"

EMPTY DISHES, drained beer bottles, and crumpled napkins littered the table between them. Eric sighed as he finished the remaining bits of his last beer. "So... what's the verdict?"

Ben grinned. "Definitely authentic, cariño. I mean, it is not my mamá's cooking, but...."

"Well, my mom wasn't much of a cook, but I doubt much would compare to the stuff Tanner's mom made me, so I get it."

"I appreciate you going to the trouble to find it."

Eric smiled. "I'm happy to." He let the smile fade. "I… I can't do what we both really need, not yet. But… if I can do other things to help our mating, I'm going to."

Ben tilted his head. "Cariño… you have not rejected me—"

"That is hardly enough," Eric said, scowling. "Look… what I had with Kim couldn't be considered much of a relationship, I get that. But I learned enough to know they take work. It's not just about us—" He paused and glanced around, then leaned in and lowered his voice. "It's not just about us biting each other and living happily ever after. Hell, even Tanner and Finley still work on things."

Ben nodded. "I do know that much, but for me… I suppose I never expected to find my… to find you. And I never talked to my mamá or papá about destined, so I did not—" He frowned. "I mean, my mamá and my papá have fights. I thought that was mostly because she is"—he lowered his voice—"human."

Eric shrugged. "I don't know about that. I'm sure that's part of it, but I doubt it's the biggest part. We're all human, when it comes down to it. With… extra abilities." He winked and Ben laughed. "But we still have the same human faults, human fears, human needs… human shortcomings. I learned that the hard way. I have no doubt I didn't do half of what I should have when it came to things with Kim. Maybe it would have gone better, but I suspect not. Either way, I was certainly not perfect. You are important. Too important for me not to try everything I can. I'll fuck up. I'm apparently good at that."

Ben scowled. "You should not talk about yourself like that."

Eric grinned. "I'll count on you to remind me."

Ben shook his head, but he was smiling again.

The waiter brought their check then, and Eric grabbed it before Ben could. Ben raised an eyebrow and Eric shrugged. "I asked, I pay. I mean… at some point, it'll all be the same money, but… it's a thing."

Ben nodded. "Okay, cariño."

Eric pulled out the card Tanner had gotten him with his name on it. It occurred to him that he was going to have to go get a state ID or something until he could get a driver's license again, in case someone asked for it when he went to pay. Eric pushed the thought off and smiled at the waiter as he took it away.

Eric sat back and considered his mate for a moment. "You know, if someone had told me ten years ago that not only did I have a destined mate, that it'd be male, *not* Tanner, and as… gorgeous as you… with the soft brown hair and beautiful brown eyes, I'd have laughed. I most definitely would not have believed them."

Ben blinked at him. "Were you in the closet then?"

"Yes, but mostly I didn't think destined mates came in the same-sex variety. But I also used to be all about reds, especially hair. That was my thing. Oh how wrong I was."

Ben blushed brightly. "Uh…."

"Well, see? There's the red," Eric teased.

Ben rolled his eyes. "You are terrible."

Eric grinned. "Yup. Are you telling me after the time we've spent together, you haven't figured this out yet?"

Ben shook his head. "You must hide it well."

Eric threw his head back and laughed. "Good reply." He picked up his glass of water and sipped it, looking around the restaurant, hoping for the waiter to come back. He wanted to get on to the next part of their date.

Just as he set the glass down, a woman walked by that Eric couldn't keep from looking at. His head swiveled of its own will as she passed. He turned back and blinked at Ben. "Oh shit! I'm so sorry, I—"

"She had a really nice ass," Ben murmured, leaning over a little.

Eric looked at the aforementioned body part, then back at his mate. "She does." Eric stopped and his eyes widened. "Wait… that didn't bother you?"

Ben blinked at him. "What?"

"I… I was just looking at a woman. While on a date with you."

"Okay?" Ben looked genuinely puzzled. "Why would that bother me? Are you planning to go chase her down and ask her out, then dump me? Or go start kissing on her?"

Eric scowled. "Of course not."

"Well, then. We're mated—even if we're not claimed yet, but mated. But we are not dead. We can appreciate a nice view." Ben hesitated. "Look, my wolf would be happy if you never even looked at another person as long as you live. That is *obviously* not going to happen. So… you were not touching her, just looking."

Eric relaxed a little and smiled. "Well… as long as *you* don't decide to dump me for her."

Ben laughed. "Hardly, cariño. She could not be you."

That comment made Eric feel ridiculously good.

The waiter returned then, and Eric turned his attention to the check.

"WE'LL BE going back toward home from here," Eric said as they settled in the car again. "There's a little place Tanner and Finley told me about that they go to sometimes. It's a bar with a decent, if small, dance floor. Finley says the music's good, and Tanner says they're gay-friendly. It's not a *gay* club, per se, they're just friendly toward LGBT people."

"That sounds good to me. You have directions?"

Eric nodded and pointed toward the way they'd come.

Ben turned the radio on, and Eric enjoyed the music as they drove, even if he couldn't understand the language. He liked the melodies and found the Spanish language really could be beautiful. He chuckled softly to himself.

"Is something funny?" Ben asked.

Eric cleared his throat. "I was just thinking I liked listening to the Spanish and, uh, was wondering… never mind," he ended up mumbling.

"No, tell me, cariño. I will not laugh at you."

Eric sighed and looked out the window. "I wondered what it would sound like if you were speaking Spanish to me. You know, like, um… when, uh…."

"I got it." Ben squeezed his hand.

Eric let out a breath. "You know, I used to try to be romantic and stuff with her. Like… flowers and stuff. And she always laughed at it." He shook his head. "I have no idea what I saw in her. I mean, I get it. Not everyone is into that stuff. I've known a few girls who were way more into sports than anything else, right?"

Ben nodded.

"But…. Kim *wasn't* like that… except with me." Eric shook his head. "I should have seen things. Tanner tried to tell me. I just wasn't willing to listen."

"Sometimes we have to learn things the hard way. I tried for so long to just hide the part of me that my mamá did not like. But eventually I figured out it was not possible. Especially if I got stressed out—you know how we are—and more than a few times, I have shifted uncontrollably."

"You'll never have to fight that again," Eric promised him. "You should never have in the first place, but now… well, you're a beautiful wolf. I'll want to see it a lot."

Ben smiled. "I am looking forward to letting him out more."

They drove without talking for a while, the silence only broken by the music and Eric's directions. When Ben pulled up in front of the small building, Eric was dubious. It didn't look like much from the outside. A squat brick building with a small awning over the single door and a few high neon-filled windows. He trusted Tanner and Finley, though, and stepped out of the car and went around to open Ben's door, happy when Ben waited for him to.

"I know it doesn't look all that great, but they said it's decent."

"I'm sure if nothing else, we can have a couple of beers before we go home."

Eric smiled. "Yeah, true."

It took a moment even for Eric's preternatural vision to adjust to the dark interior. The inside wasn't any more elaborate than the outside was. A long wooden bar stretched along the right wall. Small round tables and fragile-looking chairs filled the portion of the floor nearest the door, and a postage stamp–sized dance floor took up the space on the other end. A door in the back wall led, presumably, to the restrooms.

The music wasn't too loud, and Eric wondered if more wolves visited there than he originally thought. Most bars he'd been in back before he'd gone wolf—though he wasn't *supposed* to be in them back then, of course—had been so loud that he hadn't been able to hear himself think. But this one didn't make him want to stuff his ears with foam to block the sound.

While the bar wasn't lavishly decorated, it was clean and the furniture was in good shape. And there, above the bar, hung a neon rainbow. It wasn't exactly huge, but it was unmistakable.

A few guys sat at the bar, and one male/female couple took up a table in the corner. In the other, a couple of other guys sat together, though Eric couldn't tell if they were *together* or not.

They approached the bar and each took a stool. The bartender was younger than Eric expected for some reason, looking barely older than he was. "Evening. What can I get for you?"

Eric glanced at the taps and nodded. "Rolling Rock works for me."

"I will have the same," Ben said.

The bartender glanced from one to the other and smiled. "Be right back."

Eric relaxed, realizing he'd been interacting with people for a while and hadn't felt uncomfortable once. He looked over at Ben, sending up a silent prayer of thanks to Diana for him, because he had no doubt the vast majority of his comfort was because of his mate.

"Well, if nothing else, I don't think we'll get any crap if we want to dance." He waved a hand toward the tiny space for it.

Ben smiled. "I would like that. Do you dance?"

"I'm not exactly Fred Astaire, but I like to think I have a little bit of rhythm."

Ben laughed. "Well, then, I look forward to it."

The bartender came back and Eric paid for the drinks, which they both concentrated on for a little while, talking about mundane things like *The Force Awakens* and other movies. Eric simply enjoyed being close to Ben. Then the music changed to a dance song even Eric remembered, and he turned to Ben.

"Well, my mate, would you like to dance?"

Ben nodded. They went out onto the little dance floor, and Eric pulled Ben close.

"I have to admit something."

"What is that?"

"I've never danced with a guy like this. So, uh, if I step on your toes or something, I swear I don't mean to."

Ben laughed. "For the record, neither have I. I think we can handle it, though." He rested his hands on Eric's hips, and Eric put his on Ben's. Then they started simply moving to the music together. Despite the mostly joking comments, they danced together well, neither stepping on toes or hurting each other.

At least, not *those* kinds of problems. Before long, however, Eric was faced with a different kind. Despite his best efforts, before they'd even made it through two full songs, his formerly loose twill pants were uncomfortably tight, and it was taking all of his fortitude to fight his wolf, who was pushing him to take Ben somewhere—anywhere—pin him to the wall, fuck him within an inch of his life, then bite and claim him.

As frustrated as Eric was with his fears and hesitation, he wasn't quite in a place he could let it go completely. The memory of the pain he went through when Kim broke their bond was still way too vivid in his mind. But having Ben in his arms like this—the lean, toned body against him and Ben's own hard cock grinding into his—was making things incredibly difficult. It took all he had to keep his vision from going gray and his teeth from dropping. He hadn't smelled any other wolves and didn't need to scare the rest of the patrons half to death.

He lasted one more song, then tilted his head toward the bar. "Need a drink," he said in Ben's ear. It wasn't exactly a lie—his throat was dry—and he hoped it would help him get a better hold on his control.

Ben nodded, and they went back to the bar. They ordered fresh beers and took their seats, sipping on the brews. Except the break didn't help Eric calm down as much as he was hoping. Still, he wasn't going to cut their date short because he couldn't keep his dick from getting hard. For all his wolf was strong, he was stronger, and he *would* make this the best he could for Ben.

In hindsight, Eric should have taken a few more minutes in the shower and jacked off. He didn't know if it would have helped all that much, but considering it'd been way too long since he'd done anything with another person, a short masturbation session couldn't hurt either. In fact, he hadn't done that more than a couple of times since he'd been back either. Both times had been when Ben's scent had damned near driven him nuts. He'd closed his bedroom door and did his best to stay silent in an attempt to relieve a bit of the tension.

Regardless, he hadn't done it and was regretting that as he did his best to get control of his body. By the time he'd finished his new beer, though, he knew he wasn't going to be able to calm down much.

Still, he and Ben went back out for another couple of songs. But within a few moments, he knew it was hopeless. Having his mate in his arms, so close, the scent filling him, the feel of the hard body—and equally hard cock—grinding into him, was driving him crazy. He buried his nose in Ben's neck, inhaling deeply, unable to resist. "Gods, you smell amazing," he murmured. When he opened his eyes, he was chagrined to find everything *had* turned gray this time. He forced his teeth to retract before he lifted his face again to kiss Ben once more.

Ben was already tilting his head and kissing Eric's neck, then nuzzling him. "So do you, cariño. And you feel even better."

"Want you," Eric said, closing his eyes and struggling against the things his wolf was still pushing him to do. "Gods, I wish I was over this already. But—"

Ben reached up and put his fingers over Eric's lips. "Stop, cariño. I know. You are only going to make it worse. Kiss me, hold me. We will get to the rest. Just… maybe not tonight." He winked and Eric grinned.

"Yeah, okay." He caught Ben's lips with his, intending it to be a light kiss, but Ben opened to him and Eric couldn't resist deepening it. He let himself get lost in the feel and taste of his mate for a moment. When they broke apart, he stared into the gorgeous eyes—noting they'd bled black. "I… fuck, let's get out of here before we shift on the spot."

Ben chuckled and nodded. "Okay. Look—I do not want you to do anything you do not want to. That you are not ready for."

Eric shook his head. "No. But… if we stay here much longer, I will do something I'm not ready for. I… this was not the smartest idea for our date. I'm sorry."

"Shh," Ben said, shaking his head. "I am not unhappy."

A moment later they hurried out of the bar, hand in hand. Not long after that, they were on their way home.

Eric spent the entire time thinking of ways they could be together that wouldn't freak him out. He was determined not to ruin another of their firsts like he had their kiss. But his hard dick was making it extremely difficult to think, and touching Ben—even holding his hand—wasn't helping anymore.

He'd have to figure something out, though, because he had a feeling they weren't going to make it much longer—probably not even through the night—without doing something together.

Chapter 10

BEN COULDN'T miss the scent of Eric's arousal, and he was running the problem of what they could do through his mind as they turned off the smooth pavement onto the rough driveway leading up to the house. Having never had sex with another man, he wasn't sure exactly what they *could* do that wouldn't exchange fluids—and, thus, strengthen their bond. He'd certainly seen plenty of porn. It was the closest he'd felt safe doing to give in to that side of himself back home. But all of the porn he'd seen had either been oral to the point of orgasm or anal. Neither of which was going to work when it came to *not* strengthening their bond. He wished he'd thought to buy condoms, but it just hadn't entered his mind that they'd want to do something like this before they wanted to bond. So he was once again trying to figure something out that wouldn't strengthen it.

As much as he wanted to be with Eric, he didn't want to freak his mate out, didn't want to risk setting them back at all.

He contemplated that as he put the car into park, glad to see the blue Outlander wasn't there, which meant they had the house to themselves. They didn't speak as they stepped out of the car and turned to each other. Without a word—Ben suspected Eric didn't know what to say any more than he did—they clasped hands and walked up to the house.

Eric led him all the way in and up to the hallway outside their doors. Ben turned to him, and they stared at each other for a very long moment.

"Perhaps it would be best if we simply left it here, cariño, went to our separate beds. I… I do not want to, but I also do not want to cause you problems."

Eric tilted his head and studied Ben, tightening the hand he had around Ben's. He brushed his other thumb over Ben's cheek. "So worried about me. I care about you too, baby. I don't want to hurt you either."

It wasn't a declaration of love—though Ben was well aware he'd made no such declarations either—but Eric saying outright that he cared filled Ben with warmth. "It will not—no, I mean it," Ben hurried to add when Eric opened his mouth to interrupt. "It will not *hurt* me if we do not do anything more. Of course I want to be with you. I always want to be with you, touch you—or more. In this I think you're more important, though. You have a right to these fears."

Eric nodded. "Yeah, I do. I won't argue that. Come here," he whispered, tugging on Ben. "The least we can do is kiss good night."

Ben couldn't resist if he wanted to. His wolf—never the most insistent since he'd pushed him away so much—surprised him, pushing *back* for once. He wanted their mate. He wanted Ben to bite and claim. He didn't understand the hesitation. Ben gave in, at least a little, and poured all his want and need for Eric into the kiss. He let out the love he hadn't dared admit to out loud, sure Eric wasn't ready to hear it. But the time since he'd arrived in Pittsburgh, all the time he'd been able to spend with his mate, had given him ample opportunity to realize it wasn't just the link to Eric that made him want their mating so much. He'd fallen in love. Ben wrapped his free arm around his mate and tugged until they were flush against each other, opening to Eric's tongue touching his lips.

Eric wrapped his free arm around Ben as well, then let go of Ben's hand and lifted his to thread his fingers through Ben's hair. Eric tilted his head, his tongue sliding along Ben's and deepening the kiss even further.

Ben couldn't miss the hard length of Eric's cock against his own equally stiff length. He tried, he really did, to resist rocking into Eric, but he failed rather spectacularly. The movement brought a moan from Eric. When they broke apart, Eric rested his forehead against Ben's, both of them panting. Ben was gratified to see through the gray of his vision that Eric's eyes were now black and his teeth had dropped.

"I'm not sure I can just go to bed alone, baby." Eric swallowed. "I… I can't promise I won't freak out if we strengthen our bond, though, and I *will not* hurt you or ruin another first."

Ben closed his eyes, trying hard not to let it hurt. It shouldn't. He *did* understand Eric's fears. He might not have had the same thing happen to him, but he had his own set of fears. Still, despite that, a small stab went through him at the words. Annoyingly, it had no effect whatsoever on the state of his cock—or his vision or teeth. He took a breath to reassure his mate again, and an idea came to him.

"What if we just, uh, touched each other?" He blushed at stumbling over his words, but Eric apparently got the meaning. His eyes widened, and a slow smile spread over his face.

"Yeah, I think we could handle that." He let go of Ben, took his hand again, and backed toward Ben's room. "It's not *much* farther away from them." Eric tossed his head toward Tanner and Finley's room. "But it's at least a little more distance, if they come back before we finish."

After Eric opened Ben's door and they went inside, closing it behind them, they turned to each other, and Ben found himself more than a little anxious. *Now* his cock would choose to react—softening because of that.

Eric stepped up to him and brushed the backs of his fingers over Ben's cheek. "No need to be nervous, baby."

"You can feel that?"

Eric nodded. "You're transmitting pretty loudly." He gave a crooked smile. "I've never done anything with another guy. It's more likely you'll think I'm—"

Ben shook his head quickly. Eric raised an eyebrow, and Ben cleared his throat. "I have not been with a man either. I…. My experience is limited to my one girlfriend, and we did not do that much."

Eric's lips tilted. "My wolf wants to rip her throat out right now. He thinks she's competition for me."

Ben actually laughed. "No, cariño. Even if we were not destined, she could not compare. I did not love her."

He didn't realize what he'd let slip until Eric's eyes widened again. "Did you say…?"

Ben swallowed hard and his heart started pounding. *Shit. Shit, shit, shit.* "Um…."

"Whoa, hey, hey," Eric said, and Ben guessed he was transmitting his fear again.

"I am sorry, cariño. I know you're not ready for—"

"Shh," Eric said, putting a finger over Ben's lips. "I… I can't give those words to you yet. I'm sure I will, hopefully soon. I already care a hell of a lot about you. Losing you scares the shit out of me—losing *you*, not just my normal fears. *But* I also am sure I don't mind hearing them." He frowned. "That's not fair to you, I know."

Ben shook his head. "No. No, listen, cariño," he said when Eric looked like he wanted to argue. "Listen. That I have not freaked you out with this is what matters to me."

Eric studied him. "Really?"

Ben nodded. "I cannot lie to you, remember? What does our bond tell you?"

"That you're not lying." Eric shook his head. "I don't deserve you, Ben."

Ben took a deep breath. "I think you deserve someone who loves you. I will not say *me* exactly, but after everything you have been through, you most definitely do deserve someone who loves you. I… I do. So if that is me, then yes, you do deserve me." He swallowed and dropped his gaze to Eric's shirt collar.

"Well, then. I can't argue with that, can I?" Eric tilted Ben's chin up and covered his lips.

Ben didn't even hesitate to open to him. The kiss heated fast as Eric pulled Ben in again, crushing their bodies together, and even through two layers of twill and cotton, Eric's body felt so amazing, Ben moaned. It wasn't until they broke apart and he sucked in air that he realized he hadn't been breathing, the kiss and the feel of Eric against him taking every ounce of his thought.

Eric tilted his head, kissing a line down Ben's neck, bringing another moan from Ben. "Tell me if you don't like something," he murmured, then nipped at the spot where shoulder met neck. "Someday—I hope sooner, rather than later—I am going to bite you here and seal our bond. And I'm going to work hard to get us there."

Ben nearly whimpered at the promise. He managed to hold the sound in, but it morphed into a moan when Eric started on the buttons of Ben's shirt.

It was enough to remind Ben that *he* wasn't doing anything. He slid his hands up Eric's chest, then hesitated at the top button on the shirt. Eric looked up, and Ben met his eyes, waiting for his permission. He nodded in encouragement before going back to nipping at Ben's neck, then shoulder, as each button came undone and his shirt loosened.

Ben fumbled with Eric's shirt, then paused and took a breath to gather his wits. It was hard as hell to focus when Eric had already finished with his shirt and was running both hands over his chest.

Finally Ben managed to finish Eric's buttons, and they pushed the shirts off each other. Ben ran his hands lightly over Eric's naked chest, savoring the feel of the muscles. Eric had the lightest dusting of hair in the center of his chest, which arrowed to a treasure trail that disappeared under his waistband.

As he took in Eric's gorgeous muscles, he still worried what this might do to Eric. While it might not strengthen their bond directly, being intimate in this way was bound to change their relationship, even a little. Ben might not have had any experience in a same-sex relationship, but he didn't think they were all *that* different from opposite-sex ones. Sex meant intimacy, especially if you cared about each other.

He cleared his throat and decided to make sure one last time. "Cariño, are you sure about—"

Before he could even finish the thought, Eric caught his lips in another kiss and obliterated anything remotely resembling coherence. Eric pulled him in again, and the feel of skin against skin brought new moans from Ben. Eric's hard cock rubbed against Ben's, and the last of Ben's hesitation evaporated.

He pulled back, breaking the kiss, and fumbled with Eric's belt. His cheeks colored when he couldn't get the damned thing opened, but that faded when Eric seemed to have as much trouble with Ben's. Knowing his mate was as nervous as he was actually helped him feel better. Ben took a short breath, let it out, and finally managed to get the belt undone, then turned to the button and zipper.

Eric took that moment to kick off his shoes, and Ben did as well while he worked on Eric's pants. However, his brain was too far gone to focus on more than one thing at a time, so he concentrated on his shoes first, then opened Eric's pants.

When they dropped, he expected to see the basic Hanes he'd bought Eric when they'd gone shopping. Instead, what greeted him was black—at least, he thought so, since his vision was gray—and silky and *very* brief. Ben stared for a long moment at the snug way they fit and the lump filling them, the slight bit of the tip of Eric's dick sticking up over the top, and his mouth watered. "I do not remember seeing you buy these."

Eric gave a crooked grin. "Because I didn't buy them when you were with me. They were meant to be a surprise in case we did do something tonight."

Ben's eyes widened. "Does that mean…. *Tanner* bought them for you?" His wolf did *not* like that idea and came out a little, because the words were almost growled.

But Eric shook his head quickly. "No, no. I ordered them online a couple of days ago, after you agreed to the date. I just paid a little extra to make sure they were here on time." The wolf calmed and Eric's grin returned.

Ben let out a breath. "I'm sorry, I—"

"Oh no. I'm glad you're possessive of me."

Ben relaxed a little more. "Well, I definitely like them, cariño," he said, still staring at them, and his cock twitched and filled even further.

"I'm glad to hear it. But you are way too dressed." With that Eric finished opening Ben's pants, and they fell. Ben kicked them to the side, and both of them spent an awkward moment getting rid of their socks. But then they were kissing again as they more stumbled than walked to the bed and fell together.

Ben didn't think he'd ever get tired of the feel of Eric's lips on his, of the addictive taste of his mate. If his cock wasn't so insistent, he could spend an entire evening just kissing Eric. But his cock was hard, ridiculously so, and Ben needed more.

At that moment, though, Eric hauled him in, their legs threading and cocks lining up. Ben rocked into Eric, rubbing their lengths together through their briefs and making Ben groan. If he wasn't careful, he'd go off like some teenager, right in his underwear, and he did *not* want to embarrass himself that way.

He pushed Eric onto his back, trying to distract himself. Ben had no idea how often something like this might happen—or when it might again—and he wanted to take his time, learning as much about Eric and savoring the experience as much as he could. This time *he* caught Eric's lips and poured his want for Eric into it, making it long and thorough.

When he broke the kiss, he dove for Eric's neck, nipped along it, then made his way over Eric's chest. Eric threaded his fingers through Ben's hair, and Ben looked up to find Eric's heated, intense gaze fixed on him. Ben teased one nipple, flicking it with his tongue, bringing a shout from Eric, whose hand briefly tightened in Ben's hair.

"Fuck, baby!"

Ben grinned and, his eyes locked to Eric's, moved to the other one. He gave it the same treatment, pulling a groan from Eric this time. Then Ben turned his attention back to the chest in front of him, briefly rubbing his face over the hair. By this time Eric's sounds seemed to merge one into the other, and Ben thrilled in the evidence that he was doing the right things to pleasure his mate.

Ben followed the treasure trail but stopped to tease along the top edge of the black silk briefs. He stayed carefully away from the precum dripping from Eric's dick. He had no idea if that little bit would make a difference, but he wasn't taking chances. Instead, he brushed his lips over the silk-covered length. Eric's shout this time made Ben's cock jump. He had to pause briefly to again struggle with his wolf, who wanted so much more than he was doing. He won, of course, but his wolf was most definitely not happy about it.

He pushed the thought off and focused on going back to teasing Eric, but Eric had, apparently, had enough of that. He tugged on Ben, who moved up along Eric's body and settled in next to him.

"Much more of that, baby, and I'd be spraying the inside of those briefs."

Ben couldn't stop a chuckle at that, making Eric grin. "I had that same thought earlier."

"Yeah. Well, it's my turn," Eric said, then dove for Ben's neck, and Ben struggled to find some little bit of sanity. Eric's lips on his, then nipping a line over his neck and chest, teasing his nipples, tracing the lines of his muscles, brushing over his own treasure trail—all of it stole Ben's ability to think. His cock jumped, precum leaking copiously, and it took everything Ben had to keep from doing more than resting his hand on Eric's head. He needed that bit of touch, but it was so hard not to pull on the hair, not to nudge Eric where Ben wanted him. Because that way lay disaster and Ben couldn't forget it.

Instead, he gripped the headboard with his other hand and tried not to come when Eric ran his lips over Ben's length through the cotton. There'd just been too much touch, too much everything, and Ben was sure he was going to go off any moment. "*Cariño.* If you do not... oh *fuck,* stop, I...."

To Ben's mingled frustration and relief, Eric did, in fact, stop. He sat up and tugged on the waistband of Ben's briefs, and Ben lifted his hips to help Eric get them off. Gaze focused on Ben, Eric leaned down and very gently kissed Ben's cock.

"One day soon, I'm going to taste all of this," Eric whispered.

Ben couldn't stop the mental image of Eric's lips wrapped around his cock. Despite his best efforts, he let out a small sound while Eric wiggled out of his own briefs, cock springing free and making Ben's mouth water. It was just a little larger than his, and he wanted nothing more than to push Eric over and swallow it whole, or beg Eric to fuck him. Or something.

He was grateful when Eric effectively derailed Ben's thoughts by asking, "Do you happen to have any lube?" Ben nodded, leaned over Eric, and dug into the bedside table drawer. He emerged with the half-filled bottle and handed it over.

Before Ben could say or do anything, Eric kissed him again, their tongues sliding, the taste filling him. Ben broke the kiss when Eric wrapped his hand around Ben's cock. He moaned, lost to the feel of Eric's hand on his naked length, forgetting everything but the sensation of Eric stroking him. He bucked without meaning to, the pleasure taking all of his attention.

Eric brushed his thumb over the tip of Ben's cock, spreading the precum and sending a sharp spike of pleasure through Ben. A moment later, however, Eric let go, and Ben panted hard as Eric fumbled with the bottle. Eventually he got it open and poured some into his hand, then held it out for Ben.

It took Ben a few seconds to calm down enough to actually work the stupid bottle. He was so aroused, needed so much, his hands shook. He couldn't remember it ever being this… needy, this almost desperate before. Finally he had some of the lube in his palm and could focus once more on pleasuring Eric. He wrapped his hand around Eric's length, spreading the slick over it, then started stroking him.

Eric's "*Ben*" was almost a shout. If he'd been thinking clearly, Ben would have been embarrassed by how loud it was—but then he remembered Tanner and Finley weren't home. As it was, Eric chose that moment to reciprocate, spreading the lube over Ben's cock and stroking it, so he couldn't think enough to worry about it.

Within what could only be a minute or two, Ben was having trouble holding back. It seemed ridiculous he could be that close that fast, but he was. Maybe it was the fact that it was *Eric*, the man he'd fallen so hard for, his destined mate. Or maybe it was an entire evening of touching, kissing, feeling so much. Ben didn't know and couldn't muster enough brain power to care.

"Oh gods, cariño, so good," he moaned, and Eric's hand tightened. "So… I'm so—going to…."

"Me too, baby," Eric said, panting hard. "Feels amazing." He kissed Ben again, and the combination of the deep kiss, the hand around his cock, the feel of the length in his hand… all of it was just enough.

With a shout that Eric swallowed with their kiss, Ben's climax hit, the pleasure more than he'd ever felt. He broke the kiss, moaning Eric's name as he coated their chests and hands in his cum. Eric kept going, stroking him through the orgasm, stretching the pleasure out.

Just as Ben calmed down, Eric buried his face in Ben's neck, a long, low groan coming out as he covered them in his own cum. He rocked into Ben's hand, and Ben cobbled together enough wits to tighten it, doing his best to prolong Eric's orgasm as much as he could. Eric shook in Ben's arms, and Ben savored the knowledge of the pleasure he was giving.

They both went boneless at the same time, nearly melting into the mattress. Eric looked up at Ben and their lips met, this kiss slower but no less full than the rest. They might not have strengthened their mate bond, but there was no doubt Ben felt closer, no doubt of the emotion Eric put into the kiss. Maybe he couldn't use the word yet, couldn't say it out loud, but Ben could feel how much Eric wanted him, cared about him, through the kiss.

When they broke apart, Eric studied Ben, his eyes dancing over Ben's face. "You are... amazing and wonderful and... I... I've never been one much with words." He shook his head. "That was...."

"Incredible," Ben finished for him. Eric's smile spread and he nodded. "So are you, cariño. Thank you," he said softly, then kissed Eric, though keeping it soft and almost chaste.

They lay in silence for several long moments. Ben wasn't sure how he was going to be able to sleep surrounded by his mate's scent, yet not being close physically. Normally the scent calmed him, but the smell of sex and cum was also heavy in the air and would only serve to remind him of what he still didn't have yet.

He didn't mean to let the sigh out, and when Eric frowned at it, he wanted to kick himself for it.

"What's wrong, baby?"

Ben shook his head. He was *not* going to guilt Eric into something he wasn't ready for. He hadn't always been right about what would freak Eric out, but he really did *not* think Eric needed to hear this.

"Hey, hey." Eric lifted Ben's chin until they were looking at each other. "I might not have had the best relationship with Kim, but I learned a few things from it. One of those was that not talking about things only causes problems. I know something's wrong. Even without our bond, I know. What is it?"

Ben sighed again, then blurted, "I do not want to be without you tonight." He closed his eyes, hoping and praying—in a way he never had before—that Eric didn't freak.

"I don't want to be without you either."

Ben's eyes flew open and he stared at Eric. "You... do not?"

Eric shook his head. "No. I'm not sure I *could* sleep without you. Regardless of whether I could or not, though, I don't *want* to."

"But...." Ben swallowed.

"No, no 'buts.' We both know I'm not ready to strengthen our mate bond further, but the rest of our relationship? Yeah, I'm going to do everything I can to work on that. I'm not going to get up after we've had sex—even as limited as it was—and go to my own bed to leave you here alone."

Resting his forehead on Eric's chest, Ben closed his eyes again. "I do not want you to feel like I am pushing you."

"You're not, baby. I was trying to figure out how to bring it up, actually." Eric chuckled, and Ben looked up once more. "Really. I want to be here. I want you here, in my arms. My wolf is never calmer or happier than when your scent is so close. *I'm* calmer, happier, when you're close to me. And...." He paused and took a breath. "And that's not just the destined link either, baby."

Ben couldn't stop the smile over that. "I, we—my wolf and I—are the same."

Eric kissed him softly. "Then I suppose we should clean up a little and settle in. It's getting kind of late."

Ben chuckled. "Yes, it is."

A short while later, they were clean and had settled in a tangle of limbs under the covers. Eric's scent filled Ben, and just before he drifted off, Ben whispered, "I love you." Eric's arms tightened, and Ben fell asleep to a kiss on his forehead.

Chapter 11

ERIC LAY in the early-morning quiet, with Ben tight against him, his arms around his mate. He liked that the thought—the idea of having a mate—didn't bother him nearly as much anymore as it used to. The concept of bonding still scared him, but he could admit even that wasn't as bad as it'd been.

Everything with Ben was *so different* than what he'd had with Kim. It wasn't gender, he was sure of that. Some of it was that Ben was his destined mate, and that undoubtedly helped. But that wasn't all of it. Everything felt different, from simple touch to the pet name—and not just because it was in Spanish. She used to call him "baby," but when he compared it to "cariño," Ben's felt more… real, somehow, like there was more meaning behind it. Probably because there was.

Eric was sure, somewhere along the way, he'd loved her. While he wasn't quite ready to say the words to Ben, he already knew what he felt for Ben was different and more than he had for her.

The sad part to him was that he wasn't sure she'd ever loved him. She'd said it, at least up until he'd claimed her. But he couldn't remember her saying it more than a handful of times after. And thinking back on it now, especially when he compared it to Ben saying it, Eric was sure she hadn't meant it. She might have loved the idea of him—or what she and his parents wanted him to be—but she didn't love *him*. The him who wanted to craft leather goods for a living. Not because he *couldn't* go to college—he'd done quite well in high school and would have been fine in college—but because he loved what he did for the leather business, creating designs and pictures in the leather for them to make bags and other things with. She didn't love the him who wanted a nice small house, a few pups, and a more or less quiet life.

Ben had fallen in love with him when he hadn't even been mostly human, when he'd still been struggling to remember how to use a knife and fork, when he'd been trying to relearn how to filter basic smells and sounds. And when Ben had said those words, terrified they'd freak Eric out, there'd been nothing but real emotion behind them.

Eric closed his eyes and buried his face in Ben's short brown curls. He took a deep inhale, letting Ben's scent fill him. His cock twitched, remembering the night before, remembering Ben's lips and hands on him, the insane need and want going through him. He'd had a few good nights with Kim. But he could admit, he didn't think any of them—even though what he and Ben had done had been so basic—would compare. He'd wanted and *been* wanted, and there'd been absolutely no doubt about it.

He wanted Ben again, though he didn't want to keep suggesting sex that wouldn't allow them to bond. Once or twice might not bother Ben, but after a while, Eric was sure it would get to him. Hell, it bothered *him* that he wasn't ready to bond. *He* didn't like the idea of a lot of sex that wouldn't let them bond.

"You are thinking very hard, cariño. I can hear the gears turning from here."

Eric laughed, tightening his arms. "Good morning, baby." He kissed the top of Ben's head, and Ben looked up at him.

"Good morning. I'm glad to see you smiling. You do not regret staying, then?"

Eric shook his head. "Most definitely not. I hope you don't want the bed to yourself again." He held his breath a little, knowing what he was saying, hoping Ben would want it too. They both knew he wasn't ready to claim, so they'd be sharing a bed without bonding. He wasn't sure if Ben would even be able to handle that.

"You… want to stay with me?" Ben asked, eyes widening.

With a nod, Eric took a breath. "I'm still not sure when I will be ready to bond. But… I haven't slept this well in years, Ben. Having you here, against me, in my arms, was… almost perfect."

"Almost?" Ben raised his eyebrows.

"It will be once we claim each other. Until then, I'll take almost."

Ben's face split into a smile. "I can accept almost."

"Can you handle this? Sleeping together without being bonded? Will it hurt you?"

Ben hesitated and Eric swallowed, but he realized Ben was seriously thinking it through, not hesitating necessarily because he didn't want to. He was giving an honest answer, not just immediate platitudes that might not be true.

Finally Ben nodded. "I can handle it. I think it would be much better for me—for us—to be together."

"Then I will." Eric grinned.

Ben grinned too. "Good. I realized something last night, though. I do not know why I did not think of it before. We could buy condoms. We would be able to do—"

Before he was finished speaking, Eric was shaking his head. "Don't get me wrong, baby. I would love to do more with you. But...." He blew out a breath. "Once. *Once*, Kim and I had sex without a condom. Only once. She was terrified of getting pregnant. I understand now that she never wanted pups. At the time I didn't understand, but that didn't make it any better. She would not risk it. I think she also didn't want to bond with me beyond what she had to." He shook his head again. "But when we make love, baby, I don't want anything between us. I *want* to bond." He swallowed. "My fears are enough of a barrier."

"Then we will not use them. I am sorry, cariño. I did not know how you felt."

"Don't be sorry. Of course you didn't know. We never brought it up." Eric kissed Ben softly. "I'll work on us. I'm not going to let this go on forever." He sighed. "If we don't get up, however, I may do something we'll regret. You are a very sexy man, my mate. Besides, I need to talk to Tanner. It's time I get other parts of my—our—life moving."

"Oh?" Ben tilted his head.

Eric nodded. "Yes. I'll tell you once I talk to Tanner, though. Let me be sure of a couple of things first?"

"All right, cariño." Ben hesitated briefly, then kissed Eric. When they broke apart, with his eyes still closed, he buried his face in Eric's neck. "I like feeling like I can do that."

"Me too, baby." Eric brushed at the brown curls lightly. "I'm sorry again for—"

"You have apologized. No more." Ben looked up, and Eric considered him, then nodded.

"Okay. Well. How about some breakfast?"

Ben smiled. "Yes. But I think I might want to shower before that." He wrinkled his nose.

Eric laughed. "You can take the first one."

WHILE BEN was showering, Eric pulled his pants on from the night before and went back to his own room to get clean clothes for the day.

He considered whether or not he should actually move his few things into Ben's room, but he didn't want to assume and decided it would be a discussion for later. In the meantime he pulled on his jeans and went to find Tanner.

He found his best friend in front of the coffee maker, watching it brew. Tanner turned to him with a grin on his face. He sniffed, then raised an eyebrow. "Okay, not claimed, but his scent is all over you."

Eric scowled, though there was little heat in it. "I'm still working on that. He understands." He waved a hand when Tanner rolled his eyes. "Shaddup. We've got that part worked out for now. But...." He took a deep breath. "I would like to start trying to work with the leather tools again. And... I want to get back to working. Do you think there might be something I can do at the shop, even if I can't do the big designs yet?"

Tanner grinned. "Hell yeah. There's always a place for you there, dude."

Eric frowned. "I don't know if I'll ever get back to what I used to be able to do, but—"

"You will." Tanner nodded. "I'm sure of it. When do you want to go back?"

"Everyone's so sure," Eric muttered as he considered it for a moment. "Maybe Monday?"

"That's fine."

"Good. Um, also... I need a computer, but at this point, I have no fucking clue where to look or what to get. I'll buy it." Eric scowled, waiting for Tanner to argue, but thankfully Tanner stayed quiet, so he continued. "I just don't know where to begin. It needs to be able to run a language program, though I doubt that would take up a lot of processing power or other resources."

Tanner's grin came back. "I can pick something out if you want. Language, huh? That wouldn't be Spanish by any chance, would it?"

"Duh. What else would I want to learn?" Eric shook his head, punching Tanner in the arm, then looked away. "Hey, um... if it could run an art program, that'd be cool.... Is Photoshop still a thing?"

"Yeah. I don't know what version they're on now, but it's still out there and popular."

Eric nodded, relieved when Tanner didn't say anything more about it. His art was still a sore spot for him. "Okay, yeah. If it can run that, I'd like that. I also need to get a license or ID or something." He rubbed his face. "I've got a lot of shit to do."

"We can help with it. Let us do what we can."

Eric nodded, and Tanner put a hand on Eric's shoulder.

"Good. I'm glad to see you getting back into things, man."

"I'm trying." Eric looked up and met Tanner's eyes. "He's worth it. He's worth anything and everything I can do to get my life back. She fucked me over, man." Eric smiled when Tanner scowled. "But I refuse to let her ruin my entire life."

"I'm glad to hear that. She caused a lot of problems when she did what she did," Tanner said, then took a sip of his coffee. "To more than just you. But I can only imagine what it must have felt like. Not that I want to, mind you, but I can."

"Pure hell," Eric said succinctly. He pulled out a coffee mug, then put it in the machine, changed out the K-Cup, and hit brew. He turned around and leaned against the counter, considering his friend. "I've still got things to work on. Even recognizing all the shit she put me through, how wrong things were… I still haven't forgotten what it was like when she broke the bond. I'm still putting that away." Eric pulled the coffee out of the machine and took a sip. "But I am sick and tired of being afraid too. Yeah, she hurt me. And I fucked up. But it's past time I do something about both of those things."

ERIC LET the hot water beat down on him as he turned things over in his head. His decisions to go back to work, to get a better handle on life, felt right. It was time—past time—to stop letting what had happened control him. He'd been letting it, he could admit that, and he was better than that.

He shut the water off and gave himself a cursory pat down with the towel. Wiping the steam off the mirror, he considered himself. He needed a haircut and a good shave, but he liked what he saw. He'd always been pretty happy with himself. He was infinitely grateful Ben seemed to be too.

When his face was clear of hair, he pulled on clean jeans and T-shirt, then went in search of his mate. Ben was on the back deck, coffee cup in hand. Eric stepped up behind him and wrapped both arms around him. "Let's see if I get this right. Buenas días?"

"Buenos," Ben corrected him gently, turning in his arms.

"Buenos días," Eric said, and Ben nodded, grinning.

"*Sí.*"

Eric chuckled. "I've asked Tanner to help me get a computer. I'll start working on Spanish with it as soon as I get it." He took a breath and let it out. "I'm also going back to work."

"That's wonderful!" Ben kissed him hard. "At the shop?"

Eric nodded. "Yeah. I don't know when I might be able to do the designs I used to, but...." He shrugged.

"Have patience, cariño. It will take time, but you are capable of doing it."

"I hope you're right. I've missed it. I also wanted to ask you something." Eric took a breath, then let it out slowly. "Would you want us to, uh, have our... err... do you want us in the same room? Like...." He sighed. "Do you want me to move my things in with you?"

Ben blinked at him. "Of course, cariño. Why would I not want you to?"

Eric couldn't look up at him, instead staring at the collar on his T-shirt. "I don't know. This is all just... I've never done this before. It's all new to me. When Kim and I claimed, we lived with my folks for a long time. We'd just gotten our own place when she left. So...."

"It's new to me too. I've never lived anywhere but with my parents. But... I do not see why we should not share a room completely."

"Well...." Eric paused to try to find the right words. "It's the same reason I hesitated to say I wanted to sleep together. We're not claimed, not even bonded. I don't want to make you—"

Ben tilted Eric's chin up, and before he could even make a sound, Ben's lips covered his. Eric's eyes slid closed, and he let himself get lost in the kiss. When they broke apart, he struggled to breathe for a moment. "I love you, Eric," Ben murmured, kissing him again softly. "We'll get through this, together. We will work through your fears. I believe we are better together for it."

Eric swallowed and considered Ben, smiling when he saw nothing but determination in his mate's beautiful brown eyes. "Then I suppose we ought to spend today moving things into our room, huh?"

Ben's grin was wide. "Sí, cariño. We definitely will take the day to make it ours."

DETERMINATION WAS all well and good, but saying you're going to do something and actually doing it were two different things. Were it not for Ben holding his hand, Eric thought he might fly apart into a million tiny pieces when he stepped into the main shop building the following Monday morning. He'd been friends with many of the pack members who worked in the shop, and though he was sure Tanner or Alpha Noah had told them what happened, he'd just disappeared on them. He had no doubt at least some of them were angry over it. Eric took a deep breath, focused again on Ben's hand, then looked around.

The store itself was off in its own building next to the shop. They also sold pieces online—thanks to Tanner's insistence on a web presence—as well as on consignment to some of the nature shops around the area. Eric had rarely been in the store itself. Most of what he saw was the unfinished pieces of leather he put his designs on, then sent them off to another part of the shop to be worked into the bags, backpacks, and such for the shop to sell.

The front office only took up a small portion of the building. Most of the space was dedicated to working the leather and assembling the items to sell. The office consisted of the reception area, complete with the same lady wolf, Belinda, who'd been there for as long as Eric could remember. Behind her, the rest of the space was divided up into two other offices. Tanner had one of them, though he didn't spend all his time there, and the other would be Ben's office.

"Oh my gods, Eric!" Belinda shouted, jumping up and coming around her desk. Before Eric could brace himself, he was wrapped up in her arms, smashed against her rather ample chest, and squeezed.

His mate saved him. The growl had Belinda jumping back and blushing. "I'm so sorry! Eric, is this—"

"My mate," Eric said, grinning and turning to Ben. "Don't worry, baby. She's old enough to be my mom… and way more motherly than mine was."

Belinda smacked his arm. "Way to make me feel old."

Eric flashed her another grin. "Sorry, Bel. This is Ben, my destined mate… and our new accountant."

"Oh ho! Yes, Diana doesn't mess around with those destined mates, does she? Congratulations, honey!" Her nose twitched, and Eric was sure she was putting together that they hadn't claimed each other yet, but she was courteous enough to not ask. She turned instead to Ben. "It's nice to meet you. I'm the closest thing you'll have to an assistant, though I'm afraid I'm not good with the financial stuff beyond paying bills and depositing payments and the like."

Ben smiled at her. "It's nice to meet you too. And that's okay. I *am* good with it."

A wave of nervousness hit Eric across their bond, and Eric remembered Ben's worry about his background, especially since his accent was so recognizable. Eric didn't know what to do to help Ben feel better, other than to pull him closer and put an arm around him. It must have been the right thing, because the nervousness eased a bit and Ben's arm came around Eric, holding tight.

"Well, that's good. Noah's still doing some, but I know he's busy being the alpha prime." She shook her head. "Still getting over that."

"You and everyone else," Tanner said from behind them. "Especially him. We're going to show Ben around the place. Is his office ready?"

Belinda nodded. "Haven't done much of anything to it since Noah left."

"Good." Tanner turned to Ben. "Come on, guys."

They took the short hallway down to the shop floor itself, and before Eric could so much as look around, someone—a female with a voice he didn't readily recognize—shouted his name and the three of them were practically mobbed. Blonde hair covered his face as a pair of arms wrapped around him, and it was only the low growl from his mate—saved yet again by Ben—that had them releasing him. Eric finally recognized the woman as Annie, a girl who had been behind him a year in school and who'd been a friend, if not a close one.

"Oops!" she said, backing up quickly. "Sorry!"

Eric braced himself for the anger he expected, then took in all the faces turned toward him. But instead of anger, he saw all smiles. A few looked curiously toward Ben, then back at him.

"Hi." Eric had to clear his throat to be able to speak. "Um... I'm, uh, back. And, uh...."

Tanner waved to Ben. "This is Ben Arellano—"

"Dammit, you never pronounce his name right," Eric growled. Tanner smirked, and Eric knew Tanner had done it on purpose. He glared, promising retribution later—Tanner didn't look the least concerned—then turned back to the rest of the folks. "It's Arellano," he said, putting the correct pronunciation on it. "He's my destined mate. And our new accountant."

Chaos followed this announcement, with a lot of handshakes, back-patting, congratulations, welcomes, and "glad you're back" comments. Eric, in fact, was more than a little overwhelmed.

As was Ben, if the stunned look on his face was anything to go by—and the complete lack of *anything* across their bond. "They... they really do not care?" he whispered in Eric's ear.

Eric shook his head, not even pretending he didn't know what Ben was talking about. He wanted to say "I told you so" but instead said, "Nope. They don't. The rest of the pack won't either."

Ben shook his head as if to clear it, then turned to the people still congratulating them. "Thank you," he said, sounding more than a little stunned.

It took more time than Eric would have liked to extricate them from the well-wishers. It wasn't until Tanner made a few pointed comments about them needing to get settled that the others got the hint and went back to their workstations.

Tanner walked with them into the section where Eric's work area had been before he'd left, pointing to the exact same spot he used to occupy. "Dad wouldn't let anyone else take over. He was sure you'd come back and need your job." Tanner waved at the workbench, and despite what he'd been saying since Eric returned, Eric was surprised to see the tools in the exact places he'd put them when he'd closed up for the day the last time he'd been here. The lights were still set up just as Eric had liked them. Aside from being cleaned, it looked like nothing had been touched. There was a new addition in the form of a computer off to the side, and the bin of leather to be worked on was, of course, empty. But otherwise it was exactly as Eric had left it.

"I can't believe he kept it for me," Eric muttered, shaking his head.

"Dad was sure you leaving wasn't permanent. I don't know what made him so sure, but he was. So... there you are. I'm sure Dave—he's still in charge of the leather—can get you some scraps and such to practice with if you want to do that before starting a project."

Eric frowned. "I'm still not sure I can do all that again."

"I believe you can, cariño."

Eric glanced at Ben and smiled. "Well, maybe. I guess practicing on scraps is the best idea, yeah. Uh, is there stuff I can do besides that for work?"

Tanner didn't roll his eyes, but Eric was sure he wanted to. He sighed instead. "If you really feel the need, talk to Jack." He turned to Ben. "That's the shop... foreman, I guess you'd call him. He kinda manages everyone, though we don't really *need* to have them managed, for the most part.

Anyway." He turned back to Eric. "If you insist on doing something else, one of our shipping guys just moved out of the pack a few weeks back, so we're short a guy. If nothing else, you can package stuff to be sent out."

Eric nodded. "Okay, yeah. I can do that. I'll practice. If...." He rolled his eyes. "*If* I feel comfortable with the tools again, I'll start on simple designs."

Tanner shook his head. "Whatever. Come on, Ben. Let's get you settled."

Ben turned to Eric. "Can I kiss you here?"

Eric pulled Ben into his arms and did it without answering. When they broke apart, he smiled. "Our alpha has a same-sex mate. If the pack couldn't handle it, we'd already know."

Ben chuckled. "Okay, yeah." He paused, biting his lip, then said, "I love you." Before Eric could say or do anything in reaction, Ben gave Eric another quick kiss, and then he and Tanner disappeared through the door to the offices.

Eric stared after them for a long moment, letting the warmth of those three tiny words go through him. With a deep breath, he went in search of Jack.

Chapter 12

BEN ENDED up getting lost in accounts and numbers and ledgers and stayed late. He'd apologized profusely to Eric when he'd shown up at the end of the day, but Eric had kissed him, assured him it was fine, and went on home. Tanner had arranged for Finley to drop his car off, and then they'd left as well.

So, much later than he would have liked, Ben finally walked through the front door of Tanner and Finley's house. He still hadn't gotten to thinking of it as home yet. He hung his car keys on the hook they had by the door, then wandered through the main room. When he didn't see Eric, Ben kept going through the dining room and found him on the back deck at the table. A pouch lay off to the side, tools made a mess in front of Eric, and he held one as he pressed it into a small piece of leather.

Ben stepped up behind Eric as he worked. The lines and squiggles looked pretty basic, but Ben would be the first to admit he had no clue what was what when it came to Eric's work. Ben made a mental note to learn the names of the tools and get at least a rudimentary understanding of the process that went into setting the designs into leather. Aside from wanting to understand the company he worked for, he wanted to understand what his mate did for a living.

Eric inhaled deeply as he set the tool down, then looked up over his shoulder. He took Ben's hand and tugged until Ben moved around and was straddling Eric's lap. "I will never get tired of that scent," Eric murmured, burying his face in Ben's neck.

"That's good, cariño. Or our mating might get pretty boring." Ben wrapped his arms around Eric, then dropped a rather awkward kiss to Eric's temple when he chuckled.

"Took you a while, yeah?"

"Yes, I'm sorry. I got lost in the accounts and learning how the former alpha had things set up. But…." Ben let go of Eric and lifted a small plastic bag he held. "I did go into town for something else." He pulled a little square envelope out and held it up.

"Is that?"

"Guitar strings. I'm sorry again that I did not realize they were broken."

Eric waved that away. "While I may be a bit impatient with myself, I am not going to give you shit for something that's not your fault. I can be patient with *you*." He grinned and Ben laughed.

"Have you eaten?"

Eric nodded. "Yeah, Fin and Tanner made some meatloaf. There are leftovers in the fridge if you're hungry."

Ben shook his head. "I stopped at McDonald's drive-through on the way home." He caught Eric's lips in a soft kiss, then sat up again. "Let me go get my guitar. How is the leatherworking coming?"

Eric wrinkled his nose. "Slow, but that's to be expected. Opposable thumbs aside, it's been a long time since I've worked with the tools. It'll take a while to get used to using them again."

"I do not doubt that. I'm sure you will, though."

"You know…." Eric dropped his gaze to Ben's chest. "Your confidence in me helps. I mean, I'm beginning to believe I'll get back to doing some designs and stuff, but I'm still not sure about the really complicated stuff." He sighed. "But… knowing you believe in me helps me feel better about it."

Ben tilted Eric's face up and kissed him again. "I do believe in you. I've seen your art. Tanner has shown me pictures of some of the things you have done before. It's still in you. Some things never go away."

"I hope not." Eric tightened his arms and rested his face against Ben's chest.

Ben wrapped his arms back around Eric and buried his nose in Eric's long black hair. He took a deep inhale, savoring his mate's scent, though that caused its own problems. He hoped Eric didn't feel his cock stiffening, because he knew Eric was still hesitant about anything sexual, thanks to the fears about bonding. He didn't think he succeeded entirely, but he also thought Eric seemed to be having similar problems. When Eric didn't say anything, though, Ben started to worry. "Are you okay, cariño?"

Eric didn't speak, just nodded. Ben didn't think he was *lying* exactly—nothing came across their bond—but something was off.

"What is it?" He tried to ease back, but Eric tightened his arms.

For once Ben was right, though he wished he wasn't.

Eric sighed. "I want you," he murmured, looking up. "But I'm still not ready to bond—even partially—and it's not fair to you for us to keep doing stuff that's not going to let us bond."

Ben tilted Eric's chin up. "But we do bond, cariño." When Eric raised his eyebrows, Ben nodded. "It's not mating, not the bond that would physically hurt if something happened to me—the only way I would leave you, though I understand you're not able to trust that yet—but our relationship. We still get closer when we do sexual things together."

Eric frowned. "I never thought of it that way."

"It's one of the things I was most worried about when we were together the other night. It is still intimate, even if the bond between our wolves does not strengthen."

"That does make sense." Eric gave a small smile. "If you're sure it's not going to hurt you, then…."

"I would love to be with you tonight, cariño. But first… I have a guitar to fix and some music to play for you."

The smile turned into a grin. "Indeed." Eric pulled Ben in until their lips met, but this kiss was definitely *not* soft. When they broke apart, Ben was having quite a bit of difficulty simply breathing. "Now… how about that music?"

Ben shook his head hard. "It will be difficult to remember how to tune my guitar since you scrambled my brains."

Eric laughed. "They're not scrambled. They just… took a side trip south."

Ben snorted. "Something like that. I'll be back in a minute." With a kiss to Eric's temple, Ben went to get his guitar.

IT TOOK Ben longer than he would have liked to replace the strings and tune the guitar. But finally he had them done. The problem was, as soon as he was ready, his mind went *completely* blank. He frowned, picking lightly with his fingers as he tried to think of something he could play.

"What about something Spanish?"

Ben raised his eyebrows, but when Eric nodded, Ben smiled. "Okay." He flipped through his mental songs, then started playing softly. He had a couple of false starts, his cheeks heating. But with a glance at Eric, who was just smiling and watching him, Ben took a breath and tried once more. *This* time he picked at the strings, the song coming back quickly. He sang quietly, not even thinking about it, as he did.

He didn't look up until he finished. When he did, Eric looked downright spellbound. Ben's cheeks heated again, but the smile Eric gave him relaxed him.

"If I keep going, will you keep practicing?"

Eric gave an overdramatic sigh. "I *guess*."

Ben sighed. "Cariño, you will be much happier if you can get back to doing your leatherwork, yes?"

Eric stuck his tongue out. "Yes." He turned back to his work but then looked up at Ben again. "More in Spanish?"

That put a smile on Ben's face. "Definitely." As Ben started the next song, Eric turned back to his leather.

He—they—lost track of time. It wasn't until Ben looked up and found both Tanner and Finley sitting in the other chairs that he realized how much time had passed. It was almost dark. He'd been so wrapped up in the music. Eric had apparently put the tools away, and Ben blushed at not even noticing any of it. He'd only stopped to rest his hand.

The heat in his cheeks intensified, and he cleared his throat. "Um, hello. I, uh—"

"You play very well," Finley said, grinning.

Eric scowled. "He plays more than 'very well.'" He shook his head, rolling his eyes when Tanner laughed. "You're an asshole, now that you're alpha."

Tanner grinned. "I've always been a bit of an asshole. You're only now figuring that out?"

Eric didn't bother replying, turning instead back to Ben. "It was beautiful. It's a shame your mamá didn't want you to play."

Ben shrugged a shoulder. "Being an accountant led me here."

"Yes, and we all have work in the morning," Tanner said, standing. "I am heading to bed. Night, folks!"

"Night!" Finley called as he followed Tanner into the house.

"So, mate," Eric began, "are you up for a little nonscary bonding?"

Ben laughed at the phrasing. "Nice. Yes, cariño. Let me put my guitar away."

Eric stood and leaned over to catch Ben's lips. He kept it soft but still lingered. "I'll help. Can't wait to have you in my arms."

That did all sorts of warm and good things to Ben's insides—and made his wolf happy in the process. "Then we should hurry."

"OKAY, SO, the biggest thing you have to learn is how to trust your wolf," Eric said as he sat next to Ben. They'd just caught up to Chad and Jamie in the forest behind Tanner and Finley's place a short while ago. Now they sat together opposite the other two. Ben tried not to let it bother him that there were two other naked gay men near his mate. Only the space between them kept him from wanting to growl.

"That, I think, is what takes so long to be able to go back to being human full-time," Chad added. "It took me quite a while before I trusted him."

"It did?" Ben asked, blinking.

Chad nodded. "Yeah. It didn't help that after I'd been changed and woke up—in wolf form—he had a solid hold and would *not* let go. Everything I tried to get him to let me shift, he just got pissed at, then held on longer."

"Ugh. That must have been fun." Eric shook his head.

"Scared the shit out of me," Jamie muttered.

Chad kissed Jamie's temple. "Yeah, no. Finally Jamie and I went hunting, and when I let him do what his natural instincts called him to do… well, *then* I could shift. But I still didn't trust him for a long time. For a while I was afraid he wouldn't let go, let me shift back to human form. And I'd bet, as little time as you've spent with him, that's what's hard for you."

Ben was nodding even before Chad finished. "Yes. I've hunted some when I was back with Papá, but we did not have the opportunity to very often. We did not run with the rest of the pack, and the hunting ground where we would not be disturbed was not very plentiful."

Chad wrinkled his nose. "Yeah, I can see that being a problem."

Eric touched Ben's hand. "What you need to remember, baby, is that your wolf already knows how to do all this stuff. He can hunt, track, and all that without your help. But you have to trust in his instinct."

Ben frowned. "But how do I do that?"

"Well, that's why Eric asked me here." Chad smiled. "It takes a while for you to shift, right?"

"Yes." Ben nodded.

"That's a good place to start. One of the reasons it takes you a while is because you don't trust him. Probably, at least subconsciously, like I was early on, you're afraid he won't let the human side of you take over again."

"You think so?" Jamie asked, frowning. "Even though he's had his wolf all his life?"

Eric nodded at Jamie, then cleared his throat and turned to Ben. "You told me once your mamá used to spank you for shifting uncontrollably."

"Yes." Ben hesitated. "Do you think that's part of it?"

Chad whistled. "Really?"

Eric scowled. "Yes. Can you imagine treating your kid that way?" When Ben frowned again, Eric turned to him. "I'm sorry, it just… you shouldn't have had to go through that."

"No one should." Jamie shook his head. "As bad as my parents were about my orientation, at least I didn't have problems like that."

"Yours were both wolves, though, right?" Eric asked. When Jamie nodded, Eric did as well. "Yeah, see, they got it. Ben's mamá is human. Anyway," he said, turning once more back to Ben. "I'd bet that has something to do with it."

Ben sighed. "You're right, cariño."

Eric kissed Ben's cheek. "You are, in fact, stronger than your wolf. It is *extremely* rare that we lose control. Finley did once when his wolf thought Tanner was in trouble. I did when Kim broke the bond. So, it can happen. But as you see, once you have solid control as a human, it's not common."

Chad nodded. "Even I don't spontaneously shift much anymore."

Ben raised his eyebrows. "Anymore?"

"Yeah, for a while after I was turned, if I had any kind of extreme emotion, I spontaneously shifted. It was his way of protecting me. I once did when a jaguar shifter tried to kill Miles." Chad showed his teeth in a slightly scary grin.

"*What*?" This came from Eric.

"Yeah. Uh, the story isn't all mine to tell, but before Q and Miles mated, Q was on the run from some assholes who decided one way to make him do what they wanted was try to kill Miles."

"Uh, I don't know him all that well, but what I have gotten from him makes me think that wouldn't work."

Chad laughed. "Oh *hell* no. It took all four of us—me, Jamie, Tanner, *and* Finley, to keep him from running all the way to New York to kill the person he thought was responsible."

"Wow. Yeah, that sounds like him, from what I've seen."

"Anyway, we were going to bring Miles out here for a while, but there was a guy in his apartment who decided it would be a good idea to try to kill Miles. When I saw it, I got *pissed* and shifted on the spot." He shrugged. "It takes a lot more for me now. In fact, I haven't shifted like that in a couple of months. So you can learn too. It just takes a while."

Ben nodded and let out a breath. "So, I should practice shifting?"

"Yeah, but not too many times or you'll eat the entire contents of the fridge," Jamie said, grinning. "Chad used to go through *so much* food." He laughed when Chad glared, but it was clear he wasn't really mad.

Ben blinked. "I would eat that much?"

Jamie laughed. "Well, you might leave a steak or two." He waved a hand. "But you *would* need to refuel. Shifting takes a lot of energy."

Ben nodded. "Oh. Yes, I have had that happen a few times. It's been a while, though."

"Right, so, a few times shouldn't be too bad. Much more than that at once, though…." Jamie shrugged a shoulder.

"Okay." Ben took a deep breath, closed his eyes, and imagined stepping behind his wolf, giving control over to him. By the time he landed on four paws, he knew without looking at the others that it'd taken too long.

"He's a pretty one," Chad said, tilting his head.

Ben growled a little, surprised when Eric growled too.

Eric grinned sheepishly. "Uh, sorry. Two naked gay men near my mate…."

It felt good to hear Eric echo his own previous thoughts.

Chad raised a hand. "Say no more."

"He is, though," Eric said, turning back to Ben, who growled again.

Jamie snickered. "I think he takes exception to being called 'pretty.'"

Ben sat back, curled up, and deliberately licked his balls. Chad and Jamie started laughing like crazy. Ben sat up and looked at Eric, tilting his head.

"I have no idea," Eric replied, correctly guessing what Ben was asking.

"When…. When I…. When we…," Jamie tried, then fell back into a fit of laughter. It took another full minute before the two of them could stop laughing. Eric and Ben simply sat and waited. Finally Jamie cleared his throat. "When Chad and I first got together, I was stuck in wolf form. I think I told you that much."

Ben and Eric both nodded, making Jamie grin.

"Right, well, Chad took me to the pet store to get a collar and leash—he had *no* idea what I was, just thought I was a big dog—and when he tried to pick out a pink collar for me—"

"He curled up and licked his balls *exactly* like you just did."

Ben chuffed, then barked.

Eric laughed. "Perfect." He turned to Ben. "Now. Shift back and think about the fact that *you* control your wolf, not the other way around. You're not asking him to step back. *You* are stepping forward, okay?"

Ben considered that, then nodded. He let Eric's words go through his mind one more time, and faster than he'd shifted *to* wolf form, he shifted back. He crouched next to Eric, grinning. "That was easier!"

"See? I knew you had it in you." Eric leaned forward and kissed Ben. Ben returned it, but pulled away quickly, sending a pointed look at Eric's naked body. Eric chuckled. "Right." He sat back. "So… a few more rounds, and then we'll get back to the house."

"Okay, cariño." Ben closed his eyes and reminded himself *he* controlled his wolf. He *would* shift back and do so when *he* chose. What could only be a moment later, he was once more on four paws.

Eric grinned. "Even faster."

Ben nodded, took a breath, and mentally pulled his wolf back. It wasn't as fast as the last shift *to* his wolf form, but it wasn't any slower than his earlier shift back either. "I still need to work on it," he said, unable to keep a note of disappointment out of it.

"Dude, it took me *months* to be able to shift that fast." Chad shook his head.

"But… I've had my wolf all my life." Ben turned a confused look to Eric.

"But you haven't trusted him for most of it, have you?" Chad asked, drawing Ben's attention back.

Ben sighed and shook his head. "No, that's true."

"It's going to take time. You can't undo a lifetime of behavior in one session." Chad shrugged. "Just work at it."

"You are right. I'm sorry."

"Nothing to be sorry for. Again?"

Ben nodded and, yet again, thought about the fact that *he* controlled his wolf. But even keeping that in mind, the two more shifts to wolf form and back weren't any faster than before. When he was once more human-shaped, he sighed, frowning down at the ground as if the forest floor could help him somehow.

Eric tilted his head up and kissed him softly. "Just give it time, baby. You are already faster. I can see it. So can Chad and Jamie."

Ben looked up at them, and they both nodded. Blowing out a breath, he gave a nod too. "Very well. Now—"

Jamie and Chad both laughed when Ben's stomach growled. "Right, I think that's enough," Jamie said. "Besides, we want dinner before the full moon, so Chad doesn't empty the forest of deer."

Chad stuck his tongue out, making the rest of them laugh.

Ben had been trying not to think about the run, in fact. He was *so* not ready to meet the rest of the pack. Eric had told him many times they would accept him. It was true that the pack members at the shop had welcomed him, but that was a long way from the whole pack, in Ben's opinion.

"Right, so… how about we all shift and see who's first to get to the steaks Finley's going to have on the grill?"

Ben shook the worry off and grinned at this, because speed *hadn't* been a problem for him. "You are on, my friend!"

With a laugh he shifted—happy it was faster than the last time— though the other three were still much faster than he was. Even so, he took off at full speed, happier than he could remember being in a long time as his mate and friends ran with him.

Chapter 13

ERIC DRUMMED his fingers on his knee, staring out the window, though he wasn't seeing any of the houses, businesses, or trees they passed. He was still trying to decide how to interpret the message he'd received through Tanner earlier in the day.

"So, apparently your mom heard you were back. She said she was… upset… you hadn't been to see her."

Eric snorted at the thought. Did she really wonder why he hadn't? Or was she regretting things and worried about how he was feeling?

Somehow, Eric didn't think so, in either case. He didn't know what to believe, though. He was sure he'd known her. His mom had never been the most maternal of women, he got that, which was probably why she got along with Kim so well. But up until Kim had left him, he'd have sworn she really loved him. And he would never have thought she—and his dad—would set him up the way they had either.

He blew a breath out, and a hand landed on his other knee. Eric looked over at Ben as he put his hand over Ben's. Everything—*everything*—from the simplest of kisses to the way Ben said "I love you," was different than it had been with Kim. Eric would admit age undoubtedly had something to do with it. He and Ben were no longer young, stupid teenagers.

But all the same, he didn't once feel the need to question whether Ben was sincere. Their fledgling bond told him as much, but even without that, he could hear it in Ben's words. They sounded a hundred times more honest, more real, than Kim's had.

Eric had known, all those years ago, his parents had a hand in what happened. He hadn't wanted to really believe it, though. Buried in there had been hope that they really had wanted what was best for *him*. But after he'd shifted and taken off, and he'd seen his mother up on the mountain, he'd known that wasn't the case. When she'd looked right at him, then turned her back and walked away, he couldn't deny it anymore.

"It will be okay, cariño. Whatever happens, I will be there. And I love you."

Eric reached up and brushed a thumb over one of Ben's cheeks. His heart still skipped a beat when he heard that. "That helps. I have no idea what I'm going to find. I—" He shook his head.

"Well, we're here," Tanner said from the driver's seat. "You want Fin and I to come in?"

Eric didn't answer until Tanner had parked in front of the brick house. It was smaller than he would have expected from them, though the hints of his parent's love of money was still evident. They'd never been rich, but his father's insurance agency made enough to pay for the Mercedes in the driveway, the stained glass filling the upper half of the front door, and through the open front windows, the expensive furniture Eric could see his mother had put in the living room. He had vivid memories of spilling juice on a sofa and never being allowed out of the kitchen with anything food-related again until he was almost out of high school.

"Naw. Just, uh, keep the engine running. Or, well… be ready to go."

Tanner nodded, and Eric forced himself to let go of Ben's hand and climb out of the car. He rubbed his palms on his jeans, annoyed that southwestern Pennsylvania would pick *that* day to be unseasonably warm. He glanced at Finley as he passed, and Finley gave him a bolstering smile. Eric took a breath, nodded, then met Ben's gaze.

Ben hesitated when he came around the car. "I did not think—I just assumed—but if you do not want me with you—"

"Oh yeah, I want you with me." Eric sighed. "Let's get this over with." He took the single step up onto the cement porch and approached the door. Before he could knock, the door opened and he was faced with his mother.

He didn't know what he'd expected. She looked exactly like she had nine years before. As a wolf, of course, she wouldn't have shown any age in those few years. He supposed, if he thought about it, he would have maybe hoped her worry or something would have shown. He gave himself a mental slap for that and nodded. "Hello, Mother."

She looked him up and down, glanced over his shoulder—undoubtedly at Ben—then back to him. The smile she pulled onto her face—which didn't reach her eyes—told Eric everything he needed to know. He seriously considered simply turning around then and there. Before he could, she stepped back and held a hand out. The only thing that prodded Eric to step inside was that he was sure the rest of the neighborhood was as nosy as his mother had always been, and he had *no* wish to give them a show.

His mother didn't reply until they were in the living room. Eric wasn't sure if he was glad his father wasn't there or not. She sat, waving a hand at one of the matching chairs. Eric didn't take the invitation.

"Eric. I heard you were back. That you have been for a while."

The dig was not lost on him. He ignored it and considered how much to say. "A few weeks, yes. I had to… recover… from being in wolf form for so long."

She tilted her head. "I can believe that."

Eric wished he had the nerve to call her out on walking away from him. But now that he stood there, in the strange place that was her home, it was painfully obvious they'd never been a family. Even *if* he'd given in and gone to college, become a doctor or engineer, he'd never have been happy with them and Kim. The pretense surrounding him there just about gave him hives.

"I'm back at the shop," he said, with no idea what else to say. He hadn't forgotten Ben, but he had no idea how to introduce them with her so obviously ignoring him.

The barely contained sneer made Eric want to punch something. How had he come from this woman?

"Eric?"

Shit. Eric turned to greet his father. Like his mother, his father hadn't aged a day. Not the slightest hint that almost ten years had passed since he'd seen them last. His father's khaki pants and button-down shirt were as pristine as always. "Sir. How are you?"

"Fine. The bigger question is, how are you?"

Eric glanced at Ben, who gave him a small smile. "Better, now that I'm back."

"Where are you living?" his mom asked, drawing his attention.

Eric jumped on the question, grateful for a direction. "Tanner and Finley have given me a room while I get things going again. Speaking of…. Tanner said you guys have a couple of boxes of my stuff?"

"Yes," his dad said. He turned a polite look toward Ben, and Eric was actually glad for the opening.

"Oh, this is Ben Arellano." Eric swallowed, glancing once at his mother, then back at his father. "My destined mate and the pack's new accountant."

Eric had often heard the phrase "could hear a pin drop" over the years. He'd also heard the oft-used line "tension so thick, it could be cut with a knife." He'd never truly *understood* those until that moment. It took him a minute to get through his own emotional mess to recognize the panic and fear coming to him across the bond from Ben. He turned to Ben and took the half step closer to both offer a bit of comfort to Ben and make sure his parents couldn't misunderstand who he was talking about.

"I'm not sure I understand," his mother said anyway.

Eric didn't sigh. That would basically be useless. Instead he simply tilted his head and looked at her for a long moment. "I'm sure you do, Mother. Ben is my destined mate."

"But… you're not gay."

Eric turned back to his father, who looked genuinely confused. He could give his dad that much. He nodded. "That's true, I'm not. I'm bisexual."

His dad blinked a moment, then glanced at Eric's mother. "Let me get those boxes." And he left.

Coward. Eric turned back to his mother.

"You're… that's not possible. You're ma—you're in love with Kim. How can you be gay?"

Eric closed his eyes, counted to five, and breathed deeply. "Was. Not now. And I'm not gay. I am bi. I like both. And Ben is my destined mate. It can't be that hard to understand. You've had a gay alpha, with his destined same-sex mate, for months now."

She sniffed delicately.

Eric didn't roll his eyes, but he wanted to. Instead, he simply raised his eyebrows. "Are you arguing that Tanner and Finley are destined?"

"I'm sure they believe it."

Eric cleared his throat, fighting to keep from getting downright pissed. "Yes, they do, because they are. Just like Ben and I are. I—" He took a deep breath, then let it out. "I should have known better than to come back here."

"You know, we still keep in contact with Kim. If you've come to your senses, I'm sure she—"

Eric's mouth fell open. "Are you fucking kidding me?"

Her back straightened. "Do not talk to your mother like that!"

"You haven't been my mother in nine years, since you turned your back on me in the forest." She paled a little, and Eric guessed she didn't know he'd seen her. "Yeah, I saw you turn around and walk away from me. Ben's my mate as much as Finley is Tanner's. And I wouldn't have anything to do with Kim if she was the last person on earth." He shook his head. "I knew you'd be like this. I guess I'd kind of hoped that when you accepted Tanner...."

"Well, we sort of had to, didn't we? Not like his father was going to put his foot down and tell his son to get over that ridiculousness. *Gay*." She almost sneered it, and Eric shook his head again.

"How... where... I can't even." His father came in then, holding three file-type boxes with lids and handles.

"I will take them, sir," Ben said, stepping forward, sounding relieved to be doing something.

"Um, want to take them to the car?" Eric asked to give him an out. *He* didn't want to be there. There was no reason to force Ben to go through more.

Ben hesitated, and the nervousness that had been coming over their bond a moment ago eased. "If that is what you would like."

Eric smiled. "Yeah, it's okay. I'll be out in a minute." There was no way this was going on much longer.

"Very well." With that, Ben stepped through the door Eric's dad held open.

Eric turned back to his mother. "I seriously thought you'd accepted him."

His mother glanced at the closed door. "I kept my mouth shut when Noah was alpha. Now that *he's* my alpha...." She shrugged one shoulder. "Even if he is a... fag, well, I sort of have to, don't I?"

The door opened again, and this time Tanner stepped in. "Well, I'm glad to know exactly where I stand."

Her already pale face turned even paler. Her eyes flicked to the open windows, and she gulped, then jumped to her feet. "Uh, Alpha!" Too late, she tilted her head to the side. Eric noted his father had as well, though he, too, was a little too late. Tanner didn't even recognize the action.

"Don't bother. I'm actually glad to hear how you feel, to have it out in the open. I'm sure my father had an idea. He tends to be as nonconfrontational as I am unless he's pushed. I suppose he'd just hoped it'd never come out." Tanner shrugged. "It doesn't matter. While I learned from him... I'm *not* him." He gave a smile Eric hoped was never aimed at him. "You and your mate have thirty days to be out of Forbes territory. You have sixty to find a new pack. If you don't report in to headquarters—to my father, you know, the alpha prime—by then, you'll be labeled lone wolves."

If possible, her face went even whiter. "You can't do this!"

"I can. I am the alpha, whether you respect me or not. I am the law here. I will *not* tolerate intolerance in my pack." Tanner gave that smile again. "I don't care much what you think of me, but that kind of attitude only damages a pack known for tolerance." She opened her mouth, ostensibly to argue, but Tanner held up a hand. "Save it. Hopefully you can find a pack that aligns more toward your… attitude." He glanced at Eric, then back at Eric's mother and then father, who'd remained silent. "Thirty days." With that he stepped through the door.

Eric looked from one to the other once more. His mind was a mess, trying to put together what he'd just heard and seen. Instead, he just shook his head and stepped toward the door. He hesitated, his back still turned, then simply offered, "Goodbye." Not even waiting to see if they responded, he was out the door and off the porch in seconds.

When he got to the car, the first thing he did was pull Ben in. Ben wrapped both arms around him and held tight. "I'm… I…."

"Shhh," Ben murmured, kissing Eric's temple.

Finally Eric pulled back, kissed Ben lightly, then slipped into the car.

Ben didn't speak when he got in on his side. Instead, he simply took Eric's hand and held it.

Eric closed his eyes and tried to untangle the emotional mess going on in his head. He'd known he wouldn't like what would happen, had known, at least, it'd hurt. He wasn't sure he'd expected what he got, but at the same time, he wasn't sure it'd been entirely *un*expected either.

When the tires crunched over gravel, Eric opened his eyes. He didn't say anything until Tanner put the car in park. "I think I need some time in my fur." He turned to Ben. "Run with me?"

Ben's eyebrows went up. "You want me to run with you?"

Eric frowned, annoyed with himself that he hadn't run more with Ben besides the session with Chad and Jamie before the full moon, then that night during the full moon itself. He'd have to deal with that later, though, and make time for them to run more often together. "Yeah. I— It—" Eric swallowed. "I need you with me, so yeah. Want to?"

Ben's smile spread. "I would be *very* happy to, cariño."

"Hey, get to the mudroom first, so you're not streaking through the house naked when you come back," Finley said as they climbed out of the car.

Eric turned to him and stuck his tongue out, then turned to Tanner. "You didn't have to do that for me."

"I didn't, dude." Tanner shook his head when Eric just blinked. "I did it for the exact reason I said I did: for the pack. To a point, yeah, for you, because you're part of it. But so is your bi mate. And my gay beta and his gay mate. And our bi doctor and *his* gay mate. And the possible other gay and bi people we might take in because their packs aren't tolerant. I'm not going to put up with that here. Most of the pack *is* accepting. It only poisons a group to have someone like that in it."

"Huh." Eric considered him. The mess in his head was still a mess, but he managed a bit of humor. "And here I thought I was your best friend and you'd do anything for me."

Tanner rolled his eyes. "Asshole," he said, but he was smiling.

Eric flipped him off, then turned to Ben. "How about that run?"

"I'd like that."

"Mudroom!" Finley called as they took off to the path and the stairs that led down the hill and to the back of the house.

Eric found himself chuckling as they went down the steps.

ERIC SIGHED and nosed his snout under Ben's. Ben curled a little tighter around him, then licked at Eric's face.

The run had helped. Chasing his mate through the forest, being chased, had felt good. They'd played together, and Eric's wolf had reveled in doing something so basic with their mate. The simplicity of his wolf had helped ease some of the emotional mess.

While the scene with his parents had hurt, it hadn't been as bad as it could have been. Eric hadn't really had hopes for his family in years. Having Ben with him, even if they hadn't bonded, had helped too. He was trying not to freak out, in fact, over how much it had. *Had* they bonded more than he realized? They'd never stopped kissing, but he hadn't thought they'd bonded *more* because of it.

Eric hadn't just told Ben of the need to have him along for the run to make him feel better either. The thought of running without Ben hadn't sat well with him—or his wolf—at all. When they'd run on the full moon, facing all the old members of his pack had scared him, and it was only Ben's presence next to him that had kept him calm. Well, that and *Ben's* fear. He didn't know why it'd been so easy for him to soothe Ben's worry, why he was so convinced they wouldn't have a problem with Ben's background, yet was still so terrified of *his own* reception.

Neither of them had apparently had anything to fear, however. The pack had welcomed him back as warmly as they'd welcomed Ben—which was as warmly and happily as they welcomed everyone else. Even so, he'd been *very* grateful Ben had been there through it.

He didn't know if it meant anything, but he was starting to realize that the thought of Ben leaving scared him—and not just from the idea of breaking the bond.

When Ben started licking his face again, he realized he'd been whining. Eric sighed and returned a few of the licks. He was damned lucky to have found his destined mate, and he knew it. The frustration with his fear wasn't lessening. If anything, it was getting worse, but every time he thought about bonding, about taking that final step, his heart started pounding, his stomach twisted, and he more or less forgot how to breathe.

He did his best to suppress the fear. He didn't need to alert Ben to anything—that thought alone ratcheted the fear worse—and possibly upset him. Eric was already hurting Ben with his hesitance. That would only make it even worse.

Eric looked up at the sky, seeing how dark it was, which meant it was later than he realized. They'd been gone a while. He tilted his head in the direction of the house, and Ben nodded. Together they stood, shook, and headed back.

As they walked, Eric tried to keep from thinking, but now that his wolf had been satisfied, the worry about how much he was coming to depend on Ben grew. He focused on keeping it contained, but he couldn't stop how much it was bothering him. Would it hurt *emotionally* if Ben left, even if their preternatural bond didn't have to break the way it had with Kim?

He tried to shake the thought off as they shifted back to human form. Eric opened the door for Ben, and they both stepped into the mudroom.

Ben turned to him. "Did you still want me to cook dinner?"

"I'd love it if you're up for it." Eric managed a smile, though he was pretty sure it fell flat.

"I do not have to," Ben said, tilting his head.

Eric shook his head as he pulled his underwear and jeans on. "No, really. It's not that. Just… you know, my—uh, yeah, *them*." He sincerely hoped Ben didn't see through that. It wasn't *exactly* a lie, but it wasn't the entire truth either.

His mate considered him for a long moment but eventually nodded. Eric didn't know if Ben believed him or just let it go. "Okay, cariño. I will go get started."

Eric kissed him briefly. "I think I'm going to go take a shower." With another kiss, he left Ben to dress and started up the stairs.

Tanner happened to be coming down from the second floor as Eric got to the landing. He looked at Eric for a long moment. "What's up?"

Eric frowned. He didn't think Tanner would let it go like Ben would. Ben was still too worried Eric would reject him. Tanner had no such fears. Eric sighed, then glanced down the steps. Ben wasn't there yet, but Eric had no doubt he could hear everything. Eric waved at the stairs, then started up to the second floor. "Come on. I need to get clothes out. I'll talk upstairs."

Tanner followed him in silence until they got to the bedroom. Eric mulled over how to approach the subject as he pulled open the dresser drawer for clean underwear. "So, today sucked."

Tanner laughed. "Duh?"

Eric shook his head. "Yeah, yeah. But, I mean…." He pulled out socks and a fresh T-shirt, then turned to Tanner and leaned against the dresser. "I don't think I could have dealt as well as I did with that without Ben."

"Okay?" Tanner asked, raising an eyebrow.

Eric sighed and shook his head. "I mean… I *needed* him."

"That's what mates are supposed to be. You *do* need each other sometimes."

Frowning, Eric dropped his gaze to his toes. "Okay, so, there's no, uh, actual mate bond, I get that, but…." He swallowed, refusing to look at Tanner. "What if he leaves? Even without a bond, I mean… being— Ow!" His head whipped up as a smack landed on the back of it. He hadn't even heard Tanner move. Eric glared at his best friend. "What the fuck?"

"That's my question."

Eric was taken aback at the glare on Tanner's face. "What?"

"Has Ben given you *any* indication he'd do something like that?"

"Well…." Eric scowled harder. "No. But fuck's sake, man, it's been, what, a month? Six weeks?"

"Yeah, and?" Tanner shook his head. "He's your destined fucking mate. You know, from our patron goddess? The one you said you *met*? How many destined mates do you know that have broken up?"

Eric didn't answer because he knew Tanner was well aware that Eric knew what the answer would be.

"How many other mate pairs do you know that have broken up?" Eric sighed.

"Now, let me ask you one last question. How much is Ben like Kim?"

"Not a single gods-damned bit," Eric said without thinking.

Tanner didn't speak, simply raised an eyebrow again.

Eric blew out a breath. "Fuck."

"I get that you might not be ready to fully bond yet. But the rest of that shit, you need to let go of it. Hell, you need to accept what Ben is, what Diana gave you. *Really* accept it, because I don't think you have. If you trust our goddess, and your wolf—who knows Ben as your mate— then you need to at *least* stop hanging on to this other shit. Everyone's got fears when it comes to a relationship—no, not like you have, but fears all the same—so you're no exception to that. It's hurting him, even if he doesn't admit it. And you know this and you're fucking better than that. He deserves more, even—maybe especially—if you can't fully bond yet." Tanner shook his head and stepped out of the room.

Eric let the words roll around in his head as he went into the bathroom. He stripped out of his clothes and turned on the shower. When the water was hot only a moment later—he loved those tankless heaters—he stepped under the spray.

Was he overthinking it? He had no doubt it would hurt if Ben left, but… would Ben leave? Would Diana do that? Bring him down from the mountain, give him a destined mate, only for that *destined* mate to voluntarily leave?

He still wasn't sure he could take a chance yet on fully bonding, or even for something to happen *in*voluntarily to Ben. There were still plenty of things that could kill them. But he had to give Tanner this much: he was hurting Ben. It'd been, now, more than six weeks since he'd once again taken human form, and more than three since Ben had first said "I love you." Eric wasn't going to get any surer of his feelings in that way. He had fears, yes, but he knew how he felt about Ben and, like he'd recognized that he'd been hiding behind those fears before their date, he needed to admit he was now too.

With a sigh, Eric focused on cleaning himself up. It was time to fight harder against his fears.

Chapter 14

BEN FOUND the playlist he wanted, then set his phone in the docking station they had in the kitchen. Ricky Martin started singing about how beautiful his lover was, and Ben sang along as he pulled out pans, utensils, and ingredients. He got lost in the music as he chopped vegetables, and the spicy chicken simmered in the pan on the stove, making his stomach grumble.

Concentrating on the meal and music helped keep him from thinking. He didn't want to think too much, because he knew exactly where his mind would go: to the lie Eric had told before he'd gone upstairs. Ben shook his head at himself and stirred the meat before going back to his vegetables. Diced green peppers, onions, and tomatoes all got tossed in a bowl. He attacked the cilantro next, falling into a rhythm with the chopping. He sang, this time with Enrique Iglesias, even dancing as he dropped cutting board into the sink.

But his worries and fears wouldn't stay away for long. *Why* had Eric lied to him? That was the part that bothered him the most. Eric *knew* he would recognize the lie, so *why*? Had he, Ben, done something wrong? He frowned as he turned the meat again, but no matter what he came up with, nothing made sense to him.

Ben understood the day had been very hard for Eric. It had warmed Ben that Eric had wanted him along for the trip, and even more so when he'd asked about running together. Ben stopped and frowned as that thought hit him. Had he pushed on that somehow? Made Eric feel like he had to ask?

He shook his head at himself again, annoyed at thinking about it anyway. He couldn't know, and right then—when the scene with Eric's family was still so fresh—was not the time to ask. With a sigh he turned back to the meal.

He managed to get lost once more in music and preparation. As he was peeling the poblano peppers, he heard footsteps behind him. He sniffed, but the spices he'd used in the meat actually overpowered his nose. Before he could focus his sense of smell, arms came around him from behind.

"That better be my mate, or there will be a bloody mess in the kitchen, and I do not think Finley or Tanner will appreciate that."

Eric chuckled. "I like to think I'd tell them to take their hands off you first."

"I would hope so."

Eric stepped back and nudged Ben to turn around. He raised an eyebrow at the knife in Ben's hand and, with a smirk, took it and set it carefully on the counter. Then he tugged Ben into his arms.

Ben, confused, simply went along with it. "Car—"

"Shh," Eric said, putting a finger over Ben's lips. Ben blinked but didn't say anything more. Eric swallowed, cupped one of Ben's cheeks, then said softly, "*Te amo, mi corazon.*"

Ben stared at Eric for a very long moment, mouth hanging open. It didn't even register at first that Eric had spoken it in Spanish, only what the words meant. *I love you, my heart.* It took him another few seconds to realize he'd stopped breathing. He sucked in air before he passed out. "Cariño, do… do you know what you said?"

Eric nodded, a slightly crooked smile on his face. "I should hope so. I just spent twenty minutes researching the right way to say it to you."

Ben blinked at him again. "You… you did? You… you mean it, then?"

With another swallow Eric nodded. "Yes. I love you, Ben. I…." He blew out a breath. "I've been hurting you. Again. I know you don't think so," he said hurriedly when Ben opened his mouth. Ben closed it again, chagrined to be read so well. "But I have. It might not have been obvious, but I am *sure* going so long saying that to me, but not hearing it back… hurt."

Ben wanted to argue, but in truth, he couldn't because Eric was right. He frowned. "I…. *Mierda!*"

Eric chuckled. "I don't know exactly what that means, but I can guess. Seems like you used it once before, back when we were talking about Kim the first time."

Color tinged Ben's cheeks. "Yes. Uh, it means 'shit.'"

That brought a full laugh. "I thought it was something like that." He sighed. "Tanner, uh, smacked some sense into me."

Ben scowled. "He should not have hurt you."

"Meh. He didn't. Just my pride, which can take a few hits. Besides, I needed it. I've known I love you for a while now, but I've been letting my stupid fears get in the way again."

"Is that why you lied to me earlier?" Ben asked, dropping his gaze to Eric's T-shirt.

"Caught that, did you?" Eric asked, and Ben nodded. "Yeah, I thought you did. I was freaking out because I realized how much I'd needed you today, and I let that bother me. It was stupid, it really was—which Tanner didn't hesitate to point out—but... I've got to stop letting this shit control me." He tilted Ben's face up and caught his lips in a soft kiss. "You deserve better." He took a breath. "I love you, Ben."

Ben closed his eyes, his heart pounding. "I cannot tell you how good that feels to hear."

"I think I have an idea. You are night and day from her, and not just because your genitals are on the outside."

That made Ben chuckle. "Really?"

"Oh yeah. The times she said that to me? Never felt the way it does from you, and I really don't think that's the destined part of us either."

Ben smiled. "I... I do not think so either. I love you, cariño."

Eric grinned. "I love you. Now... can I help?" he asked, stepping back and waving a hand.

"I do not know. You won't burn it, will you?"

"Uh... maybe stick to something that doesn't involve the stove?"

Ben laughed, feeling amazingly light and hopeful. "All right. Let me show you how to peel these peppers."

BEN COULDN'T seem to stop grinning the entire evening. Eric had helped him finish making the chile rellenos; then the four of them had proceeded to clean the entire platter of them. It'd made Ben feel really good about his cooking. Now, as he readied for bed, he *still* had the grin on his face, which made brushing his teeth easier, at least. As he went back to the bedroom he shared with Eric, he more floated than walked. He still couldn't believe Eric had finally said "I love you." He'd pinched himself more than once since the scene in the kitchen.

Of course, he made sure he did that when Eric wasn't looking. Eric *had* been right: it'd hurt to say those words and not get them back. But he didn't want to make things worse by letting Eric know how he was still afraid it was a dream. They needed to move forward—and *keep* moving forward—and dwelling on the mistakes and previous problems wouldn't help either of them.

When he stepped into the room, he found Eric sitting up in bed, a book open in his hands. Ben peered closer, chuckling at the picture of two wolves on the front. "Good book, cariño?"

"Not bad," Eric said, putting a bookmark in place and closing the book. "I'm not sure how believable it is that a guy can get pregnant, but I guess, for most humans, it doesn't matter. I mean, they don't think *we* exist, so...."

Ben laughed as he slipped under the covers. "Yes, I can see that."

"And the story itself is good. I like the characters, and I have to admit some of the stuff Liam gets into—especially pregnant—is funny."

"I may have to read it when you are done."

"You should. If for no other reason than two hot guys getting it on."

Ben laughed as Eric set the book on the bedside table, then turned the light off. As he settled down on the pillow, Ben studied his mate. Something was on Eric's mind, but nothing specific came across their bond, so he couldn't figure out what it was. He didn't think it was anything *bad*, but without a more complete bond, he couldn't know for sure.

He decided it was better to simply ask. "Cariño? Is something wrong?"

Shaking his head, Eric took a breath but didn't speak. He slid across the space separating them, wrapping his arm around Ben's waist. He pulled until they were tight against each other, making Ben gasp when Eric's skin was against his. Eric reached up to cup Ben's cheek. Still without speaking, he closed the last little distance between their lips.

Ben was pretty sure he'd never get tired of the taste and feel of Eric's kisses. The spice from their dinner was still there, despite Eric brushing his teeth, not that Ben minded. But more than the taste, he loved the feel of their tongues sliding, of hearing every moan. Eric rocked into Ben, who let out his own moan at the feel of Eric's hardening dick.

When they broke apart, Ben sucked in a breath, then dove in to kiss Eric again. They rolled, Eric settling on top of Ben, and his own now hard cock against Eric's brought an even louder sound.

"Gods, you feel good," Eric muttered before catching Ben's lips again.

Ben slid his hand down Eric's back, cupped his ass, and squeezed. When Eric started rocking again, Ben brought his hands back up and threaded his fingers through Eric's hair. He got lost in the kiss, in the feel of Eric against him, but only a moment later, Eric pulled back. Ben blinked up at him—now through gray vision, thrilled to see Eric's eyes had bled black as well—but the slightly evil grin on Eric's face only confused him more.

Especially when Eric started kissing a trail down over Ben's chest. They didn't often do this—too much temptation to do the kind of thing that would allow them to bond. Usually they kissed, ground into each other, and ended with mutual hand jobs. It was fairly safe while still allowing them to share pleasure.

This… if Eric wasn't careful, this could cause all sorts of problems. But his mate's lips on his skin were making it very difficult for Ben to figure out how to think, much less speak. That got even worse when Eric settled between Ben's legs and kissed a line just above Ben's boxers. "Ca— *cariño*—" The next sound out of Ben's throat was more grunt than words.

Because Eric kissed the tip of Ben's cock where it peeked through the slit.

Ben's *very naked* dick. With precum beading on the end.

It took a near-Herculean effort, but Ben struggled to pull his wits together while Eric continued kissing the sensitive flesh. "Cariño! If you are not careful, we could—*ohfuck*—bond."

Eric looked up, his face serious. "I know, baby." Then, his gaze still on Ben's, he slid his fingers under Ben's boxers.

Ben gulped. "Car—Eric, you are not ready for this." It took everything Ben had to say that, but they'd made *so* much progress, and he was scared it would panic Eric and send them backward. Ben bit his lip, not sure what else to say.

But Eric tilted his head. "I don't know, Ben. I don't know that I'll *ever* be ready to bond. I may, someday, just have to take the leap. This isn't going to cause a full bond, though. And I'm *not* ready for *that*—I know that and so do you. And hey, it might not even cause a partial one."

Ben frowned. "But it might. I… please do not misunderstand, cariño. I would give anything for us to be ready to bond, but—"

Eric reached up and placed a finger over Ben's lips. "I promise not to freak. If we *do* bond, then we do. But I will be *damned* if I hurt you again."

Ben wanted to argue more, wanted to find some way to make sure, but he took a risk of another kind if he pushed, and he didn't want to do that either. With another hard swallow, Ben nodded. "O-okay, cariño. If you're sure."

The smile Eric gave in return caused Ben's cock to twitch. "Oh, yeah."

Before Ben could even *slightly* prepare himself, Eric pulled Ben's boxers down past his cock and balls and engulfed Ben's dick in his mouth in a single move.

Then promptly choked on it.

Were it not for the fact that he was in the process of getting his first ever blowjob, Ben might have laughed. As it was, he was more alarmed than anything. "Cari—"

Eric held up a finger, coughed a couple of times, then pulled at Ben's boxers again. "Let's take these off."

Ben nodded, lifted his hips, and kicked them aside when Eric moved. A moment later Eric was back, his own underwear now at the bottom of the bed somewhere.

"Let me try this again… maybe a little more carefully."

This time Ben did chuckle. "If you are—"

Eric looked up at him, almost frowning. "Please… I am, okay? Just…."

"I'm sorry. Um… please?" Ben rocked his hips a little, glad when Eric smiled again.

Ben wasn't sure it was the best idea, though. As Eric ran his tongue down one side of Ben's cock, then back up the other, Ben grasped the covers—pausing long enough to force his claws to retreat—and tried to keep from exploding. How could a tongue feel so damned good? *Just* a tongue ghosting over his cock?

That only got worse when Eric wrapped his lips around the tip of Ben's dick and slowly—*very* slowly, this time—moved his mouth down the length. He didn't get far, but Ben didn't care. It felt absolutely amazing, and Ben wondered how many financial statements he was going to have to make up in his head to keep from exploding down Eric's throat in three seconds flat.

Eric pulled up, then worked his way down again, a little farther this time, swallowing around Ben's cock as he did. Ben groaned, trying to keep from bucking, the feel of Eric's mouth on him stealing every bit of sanity he had. He needed a distraction, needed something else to focus on.

He put a hand on Eric's head, tugging on his hair. When Eric looked up, Ben managed to clear his throat and speak. "At least turn around? Let me…. Let me pleasure you too?"

Eric hesitated but then nodded. It took them a moment to find a comfortable way, as inexperienced as they both were, but finally they settled on their sides. Ben leaned in, ran his tongue over Eric's cock, and almost moaned at the taste. Mostly clean skin, but there was a slight salty flavor as well. He cleaned the precum dripping from the tip, then reminded himself to retract his teeth before wrapping his lips around Eric's cock. It wouldn't do to bite Eric's dick for a whole bunch of reasons, not the least of which was that he didn't want to hurt Eric.

When Eric took Ben into his mouth, Ben was *very* glad he'd suggested this. Focusing on Eric helped Ben be a little less desperate, and he could stop thinking about accounting and instead work on pleasuring his mate. He savored the feel of Eric's cock in his mouth, loved the smell—the slightly musky version of Eric that filled his senses. And every moan Eric let out when Ben did just the right thing went straight to Ben's own dick.

Despite Eric's assertions, Ben was a little afraid to let go. He needed to—more than a little desperately—but he held on with every bit of willpower he had to keep himself from coming. And he wasn't going to be able to hold back entirely.

Then Eric did something—sucked a little harder, took Ben in a little farther—and Ben couldn't hold back anymore. He pulled off Eric's cock to give warning. "Cariño! I'm…." He tried to pull at Eric's head, but Eric grabbed Ben's hand to stop him and kept bobbing his head.

Ben gave up. He swallowed Eric's cock the best he could and let go, his orgasm crashing into him hard. A few seconds later, Eric's cum flooded Ben's mouth as Eric came too.

On the heels of that, that invisible *something* that Ben had felt when they'd first kissed surrounded them, pulling them closer. Their bond! The link between them strengthened, and pleasure and love not his own filled him.

Love! That was…. Ben pulled back, looking up at Eric in awe. Eric pulled off Ben and held a hand out toward him. Ben took it, dropping his gaze to their joined hands, then back to Ben. "Is that… you, cariño?"

Eric nodded, his smile a little shaky but there all the same.

Ben probed their link, but the only fear he found was very weak. "You are not afraid."

"No. I mean, a little—you can feel that, but… not like I thought I'd be. Dear gods, Ben, this is…." Eric shook his head and tugged on Ben's hand.

Ben turned and resettled, lying against Eric and cupping his face. "It is amazing," he whispered.

Eric smiled. "Yeah, that. Gods, I… I love you, Ben. And I can feel it from you. Wow. This is going to take some getting used to."

Ben raised his eyebrows. He was loath to bring her into that moment, but he was confused. "You mean—"

Eric shook his head again. "No. Nothing like this."

Letting out a breath, Ben nodded, glad Eric understood without him having to say it. "I… I am glad."

"Me too." Eric leaned in to brush his lips over Ben's, and Ben opened to him. He tasted himself on Eric's tongue, but was too focused on the feel of their kiss, the bond between them thicker and buzzing with happiness and love, to get aroused by it. Eric wrapped his arms around Ben and pulled that tiny bit farther until there wasn't a molecule of air between them.

When they broke apart, Ben brushed his fingers over Eric's cheek. "I cannot tell you how… amazing this is for me."

Eric flashed a grin. "You don't have to. I can feel it."

That surprised a laugh out of Ben. "Indeed. And you really are okay with it?"

Eric nodded, but his smile did diminish a little. "I won't lie, Ben. I still don't want to lose you. I don't think I'm ready to bite yet, but this? This I can handle, I think." He cleared his throat and dropped a kiss on Ben's lips. The happiness faded a bit and anxiety replaced some of it. "You've been incredibly patient with me. Just keep doing that, okay?"

Ben swallowed, aware his own anxiety was coming across their bond, but there wasn't anything he could do about it. He nodded, though. "I will, cariño. I can be patient for as long as it takes."

Eric closed his eyes and rested his forehead against Ben's. Ben closed his eyes too, savoring the connection. "I like this," Eric whispered. "It's a little weird and nothing like I've ever felt before. It's a little scary—I really *can't* lie to you now—"

Ben laughed at that. "That's true."

"I don't want to anyway." Eric smiled again. "But you can't either."

"That is also true, though I would not."

Eric tilted his head. "Maybe not lie, but you try to spare my feelings a lot. Can't do that either, baby."

Ben frowned. "I guess not. I do not want—"

"You're not going to hurt me."

Ben raised an eyebrow. "How did you know what I was going to say? We are not bonded like that."

Eric chuckled. "I know you well enough by now. I don't need the bond for that." He shook his head. "You won't. And even if you do, I'm a big boy. I can deal with it. And I need to. We've got to stop tiptoeing around each other."

Ben sighed. "You're right."

That brought a grin. "Glad you recognize my—"

Ben poked him. "Do not get too full of yourself, cariño."

"I'll count on you to keep me humble," Eric said after rubbing his chest.

With a chuckle, Ben kissed him. "We should get some sleep. It's been an eventful day."

"Yeah, that it has. Thanks for being there."

"I'm happy I could be." Ben kissed Eric once more, then started to sit up.

"Where're you going?"

Ben frowned. "To get my boxers."

Eric raised an eyebrow. "Don't think that matters now, does it?"

Ben blinked at him. "I guess not."

"Besides, it's not like I'm going to accidentally fuck you in the ass… not without getting punched across the room, anyway."

Ben laughed. "Good point," he said as he lay back down against Eric.

"I'll at least get the lube out first," Eric murmured into Ben's ear.

Ben chuckled. "You better do more than that."

"Mmm. I will. For now, though…." Eric yawned.

"Yes. Good night, cariño," Ben whispered.

With a kiss to Ben's temple, Eric whispered, "Good night, baby. I love you."

Ben returned the words and fell asleep with the biggest grin he'd ever had on his face.

Chapter 15

ERIC SCOWLED at the coffee maker, willing it to go faster. Ben was up in the shower at the moment, and all Eric wanted to do was go up and join him—or, at least, get back to bed when Ben was done. He was tempted to forget the coffee, but his mate was more than a little grumpy without it, and Eric didn't think a grumpy Ben would be as open to what Eric wanted without a bit of liquid energy.

Because now that they'd taken the step to start bonding and he wasn't—yet—freaking out about it, Eric wanted to spend the day in bed, exploring the multitude of ways they could strengthen that bond. He tried not to let his imagination wander with the possibilities. He was wearing jeans, but those wouldn't hide an erection as well as he might like. And in a house full of wolves, visual was *hardly* the only way someone could sense arousal. Instead of imagining all the positions he wanted Ben in, he focused on how he hadn't freaked out yet.

He wasn't sure he *would* freak out. It felt… weird… and yet good all at the same time. Telling Ben about his fears and feelings the day before seemed to have opened something in him. It felt right, good, in a way things hadn't in a while. It felt a lot like when he'd managed to get over their first kiss and apologize… then kiss Ben for real. That had felt right.

With a sigh Eric switched mugs, put a fresh K-Cup into the machine, and started Ben's coffee. He wanted to be over the last of this—hesitation, anxiety, worry, and more—but too much fear still lurked for him of what would happen if Ben was taken from him.

That thought brought Eric up short. *If Ben was taken from me.* Not *if Ben leaves.*

Had he gotten past the idea that Ben would leave? Eric blinked into space for a long moment, trying to work that through in his mind. As he thought about it, though, it felt right. Ben, given the choice, wasn't going to take off like Kim had.

Part of his certainty, he realized, had to do with their newly strengthened bond. Nothing in all the emotions he'd sensed from Ben—especially those since the night before—had even remotely hinted at that. While the idea that he could sense Ben's feelings—and, thus, Ben could sense his—was still really weird, it wasn't *bad* either. It calmed him, quieted even more of his fears.

The bond with Kim hadn't felt like that. He wondered, yet again, if it hadn't been that strong to begin with, if Kim had held herself back and given only the part of herself she absolutely had to in order to make that bond work. Eric didn't know if that was even *possible*, but he knew other chosen mates who had a good, strong bond. Alpha Noah and his wife did. So had Kim been able to hold back and *that* was why he never sensed her the same way? He didn't think it was *entirely* the difference between destined and chosen.

Though he and Kim never had a partial bond in any way, wouldn't the emotional part still have happened with the final bond? Or, perhaps, their bond had only been as... weak as it'd been because she didn't really want it. Did that mean it would have been *worse* if they'd really, fully, bonded before she took off?

Somehow, even thinking this through, realizing the bond between him and Ben was even *stronger*... somehow that didn't scare him more, didn't lessen his frustration over the fears and the hesitation to fully bond. The fears keeping him from it were valid, and he reminded himself of that. But they still didn't need to rule him.

Gods, he really wanted to finalize that bond. Would the last of those fears, the last of this gods-awful worry, finally be laid to rest as the partial bond seemed to help with, so far?

He rested his forehead on the cabinet and closed his eyes. "Help me, Diana," he whispered.

"She will, you know," Tanner said, more gently than Eric might have expected, considering Tanner's words the day before.

Eric swallowed, struggling with his emotions. "Have I spit in her face with this?"

"Aw, hell no." Tanner crossed the room and stood next to Eric, who turned and looked at him. "I doubt she expected less. Dude, you've been living with that pain and fear for nine fucking years. That's a long time."

"Yeah, but... wouldn't the argument also stand that I had all that time to get over it?"

Tanner didn't answer right away. He frowned, then shook his head. "I don't think so. I think that might have been what brought her out to prompt you. She knew it *was* time for you to get past this."

Eric turned to the coffee maker, a little annoyed he'd let Ben's coffee sit that long. Frowning down at the now cold brew, he dumped it in the sink, then started a new cup. His own was cold too, but he didn't care as much. "I just don't know. I want to be past it, for what it's worth."

"Hey, Ben understands. It's only been a fairly short time that you've been back and in human form. Considering how we think as wolves versus how we think as humans? It's *going* to take time to deal with the human side of that."

Eric peered at Tanner. "Weren't you just poking me yesterday to deal with this?"

Tanner's nose twitched. "I know you've already taken steps to work on it."

Eric rolled his eyes. "Asshole. You didn't have to be obvious that you know."

All that got him was a snicker. "Look, I told you yesterday, I get if you're not ready for a full bond yet. That final step is *huge*. *I* was worried for myself, remember?"

With a snort Eric shook his head. "That was only because of me, though."

"Doesn't change *my* fear. I knew what that step was. I know how serious it is."

"Hey, you just didn't want to share my ass with the rest of the pack," Finley said as he came into the kitchen.

Tanner rolled his eyes. "That was hardly all of my hesitation."

Finley joined them next to the coffee maker and gave Eric a sideways hug. "You know, I was never the most devout about our gods until I met Jamie—who is scary devout."

"One of the reasons he's my beta," Tanner added.

"But he showed me our gods don't fuck around. If Diana brought you here, it's because she understands you. Sure, she prodded you, but despite her status as a deity, she's not going to expect things overnight. Neither is your mate."

Eric nodded, then smirked. "Who is currently worried, probably at why I'm taking so long."

That brought a grin to Finley's face. "So you partially bonded, then? Yes!"

Eric sighed. "Why is everyone so worried about my sex life?"

Tanner laughed. "Now you know how I felt right before Finley and I finally mated."

With a shake of his head, Eric picked up the cups. He paused to look at each of his friends. "Thanks. I needed to hear some of this—not all of it," he said at their chuckles. "Assholes. Why do I manage to have my best friends be assholes?"

Finley and Tanner just laughed at that. "Get up to your mate. We're going out for a while," Tanner said, stepping aside. "A couple of pack members are moving and we're helping. You and Ben will have the house to yourselves most of the day."

"Do you want help? I'm sure Ben would be fine with that."

"Nah. Go strengthen your bond," Tanner said, making Eric sigh.

"Yeah, right. Get lost," Eric said, heading out of the kitchen. Laughter followed him up the stairs.

He found Ben in bed, looking worried, his phone in his hand. "Something wrong?"

Ben looked up. "No, not really."

Eric raised an eyebrow. "Really?"

With a sigh, Ben set his phone on the bedside table. "Yes, really. This is just another kitten picture from Tina." He held his phone up and waved it a little. "As for you... I was a little worried—"

"Yeah, I felt it."

"—but you do not seem upset, except perhaps with me not answering you."

Eric chuckled at the scowl on Ben's face.

"That is not funny, cariño."

Eric sighed, handed Ben his coffee, then set the other mug on the table on his side of the bed. He took a seat facing Ben and took his hand. "I know you're worried about me. I get that. Last night was kind of a big step—"

"Kind of?"

"Okay, it was a big step. But I've spent some real time thinking about it since I woke up, and I'm okay with it. It feels *right*."

Ben stared at him for a long moment before nodding. "I think... I think maybe I was worried that the bond was not working right because I did not sense any fear."

Eric smiled, knowing it was a bit rueful. "Yeah, I can see that. But really, I'm okay. In fact…" He leaned forward and kissed Ben softly. "I was *more* worried about what other ways we might want to try strengthening our bond."

"Other… ways…?" Ben's eyes widened and his cheeks turned red. "Oh, you mean… other ways of having—" He gulped. "—sex?"

Eric's smile turned into a full grin. "That's exactly what I'm saying." Eric crawled over until he was straddling Ben, then leaned in to nip at Ben's ear. "You know, I've been wondering for a long time now what it'd feel like to have your cock in my ass. Think you might want to satisfy that curiosity?"

Ben gulped and Eric's grin got even wider when Ben's eyes bled black, his cock hardened against Eric's, and the scent of arousal hit Eric's nose hard.

"I'm going to take that as a yes," Eric murmured as his vision went gray. He leaned in and caught Ben's lips in a hard kiss. "Glad we just bought a new bottle of lube. If I have anything to say about it, we're going to need a *lot* of it today."

"Oh gods," Ben nearly whimpered. "But, um, are Tanner and Finley—"

"They're gone for the day. It's just us."

Ben blinked at him. "Then I *definitely* want to satisfy that curiosity. And perhaps even more, cariño."

Eric's smile turned a little bit evil. "Just don't plan to be able to do much of anything tomorrow."

Ben really did whimper that time.

BEN FLOPPED down onto the grass, laying his head on his paws. He was pouting—as much as he could in wolf form—he knew it, but he couldn't seem to pull himself out of his funk. He needed to. Eric was going to sense his emotions and wonder what was wrong, and Ben had been trying valiantly to keep him from knowing how worried Ben was.

What was worse was they'd just strengthened their bond that morning before the others had come over and they'd all gone running. Ben shied away from *that* thought process. He did *not* need to remember the feel of Eric's mouth on him or…. He shook his head at himself and forced himself to stop remembering. He wasn't interested in dealing with a wolfy hard-on, and certainly didn't want the rest to see it when they inevitably found him.

Which was what was bothering him. He still had no real skills as a wolf. He'd lost no less than four squirrels and scared away two separate deer. Clearly he couldn't hunt to save his life. If he was ever stuck in wolf form, he'd starve.

He couldn't even track the others. They'd practiced a few times since he got there, and still he was having trouble following a trail. To be fair, Eric's scent was all over the forest there. But he'd tried to cut a clear path to give Ben something to follow, and even with that, Ben hadn't been able to find him.

Ben looked up when he heard a rustle behind him. He wasn't sure what he expected, but when the black jaguar appeared, he had to remind himself that they weren't native to the region and the one in front of him wasn't wild. Quincy dipped his head in Ben's direction, then turned his attention to a tree nearby. Ben couldn't help but admire the agile leap and climb Quincy did before settling on a thick branch.

He shook his head at himself and laid his muzzle down on his paws again, turning his attention back to his problem. How could Eric want him if he was such a bad wolf? He was hardly a worthy mate to a wolf like Eric. Sure, Eric had been nothing *but* a wolf for a long time, but even so. Ben was sure Eric had been just as good before he went wolf. But Ben? Not so much.

Chad, Jamie, and Tanner had taken turns play-fighting with him too, trying to show him how to fight as a wolf, but even in that, he couldn't seem to get it. They always pinned him, always got him down.

Out of the blue, he found himself tumbling across the grass as another furry body tackled him. It took a little work, but he finally wiggled out from under the wolf. He sniffed, finding Chad's scent—he had *no* clue who was who without being able to see color—and glanced around Chad to see the others lying close by.

Ben turned his attention back to Chad and jumped at him. Annoyingly, Chad sidestepped him and knocked him over again. With a growl Ben put all his weight and effort into knocking Chad over and finally managed to get him on his back. Chad got out from under him immediately, but Ben let himself be happy over that small victory. It was the first pinning he'd managed.

Before he could be *too* happy with himself, a very light-colored blur hit him and he was, yet again, on his back. He got out from under Jamie and leaped at Chad, catching him by surprise and managing to knock him over again. Of course, Chad was right back up and pinned Ben once more.

With another sigh Ben turned his head, showing his neck in surrender. Chad backed off, nuzzled Ben's face, then sat. Jamie came up and licked him, and Ben only felt worse for the comfort they were offering.

Ben rolled, finding himself facing Eric. The riot of emotions inside him confused him, and he could see—and feel—that confusion mirrored in his mate. Eric's head was tilted, and the only thing Ben could really sense across their bond was bewilderment.

Well, he couldn't exactly explain it while they were in wolf form—not until they were fully bonded and telepathic, anyway—but he wasn't sure he could easily explain it to Eric in human form either. Even if he did, Eric would tell him their status as mates had nothing to do with Ben's weaknesses as a wolf. Eric would insist the only hang-ups were his own still-frustrating fears and that he didn't care how "weak"—he might even use air quotes—Ben thought he was as a wolf.

Ben laid his head on his paws again. Eric shook his head, then came over and lay next to him. But the one who came up next was the last person he expected: Quincy. He reached one black paw out and booped Ben on the nose, then stretched out on Ben's other side and started… purring? Not exactly. It was rougher, more of a soft growl than a purr, but Ben understood the comfort for what it was. He'd never have thought the rather aloof cat would do something like that. That made him appreciate it all the more—not that he liked that he needed it, but he certainly wouldn't push Quincy away.

Tanner, Finley, and Miles joined the rest, and before long Ben was the center of a full-on dog pile. Well, dog-and-cat pile, with Quincy. Ben didn't understand it. They were all—Chad included—good, strong wolves and a cat. How did they not think Ben pathetic?

When Eric licked his face, Ben turned to him and took a deep inhale of Eric's scent. He started calming down a little and realized that calm was in part something that was coming across their bond. He wasn't sure if he was comforted or even more upset that Eric could sense him and was trying to comfort him because of it.

Ben sighed. He would just have to work harder. After they came home in the evenings, he'd go out and practice. He'd spend time on the weekends. Maybe if he was a stronger, more capable wolf, Eric would worry less about something happening to him and be more willing to

finally claim. He put his head back on his paws and tried not to let it all
get to him. He'd just keep reminding himself Eric loved him, despite his
shortcomings, and he'd work on it more later.

BEN RAN. He knew he couldn't run *from* the frustration at his limitations,
the anger at his failings, but he couldn't stop himself from trying.

It's not going to happen overnight, dude. It took me months *to be
able to do some of this, and that's with a linked mate and a shitload of
patience from him.* Chad's words echoed in Ben's ears, but they didn't
have the effect on him he was sure Chad was going for.

He wasn't a pup. He was a grown man—wolf—and had had years,
not months, to get this stuff right. More than twenty years had passed,
in fact, since he'd been capable of learning what it meant to be a wolf.
He was smart; he knew that. Hadn't he graduated with honors from both
high school *and* college? He'd passed his CPA exam with top scores.
Why couldn't he seem to get this?

As Ben came into a clearing, he stopped to take it in, marveling at
the beauty of the tiny space. A stream came in on the east, curving and
leaving again to the south. Trees gave way to sunshine, allowing it to
warm the grass that filled the area.

He wandered over to the stream and took a drink, then turned back,
moving into the center of the clearing again. With a sigh he lay down in
the sun and closed his eyes.

Why couldn't he seem to get this? What was so different?

You believe there's so much more depending on this.

Ben opened his eyes and blinked into the sunlight. The voice in his
head had not been his own. As he sat up, a figure seemed to materialize
across the clearing. Female, that was all he could determine at first. As
she stepped forward, it seemed as if her bare feet didn't even disturb the
grass. Her long dark hair spilled over one shoulder, not quite covering
the quiver on her back. Simple clothes adorned her—a tunic and plain
pants that Ben thought were called leggings—and very little else except
for the bow that went with the quiver.

She stopped, knelt in front of him, and ran her hand over his head.
Ben closed his eyes as she petted him. Who was she? Where did she come
from? She didn't feel like other humans did, when he'd been in wolf form.
She didn't smell like them either. What was different about her?

"I know you don't know me, but I understand your struggles, little one."

When she cupped his face, Ben opened his eyes again. He considered shifting to talk to her, but as soon as he had the thought, he knew he wouldn't be able to. His wolf wasn't going to cede control in that moment. Letting that go, Ben turned his attention back to the woman and tilted his head in confusion.

"You were taught I don't exist. I understand that. But hear me now and try to believe. His fear is not because of you. His worry is not of your making. He will figure this out soon. Just have a little more patience."

Ben tried, maybe a little desperately, to accept her words. *Is that true? Is this really not the problem?*

"No, little one, it isn't. Trust in your bond, trust that I have put you together for a reason." She bent forward and kissed the top of Ben's head. Ben closed his eyes as warmth and a sense of calm filled him. "Just a little longer."

When he opened his eyes, she was gone. He sniffed, but the odd scent had disappeared as well, and there was nothing to show she'd ever been there. He lay back down, once more resting his head on his paws.

Was that who he thought it was? Had he just met their goddess? Why? *Patience, little one....*

Ben thought about what she'd said, about his own fears. Was he right to worry? Was he right to fear?

But the frustration and confusing emotions he'd had earlier had eased quite a bit. There was still a nagging doubt in the back of his mind, but he wasn't nearly as sure anymore that his own lack as a wolf was such a problem.

Could he accept that? Could he let it go and simply wait? How much longer would it be?

The feel of her kiss on his head ghosted through him, and he wondered.

Chapter 16

"RIGHT, SO if I hadn't chased it off, his very first meal would have *totally* ruined our mating."

Chad shook his head. "Hey! It was my first time out!"

Jamie grinned. "You looked so betrayed too."

"I remember thinking, 'Hey! That's my lunch!'" That brought a round of laughter. "Yeah, well, I really wouldn't have been too happy if it'd been ruined." Chad chuckled.

"You two are too funny," Eric said, grinning. "How'd you finally stop chasing skunks?"

"I eventually started reminding my wolf to *smell* it before chasing it."

Ben grinned. "I'm glad I do not, at least, chase skunks. There is an advantage to not being good at hunting."

Eric leaned over and kissed Ben. "You'll get better, baby. Seriously."

Ben didn't reply, and Eric suppressed a sigh. He wished there was some way he could help Ben feel better about his lack of wolf skills, but there wasn't much of anything he could do—help Ben practice, keep trying to reassure, but that was all. Ben *had* gotten better since his meeting with Diana, at least.

Poor Jamie had just about cried over that little meeting. *"Am I the only one she's not going to visit?"* If Chad hadn't come out then and reminded him—rather forcefully—that she'd helped him through Chad's change, Eric didn't know what Jamie would have done, but he was still bummed by not meeting her.

Eric could understand. As the most devout of all of them, Eric thought Jamie should have had a chance to meet her, but as Eric had learned, Diana had her own reasons and timing. Considering what she'd done for him, he wasn't about to question her... too closely, anyway.

"Okay, so, clean up." Finley sighed. "You," he said, pointing at Tanner, "Eric, and Quincy are cleaning up."

Eric was a little surprised all he got was a single blink from Quincy, then just one nod. The cat was still a bit of an enigma to Eric. He was so quiet but always seemed willing to offer help when it was needed, though he'd pretend he wasn't really going out of his way to give it. He'd been the one to help Eric get all his paperwork and driver's license straightened out. Tanner had told Eric not to question how, and, wisely, Eric had simply thanked Quincy and put his stuff away. Eric was pretty sure he didn't want to know, anyway.

"Good. Miles, go get the fire going. Jamie, you get the beer. Chad and Ben, since we cooked, *we* get first choice of seating for the game."

Ben grinned. "Yes!"

Eric shook his head but was glad to feel the happiness coming across their bond. Ben had been struggling, trying to hide his worry, trying not to blame himself for them being held up. Eric kissed his temple. "I'm glad you're happy. The food was amazing. We'll be out soon."

Ben returned his kiss, then stood. "I am, cariño."

Eric was rather impressed that no one said a peep at Finley's orders. He guessed it had something to do with being the alpha's mate. Or maybe that was just Finley's personality and they all simply appreciated the directness.

It didn't take long to clear the table with three of them working. Eric helped Tanner with the dishes while Quincy put away the few leftovers they had. He hummed as he worked, and Eric couldn't help but ask, "What is that?"

Quincy raised his eyebrows. "What?"

"That tune."

Eric was amused when Quincy blushed. "Uh, just something from an anime—"

"—that he's been obsessed with," Miles finished for him as he walked inside.

Quincy scowled. "I have not been obsessed!"

Miles simply grinned. "No, not at all. I mean, it's not like you haven't been drawing fan art, rewatching it a dozen times—"

"Okay!" Quincy glared at Miles, but Miles didn't even stop grinning.

Eric and Tanner laughed. "What anime?" Eric asked as he loaded the last of the silverware into the dishwasher.

"It's called *Yuri!!! on Ice!*" Quincy said, sighing. "It's an ice-skating show. Uh, males figure skating."

"I'm only giving him a hard time because I have to," Miles said, helping Quincy put the Tupperware in the refrigerator. "It's actually good. And has a canon gay couple."

Eric turned to them. "Didn't I hear that's pretty common?"

Quincy shook his head. "Only in two specific types of anime—yaoi and shounen-ai. Those are specifically about two male characters. In mainstream anime—which is what *Yuri!!!* is—it is unusual."

"Huh. Well, that's cool, then. You know, I don't think I've ever seen any."

"Oh, dear Diana," Miles muttered.

Eric raised his eyebrows. "What?"

"You've started it now. I'll see you in a few months."

Quincy elbowed him. "If you want to try it, I have a few suggestions and can loan you the DVDs."

"Sure. Ben might like it too."

"Hey!" Finley called from the living room. "You'll miss kickoff!"

Tanner hit the button on the front of the dishwasher. "We're done here anyway."

Eric went out to the living room with the rest to find Ben on one end of the couch. Eric took the seat next to him and shifted until he lay back against Ben's chest. "Wait, turn for me."

Ben raised an eyebrow but did as Eric asked, and Eric settled against him again.

"There. Better." The happiness he got across the bond filled him. He kissed Ben's hand. "Won't last. As soon as things get interesting—"

Ben laughed. "I know, cariño. This is not the first game we have watched together."

Eric chuckled. "Right." He looked up and pulled Ben to him, then kissed him. "I love you."

"I love you." Ben returned the kiss, and then Eric gave his attention to the game.

WHEN THE game ended, Finley sat up and stretched, then sighed. "Okay. I need to get moving before I pass out."

"Again?" Tanner asked from next to him.

Finley glared but otherwise ignored him. "How about a run?"

"Oh, that sounds good," Jamie said, nodding.

"I wouldn't mind stretching my muscles," Quincy added.

"I could use some fresh air too," Ben said, yawning.

"Yes!" Chad said, standing.

"I'll clean up," Eric offered, standing and starting to collect the bottles.

Ben stood as well. "I'll help." He gathered the empty chip bags, and the two of them headed toward the kitchen. It took another trip for the rest of the bottles and the dip containers before they were done.

As they came out, Finley was leading the way to the stairs, but as they got to the top, Tanner paused. "Hey, I hear someone on the road. I'll catch up."

"Want me to wait?" Jamie asked.

"Nah, go ahead. Probably nothing important." Tanner waved him off.

Jamie waved back and he, and the rest—except Ben—went down the steps.

Eric dumped the last of the bottles into the recycling bin, and then he and Ben headed for the stairs as well. Just as they got there, though, the knock sounded on the door and a scent Eric had hoped to never smell again hit him. Eric and Tanner exchanged looks as Tanner approached the door.

"Cariño?"

Eric frowned and turned to Ben. "It's Kim."

Ben blinked. "It's… *what?*"

Shaking his head, Eric frowned. "Kim."

"Why…?"

"I have no idea," Eric said, turning back as Tanner opened the door.

"Kim," Tanner greeted her, though his tone was anything but welcoming.

"Hello, Tanner!" She gave him a too-bright smile. "I heard my mate is back!"

Even with Tanner's back toward him, Eric knew Tanner's eyebrows were up. "Your mate?"

She nodded several times. "Yes. I heard Eric was back and he's staying with you."

Eric scowled, especially when anxiety and fear hit him across the mate bond. He sent calm back to Ben and looked over at him. "I got this. Don't worry. Remember, I love you."

Ben hesitated, glancing toward the door and then back at Eric. "If you're sure."

"I don't want you to have to hear her shit. I'll catch up."

With one more glance at the doorway, Ben nodded. "Okay, cariño." He sent a glare toward Kim, then leaned in and kissed Eric. If it was a little territorial, Eric wasn't going to call him on it.

When Ben was on his way down the steps, Eric turned toward Tanner and Kim. He stepped over, his scowl deepening as he crossed the distance. "What the fuck do you think you're doing here?"

She blinked at him, then glanced at Tanner. "Can we talk alone?"

"Hell no. I don't want to talk to you at all, but if you insist on standing here, Tanner can certainly hear anything you want to say."

She frowned, then brightened. Eric studied her critically. She looked... worn, frazzled and slightly... off. He ruthlessly squashed any sympathy he felt for her and scowled even harder. It didn't seem to faze her.

"That's all right! I'm so glad you came back. As soon as I heard, I hurried here to you. Get your things! I have a hotel room we can stay in until we find a house."

Eric blinked at her. "What in the gods' names would make you think I want anything to do with you, much less that I'd go with you?"

Yet again she seemed taken aback. "I'm your mate! Of course you would."

Eric shook his head. "No, you're not. First, you broke that bond, but second, I've found my destined mate. I wouldn't leave him for anything."

Her eyes got huge. "Destined mate? I thought—"

"Whatever you thought, you thought wrong. Ben's my mate."

Her nostrils flared, and Eric figured she was sniffing to find out if they were mated. In that moment he seriously regretted not claiming Ben yet so she would have had no choice but to recognize their status as mates.

"But... that can't be! I don't know who Ben is, but he can't be your mate! I am! And.... He's a guy!"

Tanner sighed and Eric echoed it. "Don't. Just don't with that."

That seemed to surprise her too, but she shook it off quickly. "Whatever. Just tell him—"

"I'm not telling him anything except that I love him." Eric paused when he sensed Ben's worry. He again sent calm back, realizing his anger was getting the better of him and Ben had sensed it. He raised his eyebrows at Kim's shock. "Just go. Get the hell out of here. I told you, I want nothing to do with you. I have Ben. We're destined and happy." Eric ignored the little voice poking him about the "happy" part. "And even if I didn't have him, I wouldn't want you." He shook his head again. "I can't believe you can think otherwise, after what you did."

"But—"

"Enough. I'm done. Have a nice life," Eric said, shutting the door in her face. He turned away, closing his eyes and taking a deep breath, then a second.

"Nicely done," Tanner said.

Eric opened his eyes again. "Thanks. It... felt good to tell her off."

"I don't doubt it. Where did she get the idea you'd want her?"

"No clue. She looked a little nuts." Eric scowled again. "She'd have to be to think that."

"Yeah, I noticed that too."

Eric frowned. "My fuckin' parents. I bet they called her. Probably told her I'd want her because they didn't believe me about Ben either."

"Imagine their faces when she tells them you didn't."

Eric grinned. "Oh, that'll be priceless. What I wouldn't give to be a fly on that wall." He paused. "Hey, did they leave like you told them?"

"Yeah. I just checked yesterday. House is empty. I called my dad to make sure he knew."

"Good. Fucking assholes." Eric struggled with himself, struggled with the fact that, aside from Ben and his friends, he was alone. He reminded himself that he had family in Tanner, Finley, and all the others, even if it was a chosen family.

Tanner looked away briefly, and the surprise on his face had Eric turning around. Kim was gone... but her clothes—torn clothes—lay in a heap on the sidewalk. "What the fuck?"

"No idea. Guess she took off."

Tanner shook his head. "Let's go run. She's not even worth your time."

"No kidding." Eric sighed, then pushed the scene out of his head. *It's time I put her completely behind me.* "I *really* need that run now. Let's go—" He was cut off when a wave of fear slammed into him. He looked up at Tanner. "Something's wrong with Ben!"

Neither hesitated, but bolted for the steps. Eric didn't even stop to strip. He shifted as he hit the doorway, his clothes falling in tatters around him, and leaped off the back porch, Tanner right behind him. *Hang on, baby. I'm coming to get you.*

WHEN HE got knocked over, Ben didn't think anything of it at first. He'd been working with the other wolves for a while on his fighting, so he'd gotten used to being randomly knocked over. His first assumption was that it was Finley. The black streak had hit him the way they always did.

It wasn't until the jaws clamped around his hind leg and bit down that he realized his mistake. The crunching sound barely registered under the pain that hit. He yelped, twisting around and trying to kick with his other hind leg. The wolf had him pinned, though, and he was having trouble even moving, much less getting out from under it.

Fear he couldn't control took over. He struggled even harder, panic threatening to make things worse. The jaws let go, and before they could find another place to bite, he managed, even with the broken leg, to get out from under it.

When he was on his feet and finally staring down his attacker, he remembered to take in the scent.

Kim?

He bared his teeth at her, the growl deep in his chest surprising even himself. What the hell was he going to do? If she wanted to, she could kill him. He couldn't fight, still hadn't even come close to mastering that.

And why was she fighting him? What did she think it would accomplish?

He wasn't getting any answers while they were in wolf form, and he didn't trust he'd be any better a fighter in human form. At least as a wolf, he had weapons. Teeth and claws he barely knew how to use, but weapons nonetheless.

To his surprise, though, she backed up, and a few seconds later, he was staring at her naked human form. He thought about shifting, but he was still slow on a good day, and with the injury, he was afraid he'd be even slower. If she shifted back before he could, she'd easily have the upper hand. So he stayed where he was, in his current form, watching her carefully.

"My mate says you're his mate. I know better." She gave a smile that sent a chill down Ben's back. Something wasn't right about it. Ben wondered about that, but he couldn't afford to let himself get distracted by it. "You can't be mated to a man. And I don't believe for one moment you're bonded, much less destined." She shook her head. "He's mine. And as soon as you're out of the way, he'll realize it."

"Kim!" Eric called.

Ben looked over at his mate, and that was a mistake. Within seconds she was on him again, her claws raking over his side. Lines of searing pain tore across his left side, and he struggled with it. He couldn't stop another yelp, but he managed to hold some of it in. He couldn't hide the pain from Eric, but he'd be damned if he let *her* know the full extent of it.

Out of the corner of his eye, Ben could see the other wolves and Quincy lined up next to Eric, all of them growling. Quincy looked frightening, and Ben was glad that wasn't aimed at him. He was equally glad to know the jaguar was backing him. They all were. *His pack.* The truth of that settled into him, and he felt better knowing that even if he couldn't do this, even if he failed, she wouldn't get away with it.

"Back off, bitch," Eric growled.

The distraction was what Ben needed to get on his feet again. She turned toward Eric, and Ben used that moment to pounce. His leg was killing him, but he managed to get his weight behind it and knocked her over, then bit down on her leg.

He would *not* give her a chance to beat him.

"Don't, guys. Just wait." Eric actually chuckled. "He's pissed and determined, I can feel it. He can do this. Let him."

Eric's words, his encouragement and confidence, filled Ben. Despite his lack of faith in his abilities, hearing that Eric had it for him flipped a switch in Ben. He let go of her and backed up, pacing around her as she got up again. She glanced at Eric and managed to look surprised, even in wolf form. She brought her attention to Ben again, though, limping as she moved, growling low in her throat.

Trust your wolf. He knows what to do. Chad's words came back to him, and Ben mentally stepped back, finally fully giving his trust to his wolf.

Let's get her.

He leaped again, aiming for her throat, but she moved and he caught her front leg instead. She let out a yelp, though, so he knew he'd at least hurt her. She struggled, snapping at him and catching his shoulder, biting down, and he heard another crunch. At this point there was so much pain, though, he couldn't separate it from the rest, so he ignored it the best he could and focused on her.

It didn't matter what she did, though. He refused to back off and moved to get a paw onto her chest. However, only a few seconds later, she managed to get out from under him somehow and moved away.

It pissed him off. He was tired of the game, tired of dancing around her. He *refused* to let her win. He would *not* leave Eric.

Making a concerted effort to put the pain away for the moment, he stalked toward her, still growling, and yet again jumped. The pain in his leg got through his block briefly, but he ignored it and knocked her over once more. This time he got his teeth around her neck.

She struggled, kicking out with her hind legs, getting a scratch across his belly, but he ignored it and squeezed his jaws. Still, she didn't give up. It took all he had to keep from snapping her neck and instead add just a little more pressure. She stared up at him, and he met her gaze. Something not quite right was in her eyes, beyond the determination, the anger. He might even say wild, but that didn't seem right either. *Off* was the best he could come up with. Not quite sane, maybe.

They held there, suspended, for an eternity. Their gazes were locked, not the slightest twitch of muscles from either of them. He wouldn't kill her—that wasn't who he was, even with the wolf in the forefront.

But he refused to back down.

He didn't know what did it, what changed, what happened, but one minute she was staring at him, and the next she went limp, baring her neck completely.

When Tanner appeared next to him a moment later, in human form, Ben released her and moved away.

As the relief hit, so did the pain, and everything went black.

Chapter 17

ERIC WASN'T sure he actually touched the ground between where he'd knelt and where Ben lay. "Miles!" he shouted, without taking his eyes off his mate. He vaguely heard Tanner telling Kim to shift, but he paid no attention to it. Ben needed him. "Baby?" If he sounded a little panicked, he doubted anyone would blame him.

He reached out to touch, but he was afraid to. Blood matted Ben's fur *everywhere*, the scratches across his side and belly looked horrible, and both his hind and front legs lay at odd angles. He didn't know where all Ben was hurt, but the pain was obviously bad, based on the unfiltered amount coming across their bond. It wasn't physical for him, but the mental was still bad enough. So Eric was terrified of making it worse.

It was only by virtue of the fact that Ben was panting, even though unconscious, that kept Eric from truly losing his shit.

When the human Miles knelt next to him, Eric pulled his hand back. Miles shook his head. "It's okay. You can touch him. His head is fine, and most of that's her blood, not his. And your touch will help."

Eric swallowed and laid his hand on Ben's head. Ben moved just a little, but it didn't do enough to stem the fear and panic in Eric—fear and panic he was sure, even unconscious, Ben was sensing, but he couldn't stop it. With a pounding heart, Eric prayed harder than he ever had before. "Diana, our divine goddess, hear my prayer. Your aid is needed, your blessings sought." A hand lay on Eric's shoulder, and he glanced over to see Jamie next to him. As he continued, more voices joined his. "See us safely through the trial ahead. Lend us your strength, your wisdom, and your fortitude. We honor you, our Goddess Divine." Eric swallowed hard, trying to stem the panic growing as Ben stayed unconscious. "Miles…."

Miles looked up, catching Eric's eye. "He's got fractured ribs, two broken legs, and a good number of scratches. But if we're careful getting him back, he should heal fine." He rested a hand on Eric's arm. "Really. He'll be okay."

Eric took another breath that wasn't deep enough. After checking with Miles, who nodded, they carefully got Ben's limp body into Eric's arms. When he was standing, he saw Miles to one side and Jamie to the other as they started walking.

"Quincy and Chad are staying to watch over Kim with Tanner," Miles said.

Eric nodded, grateful Miles and Jamie were with him. Their calming influence and the feel of Ben breathing were all that was keeping him even semicalm. Each of them had a hand on him, and that also helped, though he really was only vaguely aware of anything not Ben.

Eric couldn't care less what happened to Kim, except to hope she paid for what she'd done to Ben. He'd do whatever he had to in order to make sure of it. He didn't even care, anymore, what she'd done to him, but hurting Ben, going after him, was inexcusable.

Eric moved through the trees, both Miles and Jamie still with a hand on him. Jamie's voice continued offering prayer to Diana, and as he did, wind shook the leaves. Eric focused mostly on his steps, being careful to not jostle Ben and make the pain worse, and he appreciated the prayers on their behalf.

But when Jamie and Miles both stopped, Eric looked up in confusion. It wasn't until he saw the figure on the path just ahead that he realized what was going on.

"Holy... is that?" Jamie whispered.

Eric nodded, though he couldn't manage to reply verbally. He stared at her a long moment, desperately trying to remember how to speak. He dug around, struggled, then finally found his voice. "He'll... be okay?"

She smiled at him and stepped closer. One hand ghosted over Ben's head, and a breath shuddered out of him before his breathing calmed. The pain coming across their bond eased significantly, and Eric released a small sigh. He wouldn't be completely relieved unless and until Ben woke up and was okay. Eric looked down at the jagged, open scratches still covering Ben's side and then back up again, frowning.

"He will be fine," she said, touching Eric's cheek next. "And so will you. You are ready, no longer lost. Let go."

Then she turned to Jamie. "You didn't need to see me. Your belief is stronger than so many." She chuckled. "But know your devotion means more to me than you could begin to understand."

A few seconds later, she was gone.

"I... that was...." Jamie looked over at Eric, then back at the spot where she'd stood. "I...." He shook his head, looking somewhere between shock and tears. "Let's get Ben back. I can faint later."

That actually brought a chuckle out of Eric as he started walking again. He continued to focus on his steps, moving carefully. Diana had lessened Ben's pain, but he was still hurt, and even with her help, Eric could make things worse.

He understood why she hadn't healed Ben completely. *You are ready, no longer lost. Let go.* Ben would recover. Eric needed to see that, and he would. And it would be what he needed to know she was right about the rest.

ERIC LAID Ben on their bed, worried at how bad the scratches and breaks looked. In all his years as a wolf, he'd managed to never get more than a couple of minor injuries. Rest and food in the tiny den he'd made his home had been all he'd needed. The ones on Ben seemed horrible. He believed Diana and Miles, that Ben would be okay, but his wounds sure as hell looked bad, and the contradiction made it difficult to do anything *but* worry.

"I need clean water, towels, and something to use as a brace for each leg," Miles said, snapping Eric out of his worry for the moment. "If I don't get them set, I might have to rebreak them and that would suck."

"I'll get it," Jamie said, laying a hand on Eric's shoulder. "You need to stay close."

Eric nodded. "Thanks," he managed, his voice rough.

Miles disappeared into the bathroom, and Eric heard the water turn on. Eric couldn't take his eyes off Ben, though, and didn't pay attention to Miles. A moment later, Miles came back, followed immediately by Jamie, and Eric moved enough to let them both in. He stayed close, though, and kept one hand on Ben the whole time Miles worked, unwilling—or unable, he didn't know—to let go.

Miles used quick, efficient movements, cleaning the scratches and other cuts, then carefully setting the legs with Jamie's help. "We can recover from most infections and injuries," he said as he wrapped the bandages around the back leg. "But at best it can be rough in the process. At worst, we can actually end up dealing with infection and fever and other problems because of it. So, if I can avoid it, I'd prefer to."

"Thank you," Eric said, letting out a breath. "That makes sense. I hate to see him hurt because of—"

"Oh fuck no," Tanner said, stepping into the room.

Eric glanced up at him, then brought his gaze back to Ben. "What?"

"That's not on you. You are so not responsible for what happened to him. That's *her* fault and no one else's. Don't go blaming yourself. You've got enough issues without adding that onto the pile."

Eric snorted. "I have a few."

Jamie poked Eric in the shoulder. "Dude, you have an entire publishing company's worth."

Eric found himself smiling, and he flipped Jamie off. "Thanks so much." He shook his head, but he felt better with his friends' words. He let out a breath, then cleared his throat. "What about her?"

"Bob's got her in a room in the back of the bar. Finley called Denver for me while I stood over her, and they're sending enforcers out. They'll be here in a few hours to take her to headquarters. She's being charged with attempted murder."

Eric looked up and nodded once. "Good. She's lucky she didn't succeed or she'd be dead right now."

"And I wouldn't have blamed you one bit," Tanner said. "I'm glad she didn't, for a whole lot of reasons." He put a hand on Eric's shoulder. "He'll be fine."

"That's what everyone else keeps saying," Eric said, blowing out a breath.

"Including Diana," Jamie added.

Tanner raised his eyebrows.

Jamie grinned so wide, Eric couldn't help but chuckle. "Yes. She stopped us on the way back to the house."

Tanner whistled. "Damn. Lucky dog."

Jamie stuck his tongue out. "Wolf."

The banter eased the tight knot in Eric's chest a little. They wouldn't do that if they thought Ben wouldn't recover.

Miles tied off the bandage, and Eric cleared his throat. "Well. My mate needs rest."

"Yes," Miles agreed. He stood and gathered the towels and things. "Mine is downstairs worried about Ben. Don't tell him I told you, though. He'd skin me if he knew I told you he was worried."

Eric smiled. "Not a word."

"Yeah, so is Finley," Tanner said, moving toward the door.

"And Chad. We'll get out of your hair." Jamie put a hand on Eric's shoulder. "She wouldn't lie. Listen to her."

Eric wondered if that was just about Ben recovering or if it was also the words she'd left him with. *You are ready, lost no more. Let go.*

He settled in next to Ben, watching his breathing, and knew Diana was right. It was time—past time—and Eric was annoyed as all hell to realize he actually had Kim to thank for it. Her return and the attack on Ben was the catalyst he needed to kick his ass into gear. Eric could let go of most of the rest of his fear. He'd never completely stop the worry of losing his mate, but he could get it to a normal level.

And Ben could finally let go of *his* fears. Eric had no doubt Ben would be able to trust his wolf in a way he hadn't before and finally trust in himself that Eric would want him.

But beyond his fear, Eric wasn't the same man he was nine years ago. He wouldn't be the mate Ben needed if Kim hadn't broken the bond and he hadn't gone through what he had, the way he had.

Eric carefully curled around Ben and kissed the top of his furry head. "Get better soon, baby."

BEN SHIFTED back to human form in his sleep a few hours later, waking Eric. He hadn't meant to fall asleep, but he guessed the stress of everything had taken its toll. He frowned down at Ben's legs, hoping the change with the braces on didn't cause problems. He couldn't tell for sure himself, not positive what he should look for to be able to tell.

With a kiss to Ben's temple, Eric went downstairs in search of Miles, who he found stretched out on the couch, his eyes closed. Eric was surprised to see Quincy against him, and Chad and Jamie tangled up on the other couch. As soon as Eric came down off the last step, Miles opened his eyes and sat up, followed quickly by Quincy, Chad, and Jamie.

"Is he okay? Awake?" Miles asked, rubbing his face.

It took Eric a moment to answer, as bemused as he was by all of them there. "Uh.... He's not awake, but he shifted in his sleep. I'm worried about the braces."

Miles nodded. "Let me check," he said as he stood and stretched. "I'm sure it's fine, though. His wolf wouldn't have let go if he wasn't healing well enough."

Eric turned to the others. "You guys didn't need to stay."

Jamie rolled his eyes. "As if we'd go until he's awake."

Not knowing what to say to that, Eric simply followed Miles back up to their bedroom. He was used to a caring pack, but this was way more than just being packmates. Focusing on Ben, Eric stepped aside to let Miles check him over. He fidgeted as Miles probed the bruised leg, especially when Ben twitched over it, but let his breath out in relief when Miles started unwinding the bandages.

"He'll be fine. The braces can come off now. Unless he falls or something, it'll heal normally. I'll stay downstairs until the morning to make sure nothing happens. I cleaned the scratches, but I'll want to make sure there's no infection."

"Thanks, Miles. I appreciate it."

Miles waved a hand. "That's what I'm for. Besides, I'd want to stay anyway." He stood up and considered Eric for a moment. "I think I told you I lost my family when I came out back in high school."

Eric nodded. "I think so. Or maybe I heard it, but yeah."

"So, until I'd come to Forbes, I had no one. Over the last year, these guys have become my family. Jamie was kicked out. And while Finley and Tanner have parents and siblings, Quincy's relationship with his father is… strained, at best."

"Yeah, I kinda figured that one."

"Right. So… whether you like it or not, we've rather adopted you into it too. You and Ben, because we know quite well how rocky things are there too." Miles smiled, and Eric wondered at the expression on his face to cause it. "Just accept it," he said, patting Eric's arm. "We'll be downstairs. Let me know when he wakes up."

Eric nodded but couldn't seem to come up with anything to say. As Miles stepped through the door, Eric finally found his wits and voice. "We're a seriously weird family…." He smiled at Miles's grin. "But I'm glad to be part of it."

Miles nodded once, then closed the door behind himself.

BEN DIDN'T wake until the morning. Eric was asleep, lying against Ben. When Ben brushed his fingers over Eric's face, Eric opened his eyes and smiled.

"Good morning, cariño," Ben said, studying his mate's expression. "You did not sleep much."

It wasn't a question, it was a statement, but Eric nodded anyway. "Yeah, well, I was a little worried."

Ben smiled. "I am fine. Or, well, I will be. A couple of shifts and—" His stomach chose that moment to growl.

"And food," Eric finished for him. He leaned forward and kissed Ben's forehead. "Let me go see what we've got. I'll be right back." He climbed out of bed, but before he could get to the door, Ben called to him.

"Thank you for staying with me."

Eric tilted his head. "Of course, baby. You'll heal a lot faster if I'm close." He frowned. "If I'd claimed you, you'd be healing even faster." He considered Ben. "I wonder if you're well enough for that. I could—"

"No."

Eric blinked. He didn't think he'd ever heard Ben so firm. "Baby?"

Ben shook his head. "You will claim me when you're ready, not for this."

"But—"

"No." Ben sighed and picked at the cover over himself. "I need to know it is not just to help me heal."

Eric didn't immediately reassure Ben, and Ben appreciated that. As much as he wanted Eric to claim him, they didn't need it to be under any other circumstances than them perfectly healthy with nothing else going on. Otherwise, that worry would follow them—follow Ben—possibly for the rest of their lives.

Eric nodded. "I understand, baby." He crossed back over and kissed Ben softly. "That wouldn't be the reason, but I do understand. Let me get you that food."

"Thank you, cariño." Ben watched him go and let out a breath.

Did that mean Eric was ready? Was it because Ben had gotten hurt? Or was there something more going on? Ben tried to figure it out, but he was still tired and still hurting too much to think, so he gave up for the present. He let it go and closed his eyes.

What could only be a few moments later, Eric was back, surprisingly with the rest of their friends in tow. Ben wondered if they'd stayed or came back early, but he wasn't about to voice the question.

Miles came over first. "Let me take a look at you."

Ben nodded and moved the covers aside. "I'll be fine."

"All the same, I'd like to make sure." Miles turned his attention to the scratches on Ben's side, and Ben tried to simply ignore the man's fingers—and resulting pain—and looked up as Finley approached.

"Here," Finley said, stepping up on the other side of the bed. "Start with some of this. We'll get more in a little bit." He set a plate of breakfast sausage on the bed, and before Ben could even think about it, he had a link in his hand and had taken a bite. It wasn't until he realized Finley had left and they were all staring at him and smiling that he swallowed awkwardly.

"Uh…."

That just got him grins. "Glad you're feeling better. We were worried," Chad said. The rest nodded—even Quincy—and Ben blinked, puzzled, looking at Eric.

Eric scratched the back of his head. "Yeah, I was, uh, schooled last night about that, by the good doc there. It seems we're actually part of this weird family and we're supposed to just get used to it."

Ben had no idea what to do with that and didn't even try. Instead, he picked up another sausage and focused on eating.

"Of course you are," Finley said as he came back, another plate of sausages in his hand. "These are fastest. I can get you some steak a little later." He set the second plate next to the first and sat on the side of the bed.

Miles chose that moment to prod Ben's leg, making him wince. "Ow!" came out before he could stop himself.

"Yeah, you'll need a couple more shifts and some time before that's healed completely. The scratches will be fine sometime today, though you'll still be sore for a while."

Ben nodded. "Thank you."

Miles patted his shoulder. "Of course. Now—" He sent a pointed look at the rest of the guys. "Now that we know he's recovering just fine, we're all going to leave him alone to rest. Right?"

"Yup."

"Absolutely."

"Of course."

"I have some work to do," Quincy said, following the others out of the room.

"I'll be right down," Miles said, then turned back to Ben. "Let me know if anything gets worse. I can be here in just a few minutes." He looked at Eric. "He should be fine. He's past the window for any kind of infection for us, so don't worry. Just stay close so the soreness fades as quickly as possible."

"I will. He'll get sick of me," Eric said, grinning.

Ben rolled his eyes. "Hardly, cariño."

"Well. Let me know if you're still hungry after this and I'll get those steaks out." Finley waved, and he and Miles disappeared.

"Eat," Eric said, taking Finley's place.

Ben picked up the first plate but blinked at Eric. He held out a link. "Do you want some?"

"No, those are yours. You eat."

Ben took another bite, but when Eric kept watching him, his cheeks heated. "Are you going to watch me?"

Eric blushed and dropped his gaze. "Sorry. Just…."

"Relieved, yes. I can feel it."

"And I can feel your exasperation," Eric said. "*Really* sorry."

Ben set the plate down and reached out. "No, it's okay. I'm sorry. I would be the same if you were here."

"I'm glad to know you'd worry." Eric gave a smile that Ben knew was forced, but he didn't say anything. Instead, when Eric kissed Ben's hand, he squeezed Eric's in return, then they let go. "Eat. I'm going to go get some coffee."

BEN FOUND himself more than a little frustrated at his slow recovery. It was incredibly faster than it would be for a human, but Ben had never been patient with injury—as rarely as it happened—and he wanted himself well *now*. His bones had mended but were still weak, even after two more shifts and several pounds of meat. He wanted to move around, but the only thing Eric would let him do was go to the bathroom—and Eric even insisted on carrying him there.

On the other side of that, Ben wasn't alone and he was glad of it. Aside from carrying and doing for him, Eric also wouldn't leave. Quincy had given some suggestions of anime they could watch, and Ben and Eric had passed the time that afternoon watching it. The one Quincy said they should watch first wasn't on DVD, but it was on the internet and they'd spent the afternoon binge-watching it.

Eric's comments that morning about claiming hadn't left Ben's head all day. On one hand, he wanted to ask Eric if he really was ready to claim. Ben's determination on that hadn't wavered; he wouldn't do it until he was healthy. At the same time, he couldn't help but wonder. Would Eric have offered it if he wasn't ready? What had happened?

Eric had told Ben about the meeting with Diana. After he woke up, Ben had told Eric of his own meeting. He no longer doubted the existence of the gods, and that helped him believe more in himself and in the fact that it wasn't his shortcomings as a wolf that were holding things up. There was still some doubt, but there wasn't much he could do to rid himself of it.

So was it as Diana had said to him? Was Eric really ready?

Ben had been mentally circling most of the day, and it was driving him crazy. He thought he was going to be a candidate for the psychiatric hospital at the rate he was going.

"What's wrong?" Eric asked, pausing the video.

Ben sighed, annoyed with himself for getting so lost and frustrated that Eric could sense it. "I'm sorry, cariño."

"There's nothing to be sorry for. And that doesn't answer the question."

Ben frowned, not sure how much to say or how to put it.

"Just tell me, baby. I think I have an idea what it is, anyway. Not talking doesn't work."

With another sigh, Ben nodded. "I know. I… your… suggestion this morning."

"That's what I thought it was," Eric said, nodding.

Ben—with effort—turned to look at Eric more directly. He mulled over the best way to say it but just ended up blurting, "Did you mean it?"

Eric didn't answer right away. The hesitation worried Ben to a point, but he was also somewhat glad Eric was thinking over his reply. "I did. And no."

Ben blinked. "No?"

"No, I didn't just suggest it because you're hurt." When Ben opened his mouth to speak, Eric held up a hand. "Sure, the timing was because of that. But, Ben…." He took Ben's hand, threading their fingers together, then kissed the back softly. "Diana is right, and not just because she's a deity. This isn't because I know you're capable of fighting either."

Ben smiled in response to Eric's. "How did you know I was thinking that?"

Eric simply raised an eyebrow.

Letting out a sigh, Ben nodded. "Right. You know me."

"I'd hope, after being bonded, even in the limited way we are, that I would know you by now." Eric reached up with his free hand and brushed his fingertips over Ben's cheek. "You're so unsure of yourself, of your place, of how much people like and want you." He shook his head. "I worry about someday meeting your mamá. I may not be as polite as I should be."

Ben dropped his gaze to their hands. "She—"

"No excuses, Ben. I understand being raised a certain way, but she had evidence in front of her eyes. I assume she and your dad had the telepathy?"

"Yes." Ben nodded. "Though my understanding was she did not use it much."

Eric shrugged a shoulder. "That's on her. She had every chance to see that her religion was wrong, that what she'd been taught about us—or the idea of us—wasn't right." He waved a hand. "The point is, I get you. Your first assumption is *going* to be that it's your fault somehow."

Ben blew out a breath. "I… wish I could get past that."

Eric nodded. "Yeah, but here's the thing. I think the best way for you to do that is for us to finally claim each other."

Ben traced the veins on the back of Eric's hand. "But are you really ready for that?"

Eric put a finger under Ben's chin and tilted his head until Ben met his gaze. "Yes. And as soon as you're healthy, I want us to."

Chapter 18

IF WAITING to recover that first day—just because Ben wanted to feel better and not for any other reason—was bad, this was so much worse. Knowing their claiming was just on the other side of his recovery, he was beyond anxious, passing crazy, and getting into downright batshit territory. He was making Eric crazy too, and he could sense both Eric's agitation and his frustration as well.

Ben wasn't sure, though, if it was just frustration at his slow recovery or if it was his insistence on them waiting until he was recovered. This was one thing Ben really didn't want to let go of. He desperately wanted to claim—and be claimed—but he couldn't escape the feeling that it would always be a doubt in the back of his mind that he had, with his injury, essentially forced Eric to do so.

Claiming might put that doubt to rest. Ben didn't know how much the link would help with that. He just didn't think, considering it wouldn't be *too* long, it was worth taking the chance. Understanding all of this intellectually didn't lessen the frustration of his limitations, however.

It took two more days before he was recovered enough to get rid of the doubt. When he woke from a nap later that second day, he was happy to feel the soreness easing quite a bit. The bedside light was on and the sun was sinking. He'd slept longer than he'd meant to, but if it helped him recover, he couldn't regret it. Eric sat next to him, a book open in his lap, ignored. He seemed lost in thought.

Reaching up, Ben ran his fingertips over Eric's cheek. "Hello, cariño," he murmured.

Eric turned to him, smile spreading. "Hi, baby. How are you feeling?"

Ben gave himself a brief moment to make sure his earlier assessment was correct, then smiled back at Eric. "Better. *Much* better."

The smile widened. "Oh, that much?"

Ben didn't even try to pretend he didn't know what Eric was asking. "Yes."

In a move so fast Ben could barely follow it, Eric closed the distance between them and kissed him, hard. It took Ben a bit to catch up, but when he did, he opened his mouth, returning the kiss with everything in him. A moment later, however, he pulled back, panting at the lack of oxygen.

That's when he smelled himself. He wrinkled his nose. "I am gross."

Eric threw his head back and laughed. "Hardly. But I understand."

Ben nodded. "I also need the bathroom. Then, well…."

Eric tilted his head. "How about we shower together?"

"Oh…." Ben smiled. "I like that idea."

Waggling his eyebrows, Eric sat up. "You take care of business and let me know when you're ready to get in."

"All right, cariño." Ben stretched, then carefully stood, testing his muscles bit by bit. "I am most definitely better."

Eric came around the bed and kissed him softly. "Good. Let's get that shower, then."

Ben returned the kiss, then went into the bathroom. After taking care of business, he turned to the sink. His mouth tasted like something had died in it. He couldn't believe he'd kissed Eric with that breath. Making a face at himself, he grabbed his toothbrush, then brushed his teeth twice. He rinsed twice with mouthwash as well.

Finally he called through the door, "I am ready, cariño."

Eric wasted no time and joined him, already quite naked.

Ben couldn't stop from giving Eric a once-over. "I will never get tired of that view," he murmured, stepping close and running his hand down Eric's chest. "We have been together many times and still I love to look at you."

Eric caught his lips in another soft kiss. "And I you, baby. But I'm anxious. It's time we claim—past time. Let's get that shower."

Ben nodded and leaned into the stall, twisting the knob. "Warm, hot, or—"

"A bit north of the underworld."

Ben laughed. "Good, that's how I like it too."

Once the water was adjusted, Ben got in, then turned to Eric as soon as he was in as well. He couldn't resist another kiss and decided he didn't have to. Stepping closer, he reached up and cupped Eric's face in his hands. When their lips met this time, there was nothing soft or light about it. Ben opened when Eric ran his tongue along Ben's lip, and welcomed him in.

Eric spun them, pushing Ben against the wall and deepening the kiss even more. He leaned into Ben, and Ben moaned at the feel of their skin sliding. It'd been three days since they'd been able to be together and it felt as if Ben's wolf was trying to break through his skin to get to their mate. Need clawed at him, and it was only by sheer force of will that he kept his wolf in check and didn't bite then and there. He would *not* risk anything screwing this up for them.

Breaking the kiss, Eric bent and made a trail of them along Ben's jaw to his ear. "Te amo, mi corazon," Eric whispered before continuing down Ben's neck.

"Te amo, cariño," Ben replied, running his hands over Eric's skin. He struggled to remember why they were in the shower, and after opening his eyes to a world gone gray, he had an even harder time remembering. When Eric pulled back and his eyes were black and his teeth had dropped, Ben sucked in a breath.

"We better get clean or I'll claim you right here in the shower."

That brought Ben back a little. He reached for the soap, but Eric took it.

"I'll do this." He gave a crooked smile. "You can wash me."

"That will not help us get to the bedroom faster."

"I can hold on a *little* longer." Eric picked up the washcloth and worked up a lather with the soap. "I want to slow down a little anyway," he said, running the cloth over Ben's chest. "I want to savor this. We've had a lot of sex, but we'll only claim once. I want it something we'll remember until we're old and go wolf."

Ben swallowed, thrilling in those words. "I have no doubt we will, but I agree." He smiled. "I can control my wolf at least *some*."

That brought a chuckle as Eric turned his attention to the washcloth. Ben kept his hands on Eric, letting him move at his own pace. The slow washing was a seduction in itself, all light brushes and soft touches. Even places that weren't erotic spots suddenly became so. His stomach, arms, and hips—every touch left sensitive nerves and more need building.

Ben was actually glad when Eric finished. He wanted his turn to do the same, arousing just as much, touching everywhere. No matter how often they'd made love since they'd bonded, he still savored every moan and gasp he pulled from Eric when he touched just the right spot, teased in just the right way.

Even washing his hair turned erotic. Ben had no idea how that happened, how Eric simply running his fingers through Ben's hair and working up a lather with the shampoo could drive him even crazier. It did, though, and Ben did his damnedest to do the same for Eric. If the moans his mate let out were anything to go by, he succeeded, thrilling him all over again.

Once they were clean, despite the need to get out, to finally claim, neither could seem to stop touching and kissing long enough to do so. Every time Ben pulled back, he found another spot to kiss, the need to taste just one more place too much. Every time Eric made a move to get out, they went right back to touching.

Finally Ben managed to find his sanity. "Cariño…."

"Yeah," Eric said, voice rough. He straightened away from the wall—and Ben—and turned the water off.

When Ben reached for the towel, though, Eric shook his head and grabbed it. Without speaking, he ran the towel over Ben, drying him thoroughly. In response, Ben refused to let Eric dry himself, and yet again, by the time they were both done, they were kissing and touching.

Before they could get too lost, though, Ben took a half step back and grasped Eric's hand. As he turned toward the bedroom, his nerves and doubts kicked in, and he struggled to shove them back so Eric didn't sense them.

What if, after all this, he doesn't want me? Or worse, he changes his mind after and we are stuck together for life? What if—

ERIC COULDN'T miss Ben's anxiety and worry, tinged with fear. He was sure Ben was doing his best to hide it, but that just meant it was even worse if that was what got through. He pulled Ben back, wrapped both arms around him, and kissed a line along his neck. "Tell me, baby."

Ben let out a breath. "What if… what if you change your mind after all this? What if you realize I'm still not what you want… what you need?"

Eric stepped back and took Ben's hand. "Putting aside the fact that our goddess put us together—and wouldn't have if I wouldn't want you… well, come see for yourself." He pulled Ben with him, grateful as all hell that Tanner and Finley had gone with the enforcers and were still in Denver. Eric stepped into the bedroom and turned to watch Ben's reaction. He wasn't disappointed when Ben's eyes widened and the smile spread across his face. Ben's gaze moved around the room, and Eric was sure he was taking in the candles Eric had unearthed, set around, and lit, the carefully made bed—with fresh sheets—and even the open window, bringing in the scent of the forest they both loved so much.

"Ca-cariño?"

"I couldn't do as much as you deserve, baby." Eric went over to the dresser, woke up his phone, and touched the Play button on the music app. He'd already chosen the playlist he'd assembled earlier. Soft Spanish music floated out of the speakers he'd set up when Ben went into the bathroom earlier. "You deserve everything…." Eric held his hand out a little helplessly, unable to articulate exactly what that should be. "But…."

Ben turned to him. "You did not need to do this."

Eric shook his head. "Maybe not, but I wanted to. I want there to be no question in your mind. I want you. I want you for the rest of our lives, Ben. I would *choose* you if we weren't destined."

Ben sucked in a breath and swallowed. "Eric, you…."

"Yes." He pulled Ben in, wrapping both arms around him, then nuzzled Ben's ear. "*Eres mío. Para siempre.*" He kissed the spot on Ben's neck he'd bite in a short while. "You are a gift to me from Diana. You are mine, for always."

When Ben pulled back, Eric reached up and cupped one cheek. Ben swallowed, opened his mouth, then closed it and finally spoke. "I… I cannot… I do not… know what to say. I—"

"You don't have to, baby. I know. I feel it. Now… let's complete it."

Ben nodded, then turned, and they moved over to the bed. Eric wasted no time following him down until he lay on top of Ben, savoring the feel of their skin sliding, the need building just from touching this little bit. He caught Ben's lips in another deep kiss and promptly got lost in it.

Eric reminded himself that as much as he wanted to take this slow and savor, they had a lifetime to be together. Still, he kissed and teased, reveled in the sounds and touches. He went back to every spot he knew was sensitive and worked it over until Ben nearly begged. Then he did it all over again at the next spot and the next.

Eric's wolf pushed at him, frustrated by the pace. He didn't want to wait, didn't want to go slow. He wanted to mate, wanted to bite, wanted to claim. Now that the human side had given in, the wolf was *done* waiting. But despite all the years Eric spent in wolf form, he *was* stronger than his wolf, and he'd be damned if he rushed this.

His own cock was so hard, he was going a little crazy with his own need, but he did his damnedest to ignore it, focusing on his mate. Ben was hardly passive, however, running his hands over Eric too. Even when Eric swallowed him, working over his cock with tongue and lips, he wouldn't stop touching.

"Please, cariño," Ben more moaned than said. Eric looked up, and Ben seemed to be struggling for words. Finally he said, "More, *please*."

Eric slid up along Ben's body to kiss him again. When he pulled back, he held himself up, making sure Ben was looking at him. "I'm going to top. You know I don't normally care, but I want absolutely no question in your mind. I'm taking you. I want you, I want this, I want to *claim*."

Ben didn't speak, simply nodded. Eric knew Ben didn't mind the insistence. If he really had a problem with it, Eric would listen. But right now he wanted to show how much he wanted Ben. Eric kissed him again, then forced himself to focus on preparing Ben. They hadn't been together since before the fight, and that time, Ben had topped. So Eric wasn't going to screw up their mating by not making sure Ben was as ready as he could be for this.

So, yet again, he took it slow, ignoring his own now near-desperate need. When Ben insisted he was fine, Eric shushed him. "I will not hurt you, not for this."

"I am hardly a vir—oh *mierda*!" Ben grabbed at the headboard when Eric hit his prostate.

"You don't need to be for me to want to stretch you enough." Eric decided a bit of distraction was called for and moved his mouth down over Ben's cock as he went back to stretching. He wasn't going to overdo it, though. Ben wasn't the only one who had waited long enough—too long—for this. Eric snatched up the lube one more time and made sure he was coated, then lined up.

Their eyes met as Eric got into place. Without speaking, he pushed, easing himself into his mate, glad to feel Ben relaxed. Eric might have overworried, but he didn't care. This man, his mate, was too damned important and precious.

When he finally was fully buried in Ben's amazing body, Eric leaned forward. "I love you. I will thank Diana every day of our lives for you," he promised.

Ben cupped his face. "And I will thank her for you, cariño. I am so grateful she brought us together."

"Me too, baby. Me too. Ready to take that last step?"

Ben swallowed but nodded. "More than ready."

Eric pulled out slowly, the pushed back in just as slowly. Like the rest, as much as he wanted to bite and claim, he'd be damned if he rushed it. He refused, as well, to compare it to the last time he'd claimed. Ben didn't compare—*this* couldn't compare, and not just because he and Ben were destined.

He built it gradually, keeping his thrusts long and slow, filling Ben on every one. It was driving him a little nuts—Ben too, if the frustration coming across their bond was anything to go by—but Eric tried to drag it out, make the pleasure last as long as he could. Finally the need to feel, to give as much pleasure as he was getting, became too much. He sped up, earning himself a loud moan.

Ben's hand tightened on the headboard, and Eric briefly wondered if they were going to have to replace it. Then Ben flexed his muscles and squeezed, and any thoughts of furniture evaporated. Eric rocked faster, thrust harder as the pleasure built. He moved a little and was rewarded with another "Mierda!" Eric grinned, pulled back, and hit it again, getting a grunt this time. He did this a couple more times, pulling new sounds with each.

But a moment later, he found himself on his back. Ben straddled him, steadying his cock and sliding down onto it. When he was seated, he leaned forward, bracing himself over Eric, leaving only a few short inches between them. "Do not ever wonder if I want you as much as you do me. You *are* claiming me, but I am claiming you too. Eres mío también, cariño. Para siempre." Then he caught Eric's lips in a kiss so full, so deep, Eric wasn't sure where Ben ended and he began.

He loved it, though. He threaded his fingers through Ben's hair, pouring every bit of his love and want of this man into the kiss. That Ben wanted to prove that the claiming went both ways filled Eric with so much emotion, so *many* emotions, he couldn't begin to name them all.

Ben pulled away then and lifted himself up, then slid *slowly* back down. He set a pace guaranteed to drive Eric crazy, and it was succeeding. Eric supposed he deserved it, though, with how slow he'd gone in the beginning. Ben seemed to struggle a little—they'd never tried that position before—so Eric gripped his hips and helped steady him. Their eyes stayed locked on each other's as Ben rode him, showing how much he wanted too. Eric rocked his hips, meeting Ben's movements, and as the pleasure built, Eric knew it was time.

He moved, rolling them without pulling out—grateful for his wolf strength—and laid Ben onto his back once more. "Ready, baby?"

Ben nodded, giving a slightly strangled-sounding, "Yes!"

Eric sped up then, thrusting hard, moving fast. He sat up a little, wrapping his hand around Ben's cock and stroking it. He didn't have much rhythm, but Ben didn't seem to need it. Ben arched his back and once more reached for the headboard. The other hand, however, he kept on Eric, and still he didn't look away.

"Oh gods... going to...." Eric's voice came out low, the pleasure stealing his breath.

"Yes. Me too," Ben said, then moaned.

Eric bent then, as Ben tilted his head slightly. As his orgasm crashed into him, his cock swelling at the base, locking him inside Ben, Eric bit down, followed what could only be a few seconds later by Ben biting Eric's neck. The pleasure hit *hard*, and Eric was forced to let go of Ben's neck. As he did, his head was knocked back, causing him to look up.

There, above them, floated a beautiful ethereal form of his wolf. Next to it was the same beautiful version of Ben's. The two wolves curled around each other before moving together. The outlines turned fuzzy, then the two merged together into one before fading.

As soon as it did, the link between Eric and Ben thickened and the invisible force that drew them together before pulled them in once more, wrapping around them. As their final bond snapped into place, understanding clarified that had eluded Eric until that moment. This bond, the bond of two people who *wanted* and *loved*, wouldn't be broken, certainly not willingly.

Ben wouldn't deliberately do to Eric what had been done before. He *couldn't* because he loved Eric and would do anything and everything in his power to make sure it didn't happen accidentally either.

Ben! I... I'm so sorry—

Ben shook his head. *No. You could not know this, the way we would understand each other. Oh, cariño, this is amazing!*

Eric grinned. *It is, my mate.*

I love you. Ben reached up and cupped Eric's cheek.

I love you too. Eric bent and kissed Ben softly, savoring the happiness they shared, the love coming over their bond, so much stronger and clearer now.

While Eric's knot was swollen, they kissed lightly, just brushing their fingers over each other's faces. Eric savored the complete bond and all he felt from Ben through it. Finally the knot subsided, and he pulled out. He had to kiss Ben once more before they climbed under the covers. He settled in next to Ben, pulled him close, then wrapped an arm around him. They tangled their legs and moved that little bit closer until there wasn't the tiniest bit of air between them.

Ben yawned, making Eric grin. "It seems you are still recovering a little."

But Ben just shook his head. "No, you wore me out."

Eric raised an eyebrow. "Oh, I did, did I? You're saying I have more stamina? I can last longer? I'm—"

Ben rolled his eyes, poking Eric in the side. *Do not get too full of yourself, cariño, or you will sleep on the couch.*

Eric held a hand up. *I have no intention of ever sleeping separate from you again. I promise to behave.* He smirked. *Mostly. But you'll forgive me.*

Ben laughed. *Mostly…. So sure I will….*

You will. Eric kissed him again, keeping it soft and light.

Ben sighed and shook his head, but he was smiling. *I will.*

CARIÑO?

Downstairs, baby. Just getting coffee. Eric grinned as he waited for the cup to finish. He was being sappy as hell and didn't give a single damn.

He allowed himself a moment of regret that he'd waited so long. So much hurt could have been avoided, so much frustration—and the pain his mate went through—if he'd just listened to what everyone else had told him. He sighed. If only—

Do not do that.

Eric chuckled. Then again, knowing his mate could read him so well all the time was bound to get him in trouble. *Yeah, yeah.*

That got him a mental snort.

Just as he pulled the cup out of the coffee maker, he heard the sound of tires crunching over gravel. *They're home.*

Should I come down? Never mind, I will. I want to hear this.

I'll wait in the living room. With your coffee, so don't take too long.

A moment later Ben joined him just as Tanner and Finley came through the front door. Both noses twitched at the same time and, also at the same time, they grinned.

"Congratulations!" Finley said as he crossed the room. He hugged Ben first, then turned to Eric.

"Yeah. Congrats, man. About damned time."

"Shaddup," Eric grumbled, ignoring the snickers, and hugged each of them.

"I need coffee," Finley declared. "Then you've got to hear it all."

Tanner hung his and Finley's jackets up as Ben and Eric settled in on the couch together. Eric ignored Tanner long enough to kiss Ben thoroughly, getting a grin and blush for his trouble. He finally turned back to Tanner when he flopped down onto the other couch.

"That was… a very not fun couple of days." Tanner rubbed his face and sighed.

"What time did you get back?" Eric glanced at the clock, but it wasn't even fully ten yet.

"Oh, we got in last night," Finley said from the kitchen.

Eric raised an eyebrow at Tanner.

"Yeah, we landed at Latrobe around seven, I think. We just decided it would be more prudent to stay at a hotel. Turns out that was a good decision."

"Asshole," Eric muttered.

It is a good thing, though, cariño. We would not have wanted to claim if they could hear us. If the teasing is bad now—

Ugh, yeah. Have I mentioned this morning I love you?

Ben grinned at him. *Not in the last five minutes or so.*

Eric laughed.

"You could, you know, talk where we can all hear."

Eric scowled at his best friend, but Tanner just grinned and didn't reply to that.

"So—"

"Wait for me," Finley called. "Almost done."

"Fine," Tanner said, sighing. He closed his eyes and rested his head against the back of the couch. "The trip back wasn't fun. Even with the tea, it was rough. Hit turbulence somewhere over Ohio and my wolf was *not* happy."

Eric wrinkled his nose. "Yeah, doesn't sound too fun. I'm not sure when I'll want to try the flying thing. Glad it wasn't me."

"Be glad for a number of reasons," Finley said, coming back in. He handed Tanner one of the coffee mugs before settling in next to him.

"So… her mate broke the bond," Tanner said without preamble.

Eric blinked. "The one she left me for?"

Finley nodded. "The very same."

Eric frowned. "But she didn't shift like I did?"

Tanner shook his head. "No. I doubt she was invested in that mating as much as you were in the bond with her."

"Yeah, that wouldn't surprise me. But it still messed with her?"

"That's what she claims, and really, one look in her eyes and you can see it."

Eric thought back to that day but shook his head. "I think I was just too pissed she'd show up to notice. I mean, I saw she was off, but it didn't register how serious it was."

"I didn't either then." Tanner shrugged a shoulder. "Her arguments at the hearing were a little too… scattered, I think is a good word, to be faked."

"She most definitely wasn't right." Finley took a sip. "And… yes, it was your parents. They'd called her."

"Not my parents anymore," Eric said, scowling.

Ben put a hand on his and squeezed. "You have other family," he reminded Eric.

Eric blew out a breath. "Yeah. I do." He turned and kissed Ben's temple, sending gratitude to his mate for the calm Ben was projecting to him.

"I suspect he broke the bond with her when she took off to come back here," Tanner said, frowning.

"Or it's possible she talked about you and he broke it and that prompted her to come back here," Finley suggested.

Eric shrugged. "I don't care that much. She deserves to have the bond broken on her, not that it did a fraction to her what it did to me." He took a deep breath and let it out. "And now for the $64,000 question."

"Locked up. For life," Tanner said. "She confessed to the attempted murder—actually still seemed a little… righteous about it. Insisted all the way up to sentencing that she was your mate." He shook his head.

"Locked up?" Ben asked, blinking.

"Yeah, headquarters has the only jail we have in the United States for wolves who break laws," Eric said.

"It doesn't happen often," Finley added. "Most things are handled on the pack level. The alphas have a lot of autonomy for punishment. But some laws—well, really, only a couple of major ones—are handled on a national level."

"Murder, attempted murder, and lone wolves who refuse to join a pack," Eric said, nodding.

"And she was charged with attempted murder, so she's locked up. Not a death sentence like proven murder would be, but bad enough. The cells are... humane enough. There's a door she can use to go between inside and outside, big enough for her wolf to go through. The outside is entirely enclosed in fencing, which is buried some fifty feet underground."

Eric raised his eyebrows. "She's not digging out from under that."

"No, she's not. It's still locked up, no matter how nice."

"She'll go wild before too long," Eric said.

"Probably. But... she made the choice to go after Ben."

"I don't feel pity for her." Eric shook his head. "I guess I should, as off as she was, but... I just can't. After everything she put me through, after what she did to Ben.... Hell, I think once she does go wolf, she's almost getting off easy." He scowled.

Ben kissed his temple. "I'm just glad she is not capable of causing more harm."

"Well, she won't do that, no doubt." Tanner stood. "I'm beat, despite the sleep last night. Rough couple of days."

"We'll get a mating party planned," Finley said, standing. "If we had to go through it, so do you," he said at the frown on Eric's face.

"Hey, you're the alpha and his mate!"

"Not being the alpha just means you don't have to mate publicly," Tanner said with a smirk. "Doesn't get you out of the party."

"Asshole," Eric muttered.

Tanner and Finley both laughed as they went up the stairs.

Ben frowned. "Party?"

Eric nodded. "Yeah, kinda like a wedding reception but for matings. Oh well, at least if Finley's in charge, we don't have to worry about pink ribbons and flowers."

Ben let out a sigh of obvious relief. "That is good."

"They'll do their damnedest to embarrass us, though."

"Yay."

Ben sounded so bummed, Eric couldn't stop the chuckle. "We'll forgive them. Then get them back."

That brought a grin to Ben's face. "I like that idea."

Chapter 19

IT TOOK everything Ben had to focus on the road and not his nervousness. It was only the knowledge that if he wasn't careful they'd end up in the hospital, trying to explain why they were healing already, that made him able to concentrate. He took the turns almost on autopilot, but before they got to the last road, Eric put a hand over Ben's on the steering wheel.

"Pull over, baby."

Ben frowned but turned into the next parking lot. He let out a humorless chuckle when he realized it was the same Taco Bueno he'd eaten at when he left home before meeting Eric.

"Baby?" Eric asked, raising an eyebrow.

Ben put the car in park and turned in his seat to look at his mate. "This was the last place I stopped in Dallas before coming to Pittsburgh."

Eric took his hand. "Ah. Listen, I want you to remember something."

"Oh?" Ben stared at Eric's hand, trying to calm his pounding heart.

"Yes. First, I know you're terrified."

Ben frowned, looking back up at Eric. "Mierda. I had been—"

"You can't hide from me. You couldn't very well before we mated, and now that we're fully bonded, you can't at all."

"I... you do not need to worr—"

"Don't. That's what we're for. Do you remember when I went to see my parents for the last time?"

"Of course." Ben scowled. "How could I forget how horribly they treated you?"

Eric smiled and brushed at the hair falling over Ben's forehead. "You wouldn't. But it was your support, you being there, that kept it from being as horrible as it could have been." He put a finger under Ben's chin, and Ben looked up at him. "You know your papá will still love you. Your sister still cares about you. And we have a family in the guys back in Pittsburgh. And no matter what, I'm going to be with you." He gave a crooked smile. "You're not getting rid of me now."

"As if I would want to, cariño."

That brought a grin. "Right. So… you won't be alone, no matter what happens. But… I have a really good feeling about this."

Ben blew out a breath. "I hope you're right."

"I am. I'm right a lo—"

Ben elbowed him. "Do not get too full of yourself, cariño."

Eric laughed at the familiar words. "I'll count on you to keep me humble." He leaned in and kissed Ben softly. "Now. Take me to meet your parents."

With one more deep breath, Ben turned back in his seat and put the car once more in gear. Sending a soft prayer to Diana to help him calm down, he pulled out of the parking lot.

It was still too soon when they turned onto the gravel drive leading up to the house. The hand Eric put on Ben's leg gave him a little more calm and courage, so when he pulled to a stop at the end of the drive, he didn't, at least, feel like he was going to fly apart into a million pieces. He had to count to thirty before he could bring himself to turn off the car, but finally he managed and climbed out.

Before Ben could even take a single step, the front door opened. As his mamá stepped out, Ben's feet turned to lead and he couldn't so much as move an inch. He held his breath, vaguely aware when Eric stepped out of the car, but his entire focus was on his mamá as she stopped on the top step.

"B-Ben?"

Ben wasn't sure what it meant that she used that name instead of Jesus, but he thought it could only be a good sign. He swallowed and managed to take a step forward. It seemed to unlock something in her, and she nearly flew off the porch and launched herself into his arms.

"Mijo! Oh, mijo!"

He wrapped his arms around her as she launched into a string of rapid-fire Spanish that even *he* had trouble following, as punctuated with sobs as it was. He caught several repetitions of *I'm sorry* and at least one or two *pleases*, but he wasn't quite sure what she was asking for.

Finally he managed to extract himself from her. She took a half step back but didn't let go of his arms. Her gaze flew all over his face, tears still streaming down her cheeks.

Swallowing, he took another chance. "Mamá, my mate cannot understand you yet."

She blinked at him, then looked over at Eric as if she hadn't seen him. Ben guessed she probably *hadn't* paid attention to anyone else. "Mate? He is your... mate?"

"Sí, mamá. He is my destined mate." Ben held his breath, praying harder to Diana than he ever had in his life.

She turned to Eric. "You are... Ben's mate."

Eric glanced at Ben, and nervousness not his own came across the bond. It did good things to know Eric wanted to impress his parents so much. Ben sent calm back, though he couldn't tell Eric if it would be okay until he knew what his mother would do.

"Sí. *Me llamo* Eric." Eric swallowed. "*Mucho gusto.*"

Mamá's eyes widened. "¿Hablas español?"

Eric cleared his throat. "Uh, not much yet. But I'm learning."

She looked back at Ben, then at Eric once more, a smile spreading. "Mucho gusto. Welcome to our family."

That was all it took. Relief, joy, and a mess of other emotions filled Ben, and tears he didn't know he was holding back fell.

She welcomed me!

Yes! Ben grinned through his tears at Eric as his mamá went around the car.

"Gracias, Señora Arellano," Eric said, his voice rough.

"*Por fa*—please, call me 'mamá,'" she said, then held her arms out. A somewhat shocked-looking Eric hugged her. "Gracias."

"Come. Let's take this inside, mijo." Papá waved toward the inside of the house. Ben hadn't even seen him come out, so focused on his mamá as he was.

"Papá!" Ben followed Mamá to the porch, taking Eric's hand when they met at the bottom step. At the top, though, he stopped to hug Papá.

"So glad you're home, mijo. Welcome, Eric," his papá said, holding a hand out toward Eric, who took it and shook.

"Good to meet you, sir."

Papá waved a hand. "Papá, please, since I am yours."

Mine?

He knows what happened with... them. I told him over the phone.

Oh. Wow. Eric cleared his throat and smiled. "Uh, thank you."

Despite the welcome, Ben still wasn't entirely sure what to expect of his mamá. She'd greeted Eric, that was true, and told him to call her mamá. He figured that meant she dealt okay with the bisexual thing. But she hadn't said a word about wolves, and that, even more than the mate thing, was the problem.

He didn't get answers right away, though. Mamá insisted on getting iced tea for everyone as they found places to sit in the living room. Eric sat next to Ben, taking his hand, and Ben was glad for the closeness.

"How was the flight?" Papá asked.

"Smooth, thankfully," Ben said. "Which I was glad for, as it was my first."

"How does it work?"

Eric answered for him. "The tea Miles has makes the wolf side of us sleepy, so it's calm. He doesn't have the opportunity to get so freaked out."

At the mention of "wolf," Ben shot a look toward the kitchen. His mamá was coming out at the same time. She swallowed, but her hands were full, and Ben waited to see if she crossed herself after setting the tray down.

But… she didn't. She handed a glass to Eric, then to him and his papá before taking a seat. Papá put an arm around her, and Ben was warmed to see them touching. It wasn't that they didn't, but they seemed closer somehow than they'd been before Ben left. He wondered if it was his leaving that did it.

"I wondered…," Mamá began, glancing between them. "Um… I wondered if later, you might show me your wolf. I have not seen him since you were little. He is bigger now, yes?"

It took Ben a full minute to answer. When Eric squeezed his hand, it broke the lock on Ben's brain and he swallowed, then nodded. "Uh, yes. He's the same size I am in human form. Different shape but same mass."

She nodded. "That is what your papá said. It seemed like that with him too."

"Mamá… I… you…." Ben shook his head.

She smiled, a little shyly, but her throat worked at the same time, and Ben guessed she was trying not to cry. "Mijo… I have been so wrong. I… I thought I had lost you. I was hurt and angry."

Ben tried not to let that bother him. He still felt she'd had no right to be, and it was only Eric's hand on his that kept him from letting that frustration take over.

"Tina came home for Thanksgiving and gave me an earful too." She lowered her gaze. "It is no excuse. I know this. I was raised Catholic.

It is hard to undo a lifetime of beliefs. But I should have listened a long time ago. I should have learned, should have tried. I am so sorry."

Ben took a deep breath and had to clear his throat before he could speak, but Eric beat him to it.

"It is hard to get past something like that. I… I have to be honest, Señ—Mamá. I was ready to be angry on his behalf."

She smiled at this and nodded. "I… I believe firmly in respecting your parents, but I am glad to know you care and that you would defend him."

"I'm glad I don't have to."

They sat in silence for a moment that wasn't entirely uncomfortable, drinking their tea. For Ben, at least, he was swinging from tired to relieved and trying to deal with everything in between. But before long, his mamá put her glass down and looked up at Ben again. "Mijo?"

Ben raised his eyebrows.

"Would… would you show him to me?"

Eric squeezed Ben's hand, and Ben nodded. "If you will excuse me for a moment."

She looked puzzled.

Ben actually managed a chuckle. "I have to get naked or I'll shred my clothes. Because we're the same size, the change in our shape will tear them. I did not think you'd want to see me naked now that I'm grown."

"Ah," she said, blushing. "That is true."

Ben paused long enough to kiss Eric, then hurried into the half bathroom they had on that floor. He stripped quickly, then let his wolf take over. It felt… weird… to be in wolf form in that house. There was a minor moment of panic as he remembered that the last time had been one of those uncontrollable shifts. He pushed the thought off and left the bathroom.

When he stopped in front of Mamá, her eyes went wide. "You are huge!"

He held his breath, worried she'd still freak out. Instead, she reached out and ran her fingers over his head.

"Soft, like your papá's. And… your fur… it is the color of your hair. Is it always like this?" she asked, looking up at Eric.

He nodded. "Yeah. I'm mostly black. Our alpha has auburn hair, and his wolf's fur is dark red. The pack doctor is bright red. He stands out no matter where he is in the forest."

She chuckled. "I imagine he would." She looked back down at Ben. "You are a beautiful wolf, mijo." She petted him.

Tell her thank you.

"He says to tell you thank you," Eric said, smiling.

She raised her eyebrows. "You can talk?"

"They're mates, Alicia, just like us."

She glared at him. "I am still learning. Be patient."

Papá looked chagrined. "I'm sorry, love." He kissed her temple, and she looked mollified.

Reaching out, she touched Ben's head again. "Thank you. Now… please go change before you get wolf hair all over my living room."

Ben chuffed in amusement, making Eric grin. Then he took a chance, braced his front paw on the arm of the couch, and licked Mamá's face.

She laughed, a beautiful sound to Ben's ears. "Mijo! I prefer your kisses without slobber, now that you are grown!"

The warmth and happiness from that filled Ben. He was glad he couldn't actually cry in that form or he was afraid he would right then. Instead, he chuffed again, then stepped back. *Tell her I'll be right back.*

"He says he'll be right back. He's fast at shifting, so it won't take long."

Ben couldn't help but feel good at the note of pride in Eric's voice. He hurried into the bathroom, shifted, and redressed as quickly as he could.

"Mijo, you and Eric will be in your room," Mamá said as they headed toward the front door. "I'm sorry, but you will have to make up the bed. I only finished washing a short while ago. Eric, come with me and I will get the linen."

Eric followed her into the hallway as Ben and his papá went out to the car to collect the suitcases and gifts they'd brought. When Eric and Mamá stopped next to a wide closet, she turned to him. She swallowed, then took a breath.

"I was horrible to him when he was little, and to my shame, that did not get better. I… said things about his possible mate right before he left. I am sure he has told you, yes?"

"Yeah, he did," Eric said, nodding.

"I want you to know, separately from what I tell Ben, that I am glad he has you. His papá and I are destined, but I did not truly understand what that means, how big that is, until recently. That Ben has found his, I am happy for you both. I do not care that you are a man. Knowing what I do of him now, accepting it, I am just happy to have you in our family."

She stood up on her toes—Eric was amused to realize just how short she was—and wrapped her arms around him, like she had outside earlier. He hugged her back, still slightly bemused by the affection. When she stepped away, she opened the closet, then pulled a set of sheets and other linens from one shelf. As she handed them to him, she held his hand briefly.

"I hope you are not upset, but Alejandro told me what happened with your family. I do not understand how a mother could be like that." She actually scowled. "For all my problems, my… faults, I would not be like that." She shook her head. "I hope you will consider us your family now. I know that we can never replace what should be blood, but I want you to be comfortable… happy with us."

Eric swallowed, his heart pounding. He cleared his throat and opened his mouth to speak, but Ben must have noticed his nervousness.

Cariño?

I'm fine. Tell you in a minute.

Eric managed to focus on Mamá again. "I… I haven't felt like they were my family for a long time. My parents never were very… parental, for lack of a better word. I spent a lot of time with Tanner's family, but even so, as much as I liked Alpha Noah and Tanner's mom, Carol… they were still his parents." He blew out a breath. "I'd like that. Uh, to be part of this family."

She smiled widely, and it warmed him. "I am happy to hear that, mijo." She stood up on her toes again and kissed his cheek. "Now, we have work to do or you and Ben will be sleeping on the floor—and not in wolf form!" She walked away, muttering something in Spanish. Eric thought he heard something about a vacuum cleaner—she used the English words—and he chuckled.

Ben caught up to him as he was about to climb the stairs. "Cariño?"

Eric glanced up the steps, but she'd turned the corner. "She called me 'mijo.'"

Ben blinked. "She did?"

"Yeah." Eric nodded. "She said she wants them to be my family since mine are such dicks."

"Uh…."

Eric laughed. "No, she didn't use those words. But that was the basic idea."

Ben grinned and shook his head. "I did not expect this acceptance but...."

"Let's be glad for it. And help yo—Mamá before she yells at us."

"Eric! Benjamin! Do not make me throw my sandal!"

Ben winced, and Eric raised his eyebrows. "It's a habit she has from her own mamá. And, uh, we should go. She has a good arm."

Eric laughed as they started up the stairs. "I'll remember that."

BEN FOUND Eric in the kitchen, staring at the coffee maker. He'd clearly only started it a short while before, as the carafe hadn't filled much yet. Slipping his arms around Eric's waist, Ben murmured, "Buenos días, cariño."

Eric turned around to put his arms around Ben. "Buenos días." He kissed Ben lightly, then pulled back. "I've got to learn more. Your poor parents—your mom especially—seems to be going a little nuts trying to remember to speak English."

"I think she's too happy to have me—us—here to be upset." Ben shrugged a shoulder. "She's just not used to speaking English as much. It is not a bad thing for her to practice, though."

"Yeah. Well, when I learn more, I'll have to practice."

"I'll help. Perhaps I'll stop speaking English altogether."

"Oh yeah, no communication. *Great* idea," Eric said, chuckling.

Ben grinned. "You'll simply have to learn fast."

Eric rolled his eyes, then pulled Ben a little closer. When he kissed Ben this time, it was most definitely *not* light. Ben let himself get lost in it, let himself savor the closeness. He'd felt weird being home the night before, and thus, they hadn't made love. That was a rare thing since they'd started bonding and even rarer now that they were mated. So he took advantage of their alone time, at least kissing and touching as much as he could. Eric's arms tightened as Ben deepened the kiss even more, their shirtless chests pressed against each other.

"Ewww! Get a room!"

They broke apart, and Ben looked over to see his sister, Tina, standing in the doorway, wrinkling her nose. He could see the smile in her eyes, though, and knew she was just teasing. He'd sent her emails regularly while he and Eric had been working things out, so she had known all about Eric and hadn't even said a word about the fact that Eric was male.

"We have one. We're just more interested in kissing here and grossing you out."

She rolled her eyes but crossed the room, skirting the island. Ben let go of Eric to hug her, and she turned to Eric when they pulled back. "So. I hear you're my new brother."

Eric grinned. "Yeah, and I've never had a sister, so you're in trouble while I figure it out."

She laughed and looked over at Ben. "I like him."

Ben grinned too. "When did you get in?"

"*Late* last night. Thank you, by the way," she said, turning to Eric. "I've never flown before, and that trip would have taken *forever* otherwise."

"I'm glad you could use the tea."

Ben frowned. "Why so late?"

"The first flight was late, so I ended up missing my connection. Then *that* was delayed. I was just glad I got in before this morning."

"I'm glad you're here," Ben said, hugging her again.

"Now that we all are," Mamá said from the kitchen doorway, with a huge smile, "we can have Christmas!"

IT TOOK a little while to get coffee passed out and everyone settled, but finally they had seats in the living room around the tree. It was decorated the same as it always was, save a few new ornaments. Mamá liked to have at least one new one every year. Ben looked it over, trying to see if she'd put it on yet for this one.

When he found it, near the top in the front, he stopped breathing. He stood and crossed the room, not paying attention to anyone around him, his focus only on the tree and ornament. He reached out toward it but stopped just shy of touching it.

He couldn't tell if it was crystal or cut glass or what, but the detail on it was incredible. The wolf was in a lying pose, with its head up. Even as small as it was, he could tell the eyes were open and the wolf's expression alert. The tongue lolled, and it looked like it was smiling—as much as wolves could.

She couldn't have made a bigger statement if she'd shouted it from the rooftop.

Ben turned to see his mamá standing next to him. She stared at him, as if waiting, but he had no idea how to put it in words.

Are you okay?

Ben glanced at Eric and nodded, then turned back to his mamá. "I… that is… amazing." He swallowed the lump in his throat and pulled her against him. "Thank you."

She returned the hug, sniffled, then pulled back. "It is my ornament. You cannot have it."

Ben grinned and hugged her again. "I suppose I can live with that."

With a laugh she returned to her seat. Ben sat next to Eric again, unable to keep the grin off his face.

Eric kissed him, but they both had to pay attention when Tina yelled, "Hey! Christmas, remember?"

BEN HAD a small stack of sweaters—including a hand-knitted one with a wolf on it from his mamá. She was trying so hard, and Ben had teared up—again—when he opened it. There were books and music and several sets of guitar strings and picks. Eric had a brand-new set of leather tools—from Mamá and Papá—a bunch of drawing materials from Tina, and a handknitted scarf that Ben figured his mamá had been knitting furiously since the day before last when they'd arrived.

There were only a few gifts left under the tree. Eric handed the box they had for Tina to her and grinned when she squealed over the Amazon, iTunes, and Best Buy gift cards.

"Oh, I'm going to have *so* much fun shopping!"

Ben's gift to Eric, however, made him nervous. Eric still struggled some with his art, and Ben wanted to encourage it more but was afraid he'd push too far. Eric had seemed happy with the drawing materials and personal leather tools, though, so Ben had hopes he'd like the last gift as well.

He handed the box to Eric, then held his breath. Eric took his time opening the paper, and Ben was about to pass out from lack of oxygen by the time it was off. Eric's face was priceless. He was so stunned, nothing came across their bond. He looked up at Ben, then back at the Wacom tablet. Ben had researched himself crazy to find the right one, and he guessed he'd succeeded.

"Tanner told me how important your art and leatherwork were to you before. I want you to know how important it is to me for you to keep working on it."

Eric's smile spread slowly, and he leaned in and kissed Ben. "I've looked at them a lot—or, well, did before I went wolf—but never could bring myself to buy one. This is perfect. I've got a few ways I can make this work for my stuff at the shop too."

Ben's heart slowed for the moment, and he let out a breath of relief. But then Eric picked up a box—a not small one, in fact—and handed it to Ben, who puzzled over it. "I do not remember this being in your bags."

Eric grinned and looked over at Papá. "That's because it wasn't. Papá let me ship it ahead."

Ben blinked at him, then looked at his papá, then back to Eric. "Oh. Uh…."

"Well. Open it."

"Okay, okay." Ben pulled at the corner of the paper, but unlike Eric, he had no problems tearing. A moment later he had a sealed shipping box. He glanced at Eric, who grinned, then rolled his eyes and took the pocketknife his papá was holding out. Finally, a few moments later, he had the box opened and pulled the item out.

A leather guitar case. Ben swallowed as he turned it over, his mouth dropping open. Two wolves—which Ben immediately recognized as theirs—lay together in a forest. Trees surrounded them, grass rose around their paws, and behind them, faintly, stood a woman he recognized immediately as Diana.

"Cariño! It is… when did you do this?"

Eric smiled. "I've been working on that for weeks at the shop. I had a few false starts, for one thing. And I had to go slow. On top of that, you came to visit my station quite a bit, so I had to hide it."

Ben blushed. "I did not want to be apart."

"I didn't say I minded, but it did make it difficult to surprise you."

Ben laughed. "I love it. Thank you!"

"You didn't open it."

Raising an eyebrow at Eric, Ben turned his attention to the zipper. When he had it all the way undone, he opened it to find a small wrapped box taped to the bottom of the nylon-lined case. He blinked at it, then up at Eric, then back to the box. He didn't think for one minute it was guitar picks, even though it was the right size. With a shaky hand, he untaped it from the case and carefully put the case aside.

Eric actually took the box out of his hand. "Do you mind?"

Ben shook his head in something of a daze. "No, of course not."

With a nod Eric quickly opened the box—it turned out the lid and bottom had been wrapped separately—and upended it to dump a velvet case into his palm.

Ben's heart started pounding.

Eric opened the case and turned it to show two simple gold rings. He slid off the couch onto the floor… and onto one knee.

"Cariño?"

"Marry me, Ben."

A squeak from across the room drew Ben's attention, and he looked over to see his mamá's hands over her mouth and tears streaming. Papá had an arm around her, grinning. Tina was actually bouncing at her seat by the tree, a big smile on her face as well.

Ben turned back, swallowed hard, and nodded. "Yes. I…. Yes!" He laughed a little giddily as Eric took Ben's right hand and slipped the ring onto his finger. Ben took the box back and put the matching one on Eric's finger, then lifted the hand and kissed the ring. "Thank you, cariño. I cannot begin—"

Eric cut him off by sitting up and catching his lips with a kiss. Ben cupped Eric's face and returned it, but they broke apart when a throat cleared. Ben's cheeks heated, but he turned to his mamá.

"So… when do I get grandch—" She paused to look at Papá, then turned back. "Grandpups?"

"Um…." Ben glanced at Eric, then back to his mamá. "I… we are not equipped to have pups, Mamá. Even wolves cannot do that."

She actually rolled her eyes. "Of course not, mijo. But I am sure, like there are for human couples, there are ways for wolves, no?"

Eric laughed. "Yes, there are. We haven't talked about it, though."

You do want them, though, cariño, don't you?

Yeah, but that's a decision we both make. I always wanted pups, but—

Then we will. I certainly have nothing against them.

I'm so glad. Eric grinned, but then his smile faded and he looked serious. *One more thing, baby. Do you… are you happy with them now? Have you… have you forgiven Mamá?*

Yes. I understand how hard it was for her. I was angry, but she's trying, and I believe that's what matters.

Eric grinned. "We will have to talk about it, but… probably."

Mamá grinned. "Yes! Now… we have dinner to make," she said as she and Papá stood.

"One more thing, Mamá, Papá," Eric said, standing. He crossed the room and stood in front of them. "Would you…." He swallowed, then cleared his throat. "Would you mind if I took your name?"

Papá smiled widely. "We would love that."

Mamá hugged him, then nearly ran out of the room, her sobs—happy ones—echoing behind her.

"Oh, Papá, the pack is throwing us a mating party next month. Would you and Mamá want to come up for it?"

Papá hesitated. "I was going to wait to talk to you later, but… your mamá does not like being so far away. How would you feel if we come talk to your alpha… and consider moving? Would they welcome us?"

Ben's eyes went wide. "You would do that?"

"They'd love to have you, and we'd love to have you close," Eric said.

Papá smiled. "Then we will be there and I will talk with your alpha then."

"Ugh! That's an even *longer* flight home!" Tina grumbled. She stuck her tongue out at them, then grinned. "I guess I can put up with it. Brothers," she said, sighing, as she passed.

Is this real? Ben turned to Eric as Papá went ahead into the kitchen.

Yeah, baby. It's real. We have a family, in more ways than one. I didn't need my parents' forgiveness. I got it where it most counted. The guys in the pack, our friends. The packmates at the shop. You.

There is nothing to forgive, cariño.

Eric shook his head. *I don't agree, but I'll let it go. Let's go help our family with dinner.*

Ben grinned. *Yes. Just… do not go near the stove.*

Epilogue

Eight Years Later….

BEN PULLED Diana out of her car seat and settled her on his hip. After locking the car, Eric came around the front and kissed her nose, and then they turned toward the trees. Ben took Eric's hand, and the three of them crossed the parking area and stepped through the tree line.

The scene that greeted them had Ben laughing. Chad had his tongue out at Miles, who was grinning back at him. The three oldest wolf pups sat on the ground, heads tilted, looking up at the where jaguar cub Aubrey sat on a tree branch. Pine cones lay on the ground around them, and Ben didn't doubt for a minute at least a few of those had landed on someone's head, including the adult Chad's.

"Papá! Play!" Diana announced, then wiggled in Ben's arms.

He squatted to set her down, then had to fight with her to get her to stay still long enough to get her undressed. Within a few moments, he had her shoes and dress off. Seconds later, she'd shifted and taken off. She ran up to the other pups and immediately started chewing on the black wolf pup's tail. Eric's namesake turned around, growling at first, then stopped when he saw who it was.

Ben and Eric both grinned when Eric the pup and the other two turned to her. A few seconds later, the little cub landed next to them and they all started play-fighting. As always, the boys were quite gentle with her, even when she pounced on them.

"Hey! Glad you could make it," Chad said, turning around. Tanner, Finley, Jamie, Miles, and Quincy all turned as well, smiles on all of them.

"Finally! Diana is trying not to use sippy cups anymore. She insists she's a 'big girl,' but she hasn't gotten the hang of regular cups yet. So…." Eric sighed.

"Mess," Finley said, chuckling.

"Yeah. This one all over her dress, the table, the floor…." Eric shrugged. "Not a big deal, just a delay."

Ben nodded. "Miguel had poured her juice, but before he could get the lid onto it, she had grabbed it and… tried… to drink it."

"Oops." Finley winced.

"Yeah, Luis insisted on cleaning it up, so they're even later."

"They have time," Tanner said, looking up at the sky. He looked back at Ben and Eric, then around them. "Wait, where's your dad?"

Ben grinned. "He's staying home with Mamá tonight. She says she did not want to be alone now that Tina is mated and gone too."

Chad wrinkled his nose. "Full moon in the house? Ugh."

Eric waved at that. "Nah. He just ran the other day. So a full moon at home tonight isn't going to bother him. Last month, she had Diana. I think she just likes having her wolves around her."

"I keep telling her to go wolf so she can run with us," Chad said, shaking his head.

"She's happy that she gets to live as long as we do." Ben sighed. "I'm just surprised she does not mind the wolf hair all over the house."

"Roomba for the win," Jamie said, laughing.

Eric grinned. "Best thing we ever bought her."

Tanner chuckled. "She ought to be glad she doesn't have two pups in the house all the time. Well. Almost time to go," Tanner said, looking up again. "Will Miguel and Luis—"

"We are here!" Miguel called, running through the tree line, Luis next to him. "We made it." He was panting a little. "It is cleaned up, but then my mamá called to tell us about their flights to visit. She forgets sometimes that they are three hours behind us. Anyway, they have booked them."

"Oh?" Ben asked.

Luis nodded. "They will be here Friday." He looked over at Tanner. "I believe Papá will want to talk to you."

Ben grinned at that. "Are they coming to stay, then?"

But Miguel shook his head. "Not yet. I do think Papá has been looking at jobs here, though."

"Tell him we can help him there," Tanner said, waving a hand. "If they want to come here, we'll find a place for them."

Miguel's smile spread at that. "I think Mamá will be happy to hear that." He turned to Eric. "I'm sorry it took so long."

"Don't worry about it. Just glad you made it. Wouldn't be the same without you two." Eric said, smiling at them. "Now, the whole family is here." Miguel and Luis both blushed, but their smiles widened. Even after being with them for some four years, they still hadn't gotten used to being an important part of the Arellano family.

Eric hated what they'd gone through—being rejected by so many packs just for their sexuality—but at the same time, they'd inadvertently done so much for the entire country of wolves. Eric didn't think Noah would have been inspired to change the laws so soon if they hadn't. And, well, Eric *was* glad to have two more members of their family. Miguel's parents had more or less adopted Luis, but Eric and Ben liked having them as adopted little brothers too.

Eric patted Luis on the shoulder. "Come on. Let's run. I need time in my fur. Diana!" Eric called.

She ran back and sat, looking up at him with her head tilted.

Eric chuckled and glanced at Chad. "You really are a bad influence."

Chad feigned innocence. "Why does everyone blame me?"

Jamie snorted. "Because you're usually at fault."

Chad stuck his tongue out at Jamie, who laughed.

"Not in front of the pups!"

That brought laughter from everyone.

"Okay, we're off. We'll catch up a bit later," Miles said, waving. He, Quincy, Aubrey, and the pup Chad moved off to the side. Tanner, Finley, and their pups found a spot for the adults to change, and Chad and Jamie moved off to their own spot to strip.

Eric turned back to Diana. "It's time to run. Remember the rules. You stay with us or one of your uncles or cousins. Do *not* run off on your own. Okay?"

She nodded, then turned and... ran right off.

Ben sighed. "I will get her." He kicked his shoes off, stripped, and a few seconds later, was in wolf form, chasing after her. Miguel and Luis were right behind him.

Eric watched them run and said a prayer of thanks to Diana yet again for Ben, for their daughter, and for their whole family. As he pulled his shirt off, the warmth of a hand on his shoulder made him pause. He glanced around but didn't see anyone. Just as he decided it was his imagination, he heard words in his mind.

Not Ben's voice, no. A female one.

You are welcome.

GRACE R. DUNCAN grew up with a wild imagination. She told stories from an early age—many of which got her into trouble. Eventually, she learned to channel that imagination into less troublesome areas, including fan fiction, which is what has led her to writing male/male erotica.

A gypsy in her own right, Grace has lived all over the United States. She has currently set up camp in East Texas with her husband and children—both the human and furry kind.

As one of those rare creatures who loves research, Grace can get lost for hours on the Internet, reading up on any number of strange and different topics. She can also be found writing fan fiction, reading fantasy, crime, suspense, romance, and other erotica, or even dabbling in art.

Website: www.grace-duncan.com
Facebook: www.facebook.com/GraceRDuncan2
Twitter: @gracerduncan
E-mail: duncan.grace.r@gmail.com

F RBES
MATES
BOOK ONE

Devotion

GRACE R. DUNCAN

Forbes Mates: Book One

Finley Cooper is tired of waiting for his destined mate to be ready to claim him. In deference to human laws, he's already agreed to wait until he's eighteen. But now his birthday has come and gone—and his mate has a new set of excuses. Finley doesn't understand it any more than his wolf does, and he's beginning to wonder if fate made a mistake.

Tanner Pearce wants nothing more than to claim his mate, but he worries that Finley is too young. Tanner will never forget what happened when his best friend mated at Finley's age, only to have that mate end up feeling trapped and breaking their bond. While rare, it can happen, and the fallout Tanner witnessed as his best friend tried to deal with the break has haunted him for years.

When Finley finally has enough, he threatens to find someone who will claim him if Tanner doesn't, and Tanner realizes he needs to come to terms with his fears or risk losing his mate forever.

FORBES
MATES
BOOK TWO

Patience

GRACE R. DUNCAN

Forbes Mates: Book Two

Jamie Ryan was almost ready to accept he'd never find his destined mate. They're uncommon to begin with, and same-sex versions are downright rare. Since his gay best friend found a destined mate, Jamie figured he was out of luck. Until end-of-semester stress forces him to go through the full-moon shift early. Stuck in wolf form, he runs into none other than his destined mate. Who's human.

Chad Sutton has always had good instincts. They served him well as a detective and continued on when he went private. Those instincts tell him there's something about the dog that comes up to him while running away from animal control that isn't quite right. He works to put the pieces together, but is unsuccessful until his dog turns into a human before his eyes.

Jamie has no idea what the mate bite of a shifter will do to a human. He's terrified to try—and possibly kill his mate. They hunt for answers while working together on one of Chad's cases. It's easy to see they belong together, but Jamie fears the gods gave him someone he can't keep.

www.dreamspinnerpress.com

FORBES
MATES

BOOK THREE

Acceptance

GRACE R. DUNCAN

Forbes Mates: Book Three

Dr. Miles Grant acknowledges that his destined mate could be either gender even though his bisexuality cost him his family and his pack. Luckily he found the Forbes Pack, who happily accepts him just as he is. What he never counted on was finding his mate in Pittsburgh or for his mate to be another species entirely—a cat!

Quincy Archer isn't just any jaguar shifter. He is the heir to the leadership of his pride. Destined mates are nothing but legend to the nearly extinct and generally solitary jaguars, and Quincy certainly never expected to find one for himself, much less a male… or a wolf.

However, finding each other and coming to terms with their species is the least of their worries. Quincy is expected to select a proper female mate, father a cub, and take his place as heir to the pride. Except Quincy refuses, having no interest in women or leadership and knowing he isn't right for it. But his father will stop at nothing—not even attempting to kill Miles—to get his way. Quincy and Miles must overcome many obstacles to stay together as the destined mates they're meant to be.

www.dreamspinnerpress.com

Beautiful boy

Malcolm Tate hung up his flogger when his submissive sought out another Dom and landed in the hands of a serial killer. Convinced his lack of dominance sent his sub away, Mal has spent two years blaming himself for what happened. But when his best friend finally convinces him to go back to the local dungeon, Mal's grateful. Especially when he wins beautiful, submissive, firmly closeted Kyle Bingham in a charity slave auction.

College grad Kyle hasn't earned enough to move out of the loft his conservative, homophobic parents bought, much less to buy any of the other things still in their name. When he's won at auction by the hot, amazing Mal, he's shocked that anyone would want him. No one else seemed to—not his parents, his former Doms, or any of his disastrous dates.

But Mal does want him and Kyle lets his guard down, only to be outed to his parents. With his world crashing down, he must find a way to trust Mal—and their developing relationship—or risk losing everything.

www.dreamspinnerpress.com

WHAT
ABOUT
NOW

Grace R. Duncan

Five years ago, everything went wrong. Braden Kirk and Rafe Jessen's long-term relationship started unraveling. They stopped talking, fears mounted, then Braden walked in on Rafe and another man, completely misreading the situation. Without giving Rafe a chance to explain, Braden walks out. Out of their home, their relationship, and the game development company they started together in college.

After months of therapy to deal with the attempted rape Braden walked in on, Rafe begins to understand that his dominant tendencies in the bedroom aren't a bad thing and that Braden's submission is likely what scared his partner into silence. But Rafe isn't ready to let go of the man he loves more than life itself. He arranges for himself and Braden to end up on the same charity cruise, knowing Braden won't let his phobia—terror of vast, deep waters—rule him.

With a plan and twenty-eight days, Rafe is determined to get Braden back, make him see there's nothing wrong with being submissive, and find a way to get Braden to stay with him when they get home to LA.

www.dreamspinnerpress.com